BAD BOY

BAD BOY

A NOVEL

ELLIOT WAKE

ATRIA BOOKS

NEW YORK   LONDON   TORONTO   SYDNEY   NEW DELHI

ATRIA BOOKS

An Imprint of Simon & Schuster, Inc.
1230 Avenue of the Americas
New York, NY 10020

First Atria Books hardcover edition December 2016

ATRIA BOOKS and colophon are trademarks of Simon & Schuster, Inc.

For information about special discounts for bulk purchases, please contact Simon & Schuster Special Sales at 1-866-506-1949 or business@simonandschuster.com.

The Simon & Schuster Speakers Bureau can bring authors to your live event. For more information or to book an event, contact the Simon & Schuster Speakers Bureau at 1-866-248-3049 or visit our website at www.simonspeakers.com.

Manufactured in the United States of America

10   9   8   7   6   5   4   3   2   1

Library of Congress Cataloging-in-Publication Data

Names: Wake, Elliot author.
Title: Bad boy : a novel / Elliot Wake.
Description: New York : Atria Books, 2016.
Identifiers: LCCN 2016022111 (print) | LCCN 2016028723 (ebook) |
   ISBN 9781501115011 (hardcover) | ISBN 9781501115028 (eBook)
Classification: LCC PS3623.A356585 B34 2016 (print) | LCC PS3623.A356585
   (ebook) | DDC 813/.6—dc23
LC record available at https://lccn.loc.gov/2016022111

ISBN 978-1-5011-1501-1
ISBN 978-1-5011-1502-8 (ebook)

For the girl I was

BAD BOY

$$-\!|\!-$$

FIVE YEARS AGO

VLOG #1: FIRST DAY ON T

REN: Life is ineffably weird.

Hello, Internet. My name is Ren. Despite what my reedy voice and apple-dumpling cheeks might tell you, I'm a boy. A lost boy in the big city, trying to find myself. If you're watching this, maybe you're trying to find yourself, too.

Over the past year I've watched a thousand videos just like this one. Other guys talking to their laptops, isolated and afraid, launching their voices into the void like messages in bottles. We're all stranded on the desert islands of ourselves, sending missive after missive and hoping someone will find us, and reply:

Message received.

[Jump cut.]

Guess I'll give you the basics. I'm nineteen. College sopho-more. Gender studies major. Yep, the only boy in class. That'll be fun later, with a beard. I live with my best friend and we both live with the ghost of myself. You can't shake a haunting unless you face it, so in the interests of exorcism and YouTube view counts I'm documenting my transition.

Today was my first day on testosterone.

Here's how it works: You go to a gender therapist and say, "I feel like I've been given a life sentence, and the prison cell is my own skin." You tell them the bars make a double X pattern. The prison uniform is a pointlessly wide pelvis and unnecessary breast tissue atop your pecs. It's designed to dehumanize you. Make you feel both trapped in and disconnected from yourself. The therapist will say, "How long have you identified as a man?" And even though you don't really feel like a man inside, but more of a boy, scared and confused and alone, you'll say, "My whole life." Because you want testosterone more than anything. You *need* it. To survive.

Then, with a bit of luck, they'll sign a letter certifying you as genderfucked, and you'll get T. The wonder drug. The problem-curing, life-fixing panacea.

I'm kidding. Testosterone isn't going to fix my issues. It'll cause a hundred new ones. Male-pattern baldness, BO, acne. I've done my research. Being a man isn't all six-pack abs and sultry stubble. Honestly, manhood is pretty fucking unsexy.

But it's the only thing I have left to try before I take a razor to my wrists.

[Jump cut.]

Some trans guys count their first day of T as their new birthday. So here I am, world. Your newest baby boy, born December 13. Sprung fully formed from my own forehead, Athena-style.

I'm a mythology nerd, and there's this myth that speaks to me, haunts me . . .

This is, uh, kinda hard to talk about, actually. Maybe I—

[Clears his throat.]

My biggest issue with mythology is that it's so steeped in rape. Most of the gods and kings were total shitlords who terrorized women. Other gods took pity and transformed those women into plants so they could escape sexual assault.

Let that sink in. Better to be a *fucking plant* than a woman in ancient Greece.

My relationship with mythology is cagey, but there's this myth I'm obsessed with about a woman called Caenis. Like so many others, Caenis was raped by Poseidon. Afterward she asked to be changed into a man so she couldn't be raped again. Apparently Poseidon drew the line at sodomy.

So Caenis became Caeneus, a fearsome warrior. A man so strong he couldn't be harmed by normal weapons. To defeat him, a crafty centaur buried him beneath a mountain of logs. He's still there, tossing the trunks aside one by one, clawing his way out. Nothing can stop him. Nothing can hold him down. Someday he'll be free.

I'm Caeneus, if that wasn't obvious.

[Clears his throat.]

My voice isn't usually this hoarse. Two weeks ago, I put a belt around my neck and stepped off a chair in my closet. My best friend found me and performed CPR. No one knows how long I was deprived of oxygen. Not long enough for measurable brain damage, but long enough that I still don't have sensation in my chest. Which is actually kind of nice. Lets me forget I have breasts.

[Jump cut.]

This is probably the thousandth trans-guy-taking-T video you've watched. You're seeking answers, like me. Reassurance. Permission. You want to know if this is what you should do. If it'll really make you happy, quiet that scream inside that no one else can hear.

I don't know.

I'm not one hundred percent sure it's right for me, either.

I just know something has to change. *I* have to change.

People make ugly choices to stay sane inside prison. When your body is the cell, it feels like your only freedom is to die. But that's bullshit. There's another way out. A safe way. See a fucking therapist, okay? Don't be like me, don't wait till it nearly kills you. I spent years hurting myself, cautiously, shallowly, trying to resist that final deep cut into a vein.

I hurt myself to remember: I *am* this body. As much as I hate it, it's me.

I have to serve my time here. Make peace with it.

If I don't, if I can't—

[Jump cut.]

But I am. I'm taking back control.

No more self-harm. Now there's a silver bullet of testosterone in my bloodstream, and I didn't even have to beg a god. Thanks, Obamacare.

So this is it. The girl part dies. A little boy wakes up, confused and alone. Irrevocable changes are happening inside his cells and he's stuck on the island of himself, sailing messages out into the wide blue nothing.

This is what they say:

Somebody, please listen.

My name is Ren. I'm one day old. I'm a lost little boy.

Please find me.

–2–

PRESENT DAY

I stood on a balcony overlooking Chicago, the city lit up like a circuit board: gold wires snaking through the night, heat thickening the air into violet gel. Summer was all pulse and shimmer, a billion ones and zeroes manically flipping on and off.

A beautiful night for mayhem.

To my left was the devil herself: Blythe McKinley, inked Aussie bombshell, glitter and cigarette ash spangling her wild blond mane like dirty stars. Her scarlet strap dress showed off sleeve tats. Being near Blythe felt like hovering in the eye of a tornado. Where she went, roofs came off, lives were uprooted. Shit flipped.

On my right, her seraphic opposite: Ellis Carraway, androgynous redhead, very much a *sir* till she opened her mouth. Ellis was shy and sweet, blossoming only when she could nerd out over something. She ID'd as genderfluid: sometimes a boy, sometimes a girl, sometimes something else. Tonight she was all boy in a skinny tie and tweed blazer and Chucks.

Not only were they my angel and devil, they were also each other's exes. Right now the exes were arguing about men who played video games.

"Explain to me, Professor," Blythe said, inscribing the air with her cigarette, "the fact that ninety percent of our targets are hard-core gamers."

Ellis took an anxious hit off her vaping pen. They even smoked in good and evil ways. "Where do you get ninety percent?"

"Observation."

"You made it up."

"All statistics are made-up."

"Correlation does not imply causation, Blythe. Otherwise I'd be the biggest misogynist ever."

"Yet nearly every sexist troll loves his bloody video games. Explain that."

Ellis ruffled her short hair. "I'm not the psychiatrist. Ask Armin."

Her voice dipped into bitterness. An entire novel's worth of resentment hung in the air between us.

No, literally. The novel is called *Black Iris*. Laney wrote it.

We'll meet her in a sec.

Blythe reached past me and brushed Ellis's hand. "Just taking the piss, little bird."

The touch lingered a moment, then they jerked away simultaneously.

"Come on, kids," I said, circling their shoulders. "I'm getting too much oxygen out here. I've almost forgotten the smell of Axe body spray."

Blythe cocked an eyebrow. "Is that not what you're wearing, mate? Just standing near you raises my blood alcohol level."

"Shots fired. Actually, Ellis is wearing that delightful fragrance."

"You guys suck," Ellis said. Then, softer, "And it's not Axe. It's Ralph Lauren."

Blythe spun away from me and seized her, laughing. "Come dance, you beautiful boy."

"I can't dance. You know that. Ren, help."

"On your own, stud."

They swept into the crowd inside the club. Before they vanished I caught the flash of Ellis's engagement ring, coiled silver capped with lapis. So much condensed into something so small: a history, a promise, a future. You could take it off and on, switch fates like shirts. For a second it caught a curl of light and then was gone, breaking into bright pixels as the disco ball whirled overhead, scattering into the sea of grinding skin, sweat, want.

Welcome to Umbra: our home away from home, our glitter-flecked shadowland.

Who are we?

Like Laney says: you'll know us by the trail of our vengeance.

We call the top floor of Umbra the Aerie because up here it feels like you can fly. Music light as helium, a tinge of sugar in the crystal droplets beading on warm skin. A happy haze of prescription drugs and sexual experimentation. Blame Laney. This is basically her queertopia.

Speak of the minidevil. A voice near my elbow said, "Hey, bad boy."

"Hey yourself, bad girl."

Delaney Keating was five foot one of sheer ruthlessness. I'll be damned if I ever meet someone with as many issues—or as much badassery—per square inch. Bangs slanted across her Kewpie doll face like a feral crow's wing, above ingénue-blue eyes and the kind of heart-melting freckles you don't expect on diabolical masterminds. Laney was our boss, our dark queen. Like Dr. Evil as envisioned by Precious Moments.

"What's up?" I said. "You have that femme fatale look."

She didn't smile, but her eyes gave a schemey sparkle. "This is my resting bitch face."

"You're going to ruin someone's life tonight, aren't you?"

"Someone who deserves it."

My heart kicked into high gear. There was one person who deserved the full bore of my wrath, and Laney knew how badly I wanted to deliver it. "Who?"

"Not *him*. But he's bad enough."

It was a *he*, always. Like Blythe said, our targets tended to have certain things in common. Social isolation. Anger issues. Misogyny.

Dicks.

"I'll brief you at the meeting," Laney said, staring off at a blur of blond and ginger. "Midnight. Be there."

"Actually, I can't. I haven't vlogged in ages. I really have to put something up tonight."

"Can it wait?"

"Time goes faster on the Internet. If I disappear for a day everyone thinks I'm dead." I shrugged. "Besides, I need the money. If I'm late on rent, Ingrid'll toss my shit on the street."

She wouldn't. But things were fragile between me and my ex-BFF, and I intended to keep them from outright shattering.

"This job pays," Laney said.

I frowned.

"It pays well. In cash, and in satisfaction."

"Lane, I can't—"

She leaned closer, her voice dry ice. "I know how *the work* makes you feel. It's the same for me. Catharsis. It's something physical, animal. You need this. We both do. And we need each other to make it happen."

Despite the humid air, I shivered.

She was right.

"Midnight," she said.

"Okay."

"Tell the others. And stay sharp. I need everyone on their A game." The blue of her eyes flared like a gas flame. "This is going to be big."

When she was gone I slipped into the crowd, into the glove of shared body heat, brushing up against pretty boys with coquettish eyelashes and dashing girls with chiseled jaws. I sought that physicality Laney spoke of. Friction between skin, biochemical sparks. The thrill of touch. A guy kept bumping into me, and we danced. Still strange, the feel of my thick arms around a man more slender than me. He pressed his ass to my hips and I went hard.

I pulled away. He winked.

Once the new owner took over Umbra, everything changed. Frats and sororities phased out; Pride paraded in. Journalists came knocking. I was spokesman by default—Blythe didn't possess a social filter, and Laney's camera presence was like Wednesday Addams on downers—but I made a perfect poster boy for Umbra 2.0: Mr. Transgender Tipping Point himself, handsome, popular, palatable. Word got around. Umbra was now *the* destination for LGBT kids in the city. A safe space. A second home.

Our new owner, Armin Farhoudi, made sure of that.

I found him at the bar with Blythe. Armin looked like a model who got lost on his way to a *GQ* shoot: tall and lithely muscled, wearing a bespoke suit and wing tips, his brown hair streaked with tendrils of sunset red. That dusky complexion gave him natural eye shadow. I used to fantasize about his stubble while I peered into my bathroom mirror and painted fake facial hair with a mascara wand. Armin was my ideal male. He made masculinity seem effortless, graceful. Beautiful.

Until I learned what he had done. Then he was just another man, no god.

We nodded at each other.

"The Little Wolf sent me," I said. "Meeting tonight."

Blythe's eyes gleamed. "Finally. I'm going stir-crazy."

"You're always stir-crazy."

"I'm just plain crazy."

Armin's mouth tightened. "Don't say that."

"Let me own it. It doesn't shame me."

"Nothing shames you. That's not the point." Armin rotated the watch on his wrist, some sleek tungsten thing. "You romanticize mental illness, Blythe. Make it sound glamorous."

"I romanticize everything. I'm a bloody poet." That gleam in her eyes had become a hundred razor points. "And you medicalize everything because you're a bloody doctor."

"I'm not a doctor. I'm barely even a DJ anymore."

"A better doctor than a DJ."

"Did you just call me a bad DJ?"

"Didn't you just tell me not to romanticize rubbish?"

They both laughed. These two made an Olympic sport of insulting each other. Like Ellis, Armin was one of Blythe's exes. There was no one in our circle she *hadn't* hooked up with. Except me.

Third base notwithstanding.

"Laney says to stay sharp," I said. "Whatever she's planning, it's big."

" 'Though she be but little, she is fierce,' " Blythe said.

Armin sighed. "Please do not start quoting poetry."

"Is my pretentiousness showing?"

"At least it's not Plath."

"Oh, don't you bloody start—"

"Where's Ellis?" I interrupted.

Their good humor dropped. Blythe glanced at Armin, then said, "Fucked if I know. Try the toilet."

"That Aussie lyricism. Swoon."

She smirked, but there was an edge to it.

Once upon a time Blythe had cheated on Armin with Ellis. Still a sore spot. But it had set off the chain reaction that brought us all together, our motley crew with its fetish for justice porn. We hurt those who hurt others. Trolled harder, hit back rougher. Made them regret every shitty little hateful moment of their shitty little hateful lives. Bad begot good, somehow. If you can call cold-blooded vengeance good.

For us, it's not really about justice. There's no justice in a world like this.

It's about trolling the trolls.

I waded through the crowd, pausing when people recognized me and asked for a hug or pic. *You're Ren from YouTube, right? I love your vlog. You're so hot/inspiring/brave.* As if I were born there, online. Which I guess, in a way, I was. My boyhood was a thousand nights spent bathing in the blue glow of my laptop, watching other trans boys raise themselves into men. My stepfathers had names like Chase, Skylar, Ty. A hundred Aidens. (Seriously, what is with trans guys named Aiden?) We're self-made men. We're each other's fathers, and our mother is the Internet.

As I moved through the wash of cool light and hot shadow, I instinctively scanned the male faces around me. My brain caught false flags—a certain angle of smirk, a boldly drawn brow—and I'd stare a man down, my heart thrashing.

It was never him. In five years it hadn't been him.

But I'd never stop looking.

In the unisex bathroom Ellis stood gazing into the mirror, spooling a bang around one finger over and over till it snagged, and she jumped. Professor Carraway, a million light-years off in thought. She was the designated nerd of our little clique, always with a gadget or game controller in hand, more herself online than with real live people. We'd met in Gender in Modern Society freshman year of college. I sat beside her because she was cute. She explained with exquisite politeness that she liked girls. It was the first time I got rejected for being a boy, and it felt fucking awesome.

"How you holding up, old sport?" I said, smoothing my hair.

"Fine."

"Crowd getting to you?"

"Not the crowd. Just certain people in it."

Armin, obviously. "The Wolf's calling a meeting tonight."

Ellis stared into the mirror as if it led to Narnia.

"Space cadet."

"Sorry. I'll be there."

I touched her shoulder. "Go call her."

"I don't—"

"You do. And Vada misses you, too. Promise."

She gave me her bashful boy grin. "How do you do that?"

"Do what?"

"Know what I'm feeling before I do."

I glanced at her phone on the counter. On it was a pic of Vada, her eyes smoky and sly.

"Oh," Ellis said, blushing.

I clapped her shoulder and walked her out.

Vada was the one who'd put that ring on her finger. They lived on the East Coast, on the stone-strewn shore of Maine. Ellis was on temporary loan to us. To me, specifically. *If anything happens to her, I will end you*, Vada had said with a brightly murderous smile, and then punched my arm, printing a small purple flower there. She'd have been a perfect bruiser for our team.

Right. So now you've met us:

Me, the muscle.

Ellis, the tech genius.

Blythe, the charmer.

Armin, the profiler.

And Laney, our fearsome leader.

We are Black Iris.

———

Time to kill before midnight.

The ground level of Umbra, the Cathedral, looked like its namesake: a marble-tiled chamber lined with Gothic arches and stained glass, holy rays in shocking blue and hot pink oscillating over the crowd, their faces upturned, eyes closed in rapture. A Muse track played, the electric organ echoing up into the vaulted ceiling. I prowled toward the center of the dance floor.

I felt . . . hungry.

It wasn't real hunger. A physical craving, definitely oral, but particular. I craved the salt of human skin. The hot copper rush from a
kiss with teeth. I thought of the guy who'd grinded on me, but boys
weren't my thing. If only. At least we're utilitarian in bed.

What I really wanted was wet cherry lips and soft hands and gasps
in my ear as I held a girl against a wall.

Not like I lacked opportunity. My subscribers had a not-so-secret
Fuck Pool whose members approached me saying, *You're my favorite
vlogger, I'm your biggest fan, can I dance with you touch you kiss you*, and
I'd think, *You want that guy on the screen, the guy who looks so hot in
pixels, but IRL when our clothes come off your eyes will soften with pity*,
and so sometimes, too often, I was a preemptive asshole. Me, Mr.
Feminist. The guy who swore he'd never get privilege amnesia, never
forget how shitty it feels to be on the receiving end of misogyny. So
I made a rule:

Don't fuck fans.

Worked pretty well, except for the fact that those fans, at least, totally accepted my trans status. Same couldn't be said of the girls I met
in the real world. Girls who didn't know my history, my *specialness*.

Kinda set myself up to be screwed on both sides here.

I walked into open space as Selena Gomez cued up. This was
the closest I came to satisfying the hunger: getting into the middle
of a crowd and letting go, letting myself fully fill this shell I lived
inside. It started slow. Every other beat a snake of muscle moved
beneath my skin, tightness sliding through me as if I came alive
only in segments. When the track intensified I started hitting each
beat, throwing in a step, a snap turn, my hands playing off my body
percussively. Another guy worked in and we shuffled side by side,
white sneaker soles flashing. Sweat painted my arms with a neon
sheen. Then I stopped feeling the moves, stopped calculating the
next step. I simply existed as motion, kinesis, blur. Energy at a slow
vibration. Pure flow.

The track faded out and another thumped in and I felt eyes on me.

The guy I'd danced with gave me a bro shake. A trio of girls squeed at us. My blood burned, lasers firing in my veins.

This was what I dreamed of in those long dark nights when my body wasn't mine. Someday, I told myself, you'll stand among them and they'll see the boy you are.

It never got old, feeling like *me*.

The moment I saw *her* a thunderclap of silence filled my skull. Everything went dim, stillness spreading from the point where our gazes met. Black ringlets tumbling around her face. Pale hazel eyes, a vivid contrast against dark skin. Tight leather molding to slim curves. Gorgeous, but that wasn't what arrested my attention—it was the way she looked at me. Not coy, not like a fan who'd watched all my vids, but as if she knew me. Really knew me.

We clocked each other across the dance floor. She raised one brow and dissolved into the crowd.

I was on her heels in a heartbeat.

I lost her in the shift and sway of bodies, the ocean of hot breath and damp skin. My pulse was still amped from dancing. Not just from the dancing now. Before T I'd feel instant chemistry with certain girls—lingering eye contact, slow smiles that felt like falling. The sense that instead of air we were surrounded by some clear ether that rippled when we moved, let us feel each other without a touch. After T it became hyperintense. A hard shot of adrenaline, a spinal jolt. Girls' glances hit me physically now in a way that was impossible to ignore.

This girl's glance made me ache harder than I had in for-fucking-ever.

I caught sight of her again, the swish of dark hair gleaming, gone, like ink trickling through the crowd. There she was in the foyer, rounding a pillar. Up the stairs. Across the catwalk while the living sea surged below, movements stamped in freeze-frames as the rave lights flickered.

The girl looked over her shoulder straight at me. Smiled.

When I reached the dead end of the catwalk, she'd vanished.

How the hell?

I stood in a stream of people, scanning. I hadn't seen her double back and slip past. Either she was very good, or I was getting rusty.

And I wasn't getting fucking rusty.

She beat me, somehow. Outmaneuvered me.

Impossible.

And it was quarter to midnight.

I slunk back downstairs. Wandered into the game room with its glow-in-the-dark billiard tables, dartboards tracing the walls like luminous star charts under the black lights. Maybe a quick display of dominance to patch up my ego. There was always some drunk asshole trying to impress. I headed for the small crowd thronging around a likely candidate at the dartboards.

It was her, lobbing a dart dead center into a bull's-eye. In the ultraviolet it burned blue-white, a shooting star.

The crowd cheered.

She rolled another dart between two fingers, smiling. Her leather jacket shone.

Flick of the arm. Bull's-eye.

More cheers. An offer to buy her a drink.

I leaned on a table. Without her looking at me I could sense her awareness. She knew I'd find her here. She wanted me to.

Interesting.

I watched her toss the remaining darts in the shape of a smiley face. The bartender poured her a Guinness on the house. She murmured something, and he set another pint before the empty stool beside her.

Then she turned and looked at me again.

I took the empty seat, raised the drink.

"Cheers," we said at the same moment.

Our heads tipped back. We watched each other through thick glass. The beer was the color of coffee, and as bitter.

"You're very good," I said.

"Actually, I'm very bad."

"I meant at darts. And losing a tail. But I like bad girls."

"Are you a bad boy?"

British accent, silvery, a sterling precision to her words. London, I guessed. Her curls bounced when she moved, filled with a thousand tiny spirals of light.

"Depends who you ask," I said. "How'd you lose me on the catwalk?"

"Trade secret."

I rolled a sip in my throat, savored the taste of loamy earth. "You were a step ahead. Leading me around like a dog on a leash."

"Now, why would I do that?"

Because you know about us.

"Thanks for the drink," I said, standing.

She tapped a nail on the rim of her glass. "Leaving so soon? We've hardly met."

"Got people waiting."

"Tell you what." She took a long slug, and I could not look away from the waves of shadow cascading down her throat. "Beat me and I'll tell you how I outfoxed you."

"I don't hurt women."

"I meant at darts," she said, imitating my deep voice.

I couldn't tell if she was mocking me as a guy or a trans guy. Her tone was dry, ironic, but it had been since she started talking.

Hell with it. "Do you know who I am?"

"Should I?"

"You're new here. I'm Ren."

No reaction.

"*The* Ren. From YouTube."

"Is this the part where I'm starstruck?"

"I saw how you looked at me."

"Same as I look at any pretty boy." Her smile had a cutting quality, slicing my insides to ribbons. "So, Ren from YouTube, are you going to play?"

"We're already playing." My voice was all grit. "And I don't like your game."

As I turned to go, fingertips grazed my forearm. The hair there stirred.

"Be fair. You've charmed me with that lovely face and these exquisite arms. Allow me to return the favor."

This was starting to feel like one big mind-trip.

"Do I get your name?" I said.

"Call me Cressida. Cress, if you like."

Chaucer flickered through my head. No calling her bluff—the names we give ourselves are the truest ones. Even when they're lies.

"Cress," I said, "you seem like trouble."

"Good thing you like bad girls."

"They're my Kryptonite."

"Does that make you Superman?"

"It makes me a stupid boy."

She laughed.

Oh man. Her laugh.

"Play me," she said. "One round."

"All right."

She carried her beer to the dartboard and I tried very hard not to stare at her ass. Until she bent to retie her boot.

Nope.

I made myself count the silver Slinky rings of condensation on a tabletop.

Cress straightened, shot me a look with that crook in the corner of her mouth that never seemed to fade, and yanked the darts from the board.

"What's your game?" I said. "Round the Clock?"

"With a twist."

At a nearby table stood a bottle of Captain Morgan and two shot glasses. She filled one.

"What are you doing?" I said, my hackles rising.

"Looking for a worthy challenger."

"No thanks." I laid my palm atop the second glass before she poured. "I work tonight."

"What line of work are you in?"

"One that needs a clear head."

She shrugged and did her shot. The leather of her jacket creaked. I could smell it, a pleasant mustiness, and the scorched vanilla of the liquor, and a scent that was her, something that made me think of crushed flowers—a sweetness created by violence.

Fuck. Ren. Don't.

Cress didn't say a word about me turning down the challenge. Didn't have to. With a droll look she pivoted and flung a dart without aiming.

Bull's-eye, of course.

She refilled her glass.

I scrubbed a hand through my hair, grimacing.

"If you can't beat me with a head start," she said, "maybe you should find another line of work."

My dumb male ego bristled. I chugged the rest of my beer, belched unrepentantly, and did a shot before my frontal cortex could kick in.

"Judging by your body weight," I said, unabashedly ogling her curves, "we're equally intoxicated. Now give me a dart."

She did.

I glanced once at the board and then, holding her gaze, threw sideways, my arm snapping between our bodies. Just as precise but stronger. I kept my bicep elevated between us, watched her eyes trace the cabled muscle.

Something clattered to the floor. Her dart, dislodged by mine.

"Nicely done," she said.

Ten or fifteen throws later—I don't think either of us was counting anymore—we were soused and the score was tied and the crowd around us revolved, a carousel of weird faces, lurid in their glee. Their voices whirled dizzyingly around me.

"Are you all right?" Cress said.

If I answered, I might puke.

I fumbled for my phone. Twelve thirty-four. Ellis had texted me a wolf emoji followed by an angry face.

Uh-oh.

I was late and Laney was displeased.

Cress eyed me sympathetically. "Shall we call it a draw?"

I leaned on a table. At least I tried to, but my palm slipped and my elbow cracked the wood. "I can keep going."

"You can barely stand." She bent close, a coil of cool black silk tickling my face. Her voice was pitched for me alone. "You're good. I'll grant you that. But I'm better."

"Better at what?"

"Your job." Her fingertip brushed my cheekbone. "Go on, then. Go tend to your dark flowers, little boy."

It took a moment for her words to parse. My head snapped up, eyes clearing. Only strangers remained. I stood and lurched through the crowd, searching, but she was gone.

And that was a very, very big problem.

Because she knew about Black Iris.

"Again," Laney said.

Blythe shrugged, drew her arm back, and smacked me full across the face.

Reality cut out for a sec. When it resumed I was on my knees on a bare concrete floor. Two girls stood over me like executioners.

"Feel anything?" Laney said.

I shook my head.

Her mouth twitched, her expression otherwise placid. Laney rarely displayed anger openly. She'd sooner burn a house down than scream.

"This isn't working," Armin said. "He has to metabolize the alcohol. You can't beat it out of him."

Blythe massaged her palm. "I could try a few more times. It's quite therapeutic."

"Please." Ellis stepped between us. "Enough."

I was still in numb drunk mode, and feeling guilty. Which apparently meant wanting to get beat up by pretty girls. "I'm game. Do it again, Blythe."

"You're not supposed to enjoy this, mate."

Laney muttered and began pacing.

Our meeting chamber lay in the lowest level of Umbra, the Oubliette. The hidden dungeon. In the farthest reach of serpentine stone corridors, in this tangle of Medusa's hair, we made our lair. Dry ice slithered through the halls like viper tongues of vapor. Once upon a time, before Black Iris existed, this was the domain of a secret society at our alma mater. Now it was ours, for our own secret society.

When Laney wanted something, she took it. No matter what—or whom—she had to rip it bloodily from.

We all watched her pace. No one dared break the silence. A lone bare lightbulb threw her shadow at the wall, much bigger than she was. That shadow was jagged, toothy. It seemed about to bite.

"Can I stand?" I said.

Her eyes flicked to me.

"On second thought, I'm good down here."

But Ellis gave me a hand up, and Blythe brushed my cheek, then pecked a kiss where she'd slapped me.

"Worth it," I said.

"Is this funny?" Laney's whisper was frighteningly soft. "Is it funny, Ren?"

"No."

"Let me brief you on tonight's target."

She stopped pacing, her shadow a dark fang jabbing at us.

"He calls himself Crito." Her voice remained soft. We all breathed softer to hear. "That should tell you something. He goes after women online. Ones who talk about the ways men hurt us, threaten us. You'd know some of these girls, Ren. He doxxes them—finds out where they work and live in the real world. Then he mobilizes his troll army." Her fingers twitched. I imagined claws there. "He sends these girls *messages*. One day someone gets harassed on YouTube—typical stuff, 'Kill all feminists,' 'You should be raped until you shut up,' and so on—and then she comes home to a bouquet of flowers at her apartment door. The card inside reads, 'We love watching you.' That's the message: *they can get to her*."

I swallowed. I had my own trolls—you can't be publicly trans without attracting transphobes—but by and large my haters expressed disgust, not threats. They didn't doxx me. They just let me know how much my existence squicked them out. That was male privilege: even trans men took less abuse online than women.

"This guy is basically the leader of a domestic terrorist cell." Laney's eyes burned through me. "He's a rich little white boy with enough resentment and free time to ruin the lives of girls who'll never fuck him. Elliot Rodger is his personal hero. That guy who went on a shooting spree at UCSB and killed half a dozen people. Who wrote a misogynist manifesto saying rejections from girls made him do it. Probably the only reason Crito hasn't shot up his college yet is because he's having too much fun destroying girls' sanity."

So he targeted women who talked about toxic masculinity.

Women like my roommate.

Shit.

"Has he taken it beyond threats?" I said.

"He doesn't have to. Threats are enough. They silence those girls." Laney eyed us each in turn. "We've been letting this cancer grow in *our* city. We've let it hurt people we know. It ends tonight."

"What do we know about him?" I said. "Where does he live, work? Who is he in real life?"

"I've been tracking him. Ellis is building a dossier."

I frowned. "*You've* been tracking him? Personally?"

"I have eyes and ears in the city."

"I'm your eyes and ears. You should have sent me, Lane."

"I wanted to send you *tonight*."

I flinched.

Blythe tossed her head, hair snapping around her shoulders in golden flames. "We know where he is, right? The rest of us can take him down. Cut off the head, and the body dies."

"It's not that simple," Ellis said, eyeing her nervously. "Crito's established a hierarchy. If he goes quiet, his minions will pick up where he left off."

"Not if we make an example of him. What's that phrase you Yanks love? 'Shock and awe.'"

"We're not taking it that far," Armin said. "We don't kill."

Laney stared at him a long moment. "Right. We don't."

Then her gaze flashed again to me.

I averted mine. Faked a groan, collapsed into a cracked leather armchair. Put a hand to my head.

Armin said, "It's no use. We have to reschedule, Lane."

"We can't. I paid people off."

"We'll pay them off again."

"The mousetrap is set for *tonight*. His roommate's out of town. Things won't line up like this for months." I could almost hear her teeth gritting. "I planned this out perfectly."

"And I fucked it all up," I said. "Because I'm not perfect, like you."

Laney didn't respond, which was response enough.

"He made a mistake," Armin said. "This is why there's a plan B."

Fraternal solidarity. How nice.

"What's plan B?" I said.

Laney looked at me, expressionless, then headed for the door. Before it opened she said, "Reconvene tomorrow. Same time. Show up sober, or don't show up again."

Heavy steel creaked and slammed, so loud it made my teeth ring.

And then there were four. I sank deeper into the chair. Blythe turned to go and Armin caught her hand.

"I'll talk to Lane," he said.

"She needs me."

"You'll just set each other off. Let me defuse her."

There was a weird bond between those three. Laney and Blythe were girlfriends, madly in love; Armin was the pseudo-platonic ex who arbitrated their fights, smoothed their jagged edges, kept them together while he lived through them vicariously. Blythe called it a two-and-a-half-sided love triangle. It was sad, clinging to something dead like that.

To someone who didn't love you the way you loved them.

Blythe scrunched Armin's sleeve in her fist and let go. The door opened and closed again, gentler.

"Bloody hell," she said when he was gone. "I wouldn't mind dismantling the shit out of that bloke."

"Armin?" Ellis said, looking horrified. But not too horrified.

"No, little bird. That arsehole, 'Crito.' Talk about bloody pretentiousness." Blythe sank her nails into a leather chair back. "Every men's-rights fuckwit fancies himself some Greek philosopher. A beacon of pure reason, shining a light on our womanly hysteria."

"You know," Ellis said, "that word itself is sexist. 'Hysteria' literally means 'suffering in the womb.' The ancient Greeks actually thought the uterus drove women crazy."

"Here we are two thousand years later, and some blokes still think it does."

I shifted uncomfortably.

Thing is, some blokes *have* a uterus.

"So what's this plan B?" I said, changing the subject.

"Who bloody knows. Lane never tells me anything."

"She's been watching this guy for a while, but never mentioned him before."

Ellis cleared her throat. "Actually, we've kind of known about him the whole time."

" 'We'?" I said.

"Well, me. I mean, obviously all our missions lately were connected. The flower bouquets, the threatening cards. It's his signature move. We just didn't know who was behind them."

"Crito," I muttered, stroking my stubble.

Ellis eyed me. Then she eyed Blythe. Then she bit her lip.

"You have that thinky look," I said.

"It's nothing."

"That means it's definitely something."

Ellis took a step back, loosening her tie. Behind those Buddy Holly glasses, her clear green eyes bounced between us.

"What do you know, E?" I said. "Laney said you've built a dossier."

"She'd kill me if I shared it."

"We're all on the same side here." I stood. "I want to see that data, Ellis."

She looked pleadingly at Blythe. Blythe merely shrugged.

"I can't, Ren."

"Then just give me the address. That's all I need. I can take this scumbag out myself."

"Laney set everything up a particular way. If we mess with it, who knows what could happen."

I could redeem myself, I thought. And then ask for the favor I wanted. "We go way back, old sport. Do me a solid."

Ellis was grimacing. "Let's wait till tomorrow. Ren, you're not sober. Maybe that's a sign this wasn't supposed to happen."

"Since when do you believe in signs, Professor?"

"I don't. I'm just saying—" She sighed and glared at Blythe. "Could you back me up here?"

"Mate, Laney doesn't like anyone fucking with her plans. She's allergic to the unexpected. It makes her bite people's heads off."

"If I didn't know better, I'd say you two know something you're not telling me."

Ellis tossed her hands up. "We're just trying to keep you out of trouble."

"Blythe's middle name is trouble."

"It's Spencer, actually." Ellis sighed again, but with resignation. "This is a really bad idea. If you mess up—"

"Give me an hour and I'll be fine. I'm a professional, E. I don't mess up."

Blythe cackled and said, "Famous last words."

———

An hour later I clung to a rusty fire escape on the side of an apartment complex, gazing out over the sleeping city. From far away the lights were a swarm of gold fireflies, flickering as if a finger stirred them. When a breeze broke through the thick heat, tinged with the lake's coolness and a freckling of raindrops, I felt a wild impulse to swing over the rail, swan dive to the pavement.

Testosterone was supposed to toughen me up. But sometimes it gave me just enough edge to make me a danger to myself.

And to others? Always.

I climbed to the top floor. Night sky above, clouds crumpled like foil paper. The window before me was a grimy mirror. In it, a man clad in Kevlar met my stare. Raindrops spattered his masked face, tiny globes of mercury.

I slid a shim into the window frame, caught the lock and lifted. Chilled air rolled out. No movement. Down in the alley Blythe flicked her flashlight, two blinks. All clear.

I whispered into my headset.

REN: I'm in. No sign of target.
ELLIS: His IP traces there. He's inside. Be careful.

Inside the bedroom the cool blooms of LEDs pulsed in the darkness. I slunk through the shadows, listening. Dead silence. A too-pure, too-still silence, like something that lay tightened, waiting.

The computer showed a black screen saver. I bumped the mouse. Some online video game. I aimed my body cam at it.

ELLIS: Something's wrong.
REN: What?
ELLIS: Look at the screen.

I tilted my chest to give them a clearer view.

BLYTHE: That creature is hitting him.
ELLIS: He's just standing there in a dangerous area.
REN: Why would he do that?
ELLIS: Because he was interrupted. I think we should abort, guys.
REN: Relax. We just got here.

I pulled the .40 from my rib holster and screwed on the suppressor.

My muscles flexed, every fiber coiling, ready. I sidled through the apartment and paused at each door. Bathroom, kitchen, living room: all empty.

ELLIS: I don't like this. I've got a bad feeling.
BLYTHE: Go back to the bedroom. Now.
ELLIS: Why?
BLYTHE: Because I just saw a shadow in the window.

Goose bumps stippled my arms. I gripped the gun tighter.

When I returned to the bedroom I felt that tension in the air, an elusive vibration. Higher now.

The closet door was wide open. It had been closed when I arrived.

I raised my weapon and stalked toward it. Switched the gun light on, prepared to shoot.

No one. Oxfords and chinos, hanging still.

My shoulders unknit. Light off. I began to turn.

And the shadows in the corner *breathed*.

My spine snapped straight. I aimed and at the same time heard the swoop of displaced air, saw the darkness arc with motion.

Someone was aiming at me.

"Drop your weapon," I barked.

Something clicked.

I was a hair from firing when light exploded in my face. It swiveled aside, and the afterimage cleared. There was a woman.

"Drop yours," she said.

A woman with a smart British accent. The very same one who'd baited me at Umbra.

Cressida.

BLYTHE: Who the bloody hell?

ELLIS: She's got our target.

A mass of shadow sprawled on the bed behind her. Two faint white gleams. Eyes. The rest of the man appeared to be thoroughly duct-taped.

"What are you doing here?" I demanded of Cress.

"Lower your weapon. Then we'll talk."

"No chance. You first."

"Count of three, then."

BLYTHE: Don't trust her.

ELLIS: You don't have a choice. Just do it.

BLYTHE: I'm coming up.

ELLIS: No. Artemis, stay put. If you barge in she'll shoot you.

"One," Cress said.

Our code names represented our primal selves. Blythe was Artemis, the wild huntress, fierce and indomitable, beholden to no man. Ellis was Blue, the boy she was inside. The part of her she'd hidden for so long.

And I was Cane. You know why.

"Two."

Metal creaked on the fire escape. The duct-taped mummy moaned through his gag.

"Three."

And this was where I made a mistake.

I trusted my gut and lowered the gun. "What are—"

"Wrong move," Cress said.

Before I could blink, something struck me in the face.

If I weren't still battling the dregs of my drunkenness I would've taken it like a champ and struck back, but instead I staggered, fell. Flailed wildly and shattered the computer screen, glass talons slashing at my skin. I rolled with the impact. Cressida's boot stomped an inch from my head and I seized a handful of debris and hurled it, blind. A nebula of shards and dust spun around us.

Cress recoiled. My gun was on her instantly.

"Lower your weapon," I growled.

She took aim.

I hurled myself forward and dragged her to the floor. Our limbs locked, her leather groaning under my grip, her nails skittering for purchase on my body armor. We twined together and rolled through the glass and for a moment the violence was almost elegant, like some full-contact ballet. We moved the same way. All grace and flow. Absurdly I thought: she's a dancer, too. Then we paused and she crouched over me, panting, and I hesitated. She didn't.

An elbow decked my jaw. I flipped her, pinned her to the hardwood.

Our faces were inches apart. Summer rain and warm sweat filled my senses.

"Stop," I rasped. "I'm not here for you."

"You're good, bad boy. But you hold back too much. That's why you're going to lose."

Her knee swung straight between my legs.

It hurt—getting hit that hard anywhere hurts—and I slammed her down, knocking her breathless. Cress lay limp. Confusion reeled across her face. She hadn't braced for impact, assuming she'd crushed my balls.

For a second I actually felt shitty for winning this fight. Because of the way I won. Because of what it meant.

I stood, confiscating her weapon. Same caliber, suppressed. She swayed to her feet.

"Get out of here," I said. "Last chance."

A steel fang ripped through the darkness. Her knife. Instead of firing I flung my arm out, to catch blade on bone.

Don't hurt her, don't hurt her.

Then Blythe flew through the window and tackled us both.

The knife spun away in a fan of silver. The two girls thrashed across the floor, knocking lamps over, a bookshelf they both deftly avoided, a TV neither of them did. I trained my light on them, a blur of slender bodies twisting around and around in vicious helixes.

"Freeze," I bellowed.

Cress perched over Blythe, but she'd paid for it. Red stripes raked down her neck.

And then it happened.

The knock at the front door.

"Hello?" a woman called.

ELLIS: Oh, *shit*.

Prim-and-proper Ellis rarely swore. This was bad.

I moved toward the guy on the bed.

"Stop," Cress hissed. "You take that gag off, he'll scream for help."

Tapeface shook his head *no* emphatically.

Another knock.

"Hello? I live below you. I heard things breaking. Are you okay?"

"Oh, for Christ's—" Blythe shouldered Cress off and sat up. Her voice turned saccharine. "Er, we're a little *busy* right now."

And she gave a low moan.

And giggled.

From the hall, a pause, then, "Oh. Sorry. I didn't mean to—sorry."

Footsteps, receding.

I gestured at Cress with my gun. "Stand up."

Slowly she rose, eyes locked on me. Glass cascaded off her jacket and plinked musically on the floor. Blythe pursed her lips and spit a mouthful of blood, dark as wine.

ELLIS: Are you guys hurt?

REN: I'm fine. Artemis?

BLYTHE: Think she broke my bloody rib.

ELLIS: Can you breathe okay?

BLYTHE: I'll live. Especially if I can hit her again.

ELLIS: You need to get *out* of there.

REN: And how do we do that with two hostile captives?

ELLIS: I don't know. I think . . . maybe we should leave Crito to her.

BLYTHE: You're joking.

ELLIS: No, I'm not. We're not supposed to be here, Artemis. Who knows what we're *interfering* with.

Cressida watched us as we spoke, not missing a word. Her gaze ricocheted around the room. Planning a move. She was trained, very well trained, but those eyes filled with curiosity when they landed on me. I'd surprised her.

You were wrong, I thought. I'm not some cocky prick who throws his strength around carelessly. I learned how to survive just like you did.

In a female body.

Crito squirmed and mumbled into his gag. It almost sounded like "She's going to kill me."

"What are you doing here?" I asked Cress. "Who are you?"

"How amusing. I know who you are, yet you don't know me."

"You know a lot of things you shouldn't. That's not good for your long-term health."

Blythe kneaded her side. "Let me beat the truth out of her."

ELLIS: [Mutters inaudibly.]
BLYTHE: What?
ELLIS: I said, "Don't you think that's kind of overkill, Artemis?"
BLYTHE: Me, taking it too far? Never.

I circled closer, putting Cress between me and Blythe. "I don't want to hurt you. But if you don't start talking, I'll have no choice."

Blythe's hand crawled toward the knife strapped to her thigh.

Cressida stood there calmly, loose limbed. In the harsh white beam her eyes were pale gold. Small galaxies of crushed glass sparkled around us, dusting the tumbled books like snow.

"You won't hurt me," she said. "You've had three chances and failed."

"I didn't fail. I was trying *not* to hurt you."

"How noble. So chivalry isn't dead."

"What do you want with this guy?"

"Same as you." She glanced at him icily. "To give him a taste of true fear."

Crito's eyes bugged.

REN: Anyone else bother to notice that this girl's not wearing a mask?
ELLIS: So?
REN: So she's not worried who sees her face. Because she's not
      planning to leave witnesses.

Something flashed in Cress's gaze like the flick of a switchblade.
Light carved through the shadows. Cress hooked a foot around

Blythe's ankle just as Blythe swung her knife. I fired low, a disabling shot, but Cress anticipated and juked. She barreled at me and I braced for it, which was just what she wanted, because I felt her wrench the gun from my hand.

I couldn't shoot at point-blank range. Not her.

Not a woman.

So instead I let her disarm me and thought: This is the way I die.

She dropped the muzzle in line with my heart.

Then pivoted neatly and fired at the bed.

Crito heaved himself away, and Cress kept firing, a sound like giant needles puncturing the air. Feathers jetted up from the quilt. On the white wall above us burst a Rorschach rose painted in blood.

I flung myself at Cress, smothered her against the bed. Her body beneath me was toned and tight, but small. Easy to overpower when I gave myself free rein. Blythe darted in to disarm her.

"You damned idiot," Cress said. "I'm—"

I pressed her face into the mattress as Blythe cuffed her with a zip tie.

"Shut up," I said, "or I'll gag you, too."

When I released her she shot me a cold glower but didn't speak.

Quiet permeated the room. Only the redness and rain were alive, falling.

ELLIS: Oh my god. Is he—

Crito flopped onto his back, groaning.

BLYTHE: Much as it pains me to be thankful for this, he survived.

Heavy pounding on the front door. Now a man's voice said, "Open up. I know there's a lady in there with you, asshole. What have you done to her?"

"And the shit just got deeper," Blythe said.

Cress smiled. "Could you have fucked this up any more thoroughly?"

"What did I tell you about talking?"

She kept smiling till I fished the roll of duct tape from my field pack.

"Listen," she said. "We're on the same side."

"Why is your mouth still moving?"

"You don't want to do this." I stepped closer, and she blurted, "The Little Wolf sent me, you oaf. *I'm* plan B."

Blythe and I stared at each other, startled.

ELLIS: Oh. Huh. I . . . hmm.

"If the Wolf really sent you," I said, "you'd know this is a nonlethal takedown."

"And if *you* could hold your bloody rum," she spat back, "you'd know I'm here to do the job you couldn't. She sent me to knock the stuffing out of him and record it. We put that on the Internet, it'll scare his lackeys shitless."

Footsteps thumped in the hall. More voices.

"There's no time for this," Cressida said. "Untie me."

"No." I hauled her to her feet. "You're coming with us."

When I tugged, she resisted.

"You can't leave this unfinished," she said.

We both looked at the bleeding man.

I handed Cress off to Blythe. Knelt on the bed, took Crito's jaw in my hand. From the hall, someone called, "The police are on their way."

Weight hurled at the door. They were trying to break it down.

"Wake up, fuckboy." I shook Crito till his eyes opened. On his shoulder was a wet red welt, fragrantly sweet. Burnt goose down and gunpowder tinged the air bitter. "Look at me."

His eyes focused.

In the darkness, with his face bloodied and taped and distorted by fear, I hadn't realized what I'd been seeing.

I knew him.

My body went cold. We stared at each other and in horror I waited for him to recognize me, but his fear remained solid, unwavering.

My mask, my voice. The stubble shading my jaw.

Of course. He wouldn't know me like this.

I felt Cress's gaze and swallowed. "You got lucky tonight." The words grated from my throat, but in my mind I heard my old self narrating in her thin, fluting voice. "Time to make some life changes, buddy. You know what I'm talking about. If I ever see your face again, I'll put a bullet in it. Clear?"

Another shake, for good measure. He groaned. It might've been *yes*.

A splintery crash from the front room.

"Cane, *now*," Blythe called from the window.

Gauzy light drifted through the glass, setting the raindrops aglitter like sequins. I ducked beneath the sash as the door banged open behind me.

We fled down the fire escape, skidding on slick iron. Reached the alley just as police sirens sounded. Red and blue lights raced over rainbright asphalt like jags of electricity. We dragged Cress between us and she fought and we stumbled and it kept coming back in flashes: The sting of her bullets piercing the air. Plumes of pale fire. The wet sound of blood slapping the wall.

She tried to kill him.

A man I knew. One I'd have killed to forget.

Rain needled the top of my head, stitching a chill all the way down my spine.

Ellis had the SUV running. We scrambled inside as the crunch of cruiser doors echoed, hustled Cress into the backseat between us. Ellis pumped the gas and drove with controlled franticness, and we all held our breath, staring through a veil of neon haze and falling diamonds, waiting for the sirens to catch up. They never did. We hit every green on the way back to Umbra, but all I saw was red.

———

The Little Wolf was waiting.

As we walked into the meeting chamber, her expression went from studiously blank—Laney's version of furious—to bewildered. She touched Blythe's mouth. Blood transferred to her fingertips.

"Please tell your thug to unhand me," Cress said dryly.

Laney blinked. "Untie her, Ren."

I slid my knife against Cress's wrist and paused, touching cold carbon to her skin. Then I cut her loose.

If she made a wrong move, she'd regret it.

Laney regarded us each in turn and settled on me. Those big eyes were luminously blue, teal marbled with aqua, little schisms of sea light. They seemed innocent, artless, but she always stared too long until you felt your layers peeling, your tendernesses rising to the surface. She left you feeling soft and raw, exposed. Laney said she learned that look from her mother.

Ordinarily I would've thrown myself at her feet and begged for mercy. Now I faced her with reserve, picturing Crito's face.

"I can explain," Ellis began.

"Just tell me: Is Crito dead?"

"No," Cress said, elongating the vowel. "But he *is* bleeding quite profusely, so it's certainly a possibility."

Ellis fidgeted. "This is all my fault. I'm sorry."

"No, it's my fault," Blythe said.

I said nothing.

Cressida raised her eyebrows, amused.

"I don't care whose fault it is," Laney said. "I care that you went behind my back. All three of you."

Blythe crossed her arms. "Technically, you went behind *our* backs. Trusting an outsider, sending her out alone—"

"Blythe," Armin said sharply.

"What? I'm saying what we're all thinking. Right?" Blythe cocked her chin at Cress and I. "You sent *her* when you should have sent *him*."

Laney's mouth tightened. "*He* was drunk."

"Off his arse," Cress said cheerfully.

"But he's one of us," Blythe said. "And he deserved to be a part of it. Drunk or not."

I suddenly had the uncanny sense that two conversations were occurring: one I understood, and one lying beneath that, full of allusions and riddles.

"What are you—" I began.

"Don't." Laney stared stonily at Blythe. "Don't question me, either of you. That's not how this works. I run the show."

"You deliberately withheld information from him."

"I did what needed to be done to protect us all, Blythe."

"You're keeping secrets from us. From your friends."

"For good reason. Because otherwise you'll fly off the handle and do something stupid, like you did tonight."

"Oh, sure. Blame it on good old manic Blythe, and hothead Ren, and tagalong Ellis."

Ellis winced. Blythe could be brutally blunt, especially when pissed.

I shifted my weight and Laney looked at me, and I almost said, *So when were you going to tell me I know Crito? That you're going after someone from my past?*

But something stayed my tongue. Some inarticulable misgiving. The air pulled taut around me, thickening like a web.

He deserved to be a part of it.

Armin spread his hands. "Let's not character-assassinate each other, okay? Laney knows what she's doing. Tonight was our window of opportunity. We had to take action."

"Besides," Cress said crisply, "I needn't have shot him if you bumbling twits hadn't cocked the whole thing up. You weren't supposed to be there."

My jaw tensed. "If you hadn't tried so hard to prove you're better than me, it might've gone smoother."

"If you weren't so butthurt about losing to a girl, perhaps it might have."

"I didn't lose. And it makes no difference that you're a girl."

"You certainly seem to resent the comparison."

"Stop putting words in my mouth."

Cress merely gave me that cool, sardonic look.

Hothead Ren indeed. I made myself unclench my fists.

No comment from Laney, but her expression silenced us. A bar ran along the back of the room and Blythe stomped over and sifted through bottles, tossing empties. Shards burst across the floor, amber, tourmaline, crystal, a jagged jewel puzzle. Eventually I realized she didn't want a drink but simply to break stuff. No one stopped her. That was Blythe: her emotions manifested physically, whirling around her like debris in a cyclone.

"Where does this leave us?" I said.

Armin answered calmly over the shattering glass. "It depends. Gunshot wounds have to be reported to the police. He might seek discreet care to stay off their radar. Last thing he wants is police attention."

"So we lay low," I said. "See how it plays out."

Laney wrapped her small hands around a wooden chair. "And tell all the people we've promised to help that we can't help them now."

She stood very still for a moment. Then she flipped the chair over.

Everyone froze. Blythe clutched a bottle in her fist, light skittering over it as she trembled.

"This is on you," Laney said, not looking at anyone. "You tell them that we can't help. That we got their hopes up for nothing. That we lied to them."

If that misgiving hadn't taken root in me, I would've stayed silent. Cowed.

But now I said, "You lied to *me*."

Her head swiveled slowly.

"You knew," I said, trying to steel my voice. "You knew that *I* knew Crito."

The others watched us, tense.

"Why didn't you tell me, Laney?"

"Why do you think?" No rise in her tone. Totally calm. "Because I didn't want you to worry. Not until I knew what he was up to."

"So you sent this—this *outsider* after him." Blythe's word fit well. "You didn't trust me to handle him."

"I didn't trust you not to make it personal. I didn't trust you not to get emotional. Like you are right now."

Her words stung like a slap.

"I'm not emotional," I said, my voice quavering.

Perfect.

Laney shrugged. "This is what I mean. I'm sorry, Ren, but you're off the Crito case. Cressida will take your place."

"Laney—"

"Take some time to unwind. Clear your head."

I watched her walk to the door. The air in her wake seemed to scintillate with cold. Before she left she paused, glancing back at me.

"And tell your roommate to be careful. Because you woke a sleeping dog. Now he's hurt, and pissed off. And he'll want blood."

-3-

It was dawn by the time I got home. Soft lilac shadow filled the apartment, vines of sunlight curling through the pastel gloom as the city woke. Ingrid's cat wove infinity symbols around my feet.

I washed the dishes in the sink. Took out the garbage. Fed the cat. Kept moving, moving. There was a rabid energy in me, an anxiety I hadn't felt in ages. It wasn't only the fact that I had twelve dollars in my bank account and owed seven hundred for this month's rent. It wasn't that I started recording a vlog and stopped it three, four times before finally giving up. It wasn't that I'd fucked up Laney's plans, got myself put on involuntary hiatus from Black Iris.

It was *him*.

That face from my past. A link to all I'd left behind.

To the girl I was.

I stood in the living room and stared at a painting hanging in a pool of pale sun. Vada and I used to geek out over myths, and one time I told her the legend of Caeneus. Weeks later I came home to a canvas wrapped in brown paper leaning against the front door.

The note read *For when it's hard to keep your head above water.* My hands shook as they tore the wrapping. In the painting a boy stood at the edge of the ocean, his back to a towering tsunami wave. Water slammed against him and sprayed outward in a halo of foam and salt, but he held strong. In the froth above him was a face, Poseidon screaming, dissolving, powerless. I cried for the first time in a year on T.

She'd titled it *He's Still Breathing.*

The painting blurred.

Sunlight filled my tears, blinded me with liquid gold. Morning. Time for my daily dose.

I fumbled a packet of T gel out of the medicine cabinet, stripped my shirt off. Stared at the man in the mirror. Sometimes I still saw her—the girl I'd been born from, the body I broke through like a chrysalis. At my lowest, in my ugliest moments of sorrow and fear, she'd bleed through and I'd see the skinny chest crammed into a binder, the smooth cheeks flocked with fuzz. Not a girl. Barely a boy. Mostly a child, full of terror.

Still there, beneath the hard muscle and coarse skin. Still haunting me.

I unzipped my jeans. Cupped the bulge in my boxer briefs.

After all this time, part of me was still *her.* Part of me could still be hurt the way men hurt women.

You mean you never put it in? Crito had said. IRL, his name was Jay. I was standing in a hallway, hidden, listening to him talk. *Her blowjob is that good, huh?*

So?

So I'm just saying, it's kind of gay. All she does is suck your dick and jerk you off. That's so faggy.

Shut up, Jay.

C'mon, man. Look at her. She looks like a dude. You're fucking a dude.

I said shut the hell up.

It always came down to this. This fucking broken part of me.

I sank to the edge of the bathtub. Water, all over my face. Couldn't breathe.

"Hey, you."

A hand fell on my shoulder.

Ingrid, my roommate. Touching me. Touching the wet testosterone gel on my shoulder.

I shoved her away, too hard. Then I was on my feet, turning the tap to hot. "Wash it off. Immediately."

Her arm rose, as if she feared I'd hit her.

"What the hell is wrong with you, Inge? Wash it off."

"What the hell is wrong with *you*?"

I made myself inhale, exhale, counting each. "Please rinse it off before it's absorbed. It's highly potent. You don't want it in you."

"I know. But you're kind of *freaking me the fuck out*. Will you calm down?"

I gave her space at the sink and an imploring look. She eyed me strangely.

"Uh, dude."

My fucking pants, halfway down my thighs.

I zipped up as she washed the gel off.

"What is going on?" she said, toweling her hands. "Were you crying?"

"I'm fine."

"What happened? You woke me up with all that noise."

"Sorry. Anxiety cleaning."

Ingrid leaned on the counter. "You are being totally weird. Talk to me, caveman."

You can't hide shit from your best friend. Even if she's not really your best friend anymore.

We'd been thick as thieves in high school. Girls' basketball, all four years—I was the one to her two, running point for the Nordic queen with the glacier-blue eyes. Svensson and Khoury, the demon duo. No one fucked with us on or off the court. In college things changed. I started my transition, and the tightness between us unraveled. *All you ever talk about is hormones*, she said, *and we just finished being teenagers.* Inge was witheringly sarcastic, but one night she looked at me with abject sincerity and said, *It's like we're not on the same team anymore.* We stayed together to save rent. Exchanged inanities, like hostel guests. *Is it raining today? I bought milk. It's your turn to clean the shower.* I didn't know who she was dating, what her plans were. What she thought of the man I'd become. It was too painful to part ways and too painful to keep up with each other's ephemera, so we fell into friendship purgatory. Ghosting in and out of rooms, starting sentences with *Do you remember when* and then trailing off, grieved. Once, when a Black Iris escapade made the news—we exposed a date-rape drug ring in a notorious frat by drugging the ringleaders with their own product and tying them up, naked, on the campus common—Inge watched, and said, "Social fucking justice."

She was still my sister-in-arms. If only she knew.

"I'm broke," I said, and more words followed, in a flood. "I'm broke, and I can't record a video for shit, and I fucked up this . . . big project a friend was working on, and I almost—" I caught myself, laughed.

"You almost what?"

"I almost feel like I'm PMSing again. How crazy is that?"

Ingrid studied my face. Same age, but I looked years older now. T carved the softness off. "Are you seriously broke?"

"I'm sorry. I'll have rent, just a little late."

She sighed. "Again."

"I can probably borrow it from Ar—"

"What about this?" Inge jabbed a hand at my shoulder. "You have the money to pay for this shit, but not the roof over our heads."

"Ingrid. This is a medical necessity for me."

"Give me a fucking break. You won't die without testosterone. You might even be tolerable to be around."

At first I hardened. It was always like this now: All emotions started as resistance. A fight inside me. Flare of acid in my throat, a chemical fuse between gut and mouth. Brace against it. Hold it back. This is why men are quick to anger—everything we feel is an assault.

In the past, my dead self would have taken her words right into the soft pulp of my heart. I would have let them hurt me. I would have *felt* them.

Now my mind filled with cruelties like *Sorry that you don't like me now that I like myself* and *You've kinda been a cunt these days, too*. Words I used to say to her with impunity. I couldn't say them now, in a man's voice. It was different. Everything was different.

"I'll have the money on the first," I said.

"Oh, come on." She flung her hands up. "I'll cover you. Just pay me back when you can."

"I don't want your charity."

"It's not charity, asshole. It's having your back."

Neither of us quite looked at the other. Silence stretched, twisted. Then, simultaneously, we both made fists and bumped them: one-two, switch sides, three-four. In the back of my head I heard the crowd chant our names. *Svens-SON. Khou-RY.* Sneakers squeaking on glazed hardwood. The buzzer blaring as my feet left the floor.

Something knotted unpleasantly in my chest.

"I'm making breakfast," Ingrid said. "Want some?"

"I'm good."

"Gonna stop by your parents' this week."

"Okay."

"Any presents for the princesses?"

"I really am broke, Inge."

"Then I'll pick something up. Say it's from you."

Water welled in my throat.

When I didn't respond she shrugged, turned to go. My hand half rose. I wanted those fingertips back on my skin, dangerous or not. I wanted human contact. Her contact.

"Ingrid."

"Yeah?"

There were a million things I wanted to ask. *Are you happy? Do you miss what we had? Do you miss me?* Instead what left my mouth was "Are you still writing for that site?"

"Which?"

"That feminist one. Where you talk about toxic masculinity and shit."

"'And shit,'" she echoed drolly. "I write for lots of feminist sites. How else do you think I pay rent, meathead?"

Half-truth. Ingrid sat on a very cozy trust fund. "Could you maybe . . . take a break? At least from your more incendiary pieces. It's dangerous to associate your real name with that stuff right now."

"I've got a brand to maintain. You know how it is—you do the same on YouTube."

"Maintaining that brand is much more dangerous for you than me, Inge."

"Why's that?"

"Because women like you are being targeted by the men's-rights lynch mob. And I'm worried."

She held my gaze. Inge's intelligence was implacable, and somewhat predatory. A Venus flytrap patiently closing around each thought. I could never ask her an innocent question—in seconds she'd discover what I really meant, unearth every ulterior motive.

"Women like me," she said, "are always being targeted by men. I'll be fine, Boy Scout."

Unlike Cressida, there was no mistaking her mockery. The words "men" and "boy" dripped with irony.

Another moment of silent eye contact. The air between us teemed with all we'd left unsaid.

Ingrid touched the door and I said, "Wait."

Her head half turned.

I miss you. "Tell my princesses I love them."

Her face was pale and smooth as milk glass, her eyes empty. But finally she cracked that conspiratorial smile I knew so well.

When she left I locked the door behind her. My palm stung. I was crushing the gel packet, wasting my precious T. The drug I had to take every single day for the rest of my life.

Or else die.

Not directly. Inge was right about that. But my life wasn't worth living without it. Testosterone was a medical necessity because it was all that made living inside this body bearable.

She didn't get that. Nobody did.

If only they knew what it felt like, being held hostage by your own skin.

TODAY

DELETED VLOG: DEPRESSION

REN: This is the fifth time I've tried to make this video. Fuck it. Fuck putting a brave face on things. I'm not well, Internet. I'm telling one million strangers instead of telling my therapist, because I can't afford him right now and what is therapy, really, but reflecting ourselves at another person and seeing what bounces back? Maybe I'll find myself scattered somewhere in these million shards. Maybe all the pixels will come together, coalesce into a portrait of a sad, lost boy.

I'm depressed.

I haven't said that out loud for years. It feels . . . terrifying.

Last time I owned my depression was before I started T. Back then I thought it was just part of dysphoria. Once I fixed my body, once my brain soaked up the right hormone, I thought it'd stop. And for a while it did. Or at least transition kept me busy, distracted. There was always the next milestone to look forward to: My voice dropping, my beard coming in, my curves flattening out. Top surgery. Official document changes.

I mean, just look. Look at how I used to be.

[Cut to an older video clip.]

. . . and my voice is *still* dropping. It feels like roots growing up through my chest, tangling around my throat. I can't sing for shit. Like, it's seriously bad. My roomie imposed a moratorium on shower singing. She'll freeze me out—she flushes the toilet if I so much as hum. Thinks it's funny when I scream in my new man voice. I kinda hoped I'd be a tenor, but I guess I'll never have to worry about passing vocally now . . .

[Cut to another clip.]

You guys. You see this? This is my brand-spanking-new Illinois driver's license. And that, right there, under *Sex*? That says *Male*.

[Cut to another clip.]

So, I did it. I scheduled top surgery. Three months from now, I'll let a man in a mask drug me and touch my tits. When I wake up, I'll have the adolescent boy-chest of my wildest dreams. This is happening. Really, truly happening. I feel . . . terrified. In a good way. I feel hopeful.

[Cut to the present.]

That was my life. Milestone to milestone.

Now I'm all out of goals. Transition goals, anyway. All I've got left is to *live*.

And I'm fucking miserable.

I don't get it. How was I more hopeful back then, before I passed, before people called me "sir" without snickering, before they shut up when I spoke and treated me with basic human decency because they assume I have a dick?

My therapist calls it post-transition depression. It's sort of like postpartum: You've done something big, something life-changing. You've given a piece of yourself away to make something new. Birth hurts; rebirth hurts, too.

The weird thing is you can grow fond of pain. Of the sense

of meaning it gives your stress and anxiety. When it's gone, you drift. There's no context anymore for why you feel down. You're just empty. There's an inexplicable ache, a hollowness that hungers for a cause. There should be something there, a knife, a thorn, something causing you to bleed. But there's nothing.

You just hurt, for no fucking reason at all.

God, what is wrong with me?

I can't upload this. I can't. It's career suicide. I've got a *brand* to maintain, after all. The Internet pays to hear my oh-so-inspirational story of overcoming adversity. Nobody wants to hear how sad I am—you're all fucking sad, too. The world is a cold, ugly place and you want me to be the shining light, the warm fuzzy feeling that gets you through the day. The Little Boy Who Could. I'm a trained fucking monkey, and all these likes and comments are the peanuts you throw to make me do tricks.

What a joke. I can't be real. I'm playing another role, Mr. Happy, Well-Adjusted Trans Guy. Because that's the narrative. The only story I'm allowed to tell is how much I hated myself before transition, how happy I am now.

I'm alone. One million people are watching my every move, and I'm utterly alone.

Fuck this.

[Reaches to turn off the camera.]

TODAY

VLOG #344: GIVEAWAY!

REN: Hey, Internet! It's your boy Ren here. Excuse the dark circles beneath my eyes—been a long night. Nothing exciting, I promise. I'm not on drugs. I'm not in love. Still Ren Solo.

That's . . . that's fucking terrible. Sorry. Fuck, should I start over? Cut!

[Jump cut.]

So I promised you guys I'd have something awesome for you today, and here it is. Are you sitting down? At your resting heart rate? Okay. Today I'm doing an *epic* giveaway.

[Ren tilts the camera to show a cardboard box stamped with logos.]

My sponsor, Windy City Fitness, sent this *huge* crate of goodies to review. There's way more product than I can use, so I'm gonna share the love. Check this out: whey protein powder, creatine, natural testosterone boosters, the works. Everything you need to get ripped like yours truly here. Shout-out to Windy City Fitness for making what I do possible.

Guys, real talk: You don't get rich slapping your face on the 'Tube. I earn *pennies* for every video I put up. And making videos isn't easy—it takes time, energy, skill. I rely on sponsors to fill in the gaps: everything from the food I eat to the clothes on my back. It all comes from the support of companies like this. So show them some love and hit that link in the description below. They keep my electricity and Wi-Fi on.

Now, let's get to the nitty-gritty. I've been taking this whey protein for a while, and . . .

———

For weeks Black Iris lay low. Laney didn't want to ping Crito's radar. Neither of us spoke of my connection to him—it felt tense, furled, like something I had to wait out till it unraveled. So I waited. Ellis and I sat on the roof of Umbra beneath a summer sky molting into autumn, shedding blue scales for silver. Leaves laureled our feet, the green slowly bronzing. Fall cast the city in precious metal, but soon the cold would tarnish away all color. Sometimes Blythe joined us, and it felt like sitting between my sweet little brother and wild older sister. I thought of Mina and Kari, my princesses, till my throat went tight like a wire. *How are your sisters?* Ellis said, and I could only shrug. In the distance the lake rippled. Somewhere two tiny pairs of pale olive feet would dip into the water, dash through sand. I imagined it sticking to their damp skin like brown sugar.

At Umbra I spotted Cress slinking through the shadows. When I danced I felt the slide of her gaze over my body, sinuous and sly. For the first time in forever I was conscious of my hips, the femmey movements I made. Unlike Ellis, I'd never learned to own my girliness. So in typical male fashion, I overcompensated. Flirted. Drank. Hooked up. My mouth was a mash of musky rum and smeared lipstick. Then I got pissed that Cress could affect me like this, and put on guyliner and Blythe's fuchsia eye shadow and a spandex muscle tee, because fuck gender stereotypes. I could be feminine if I wanted to. It didn't make me any less a man. Besides, Cress would've seen my YouTube channel by now. She'd know what was in my pants. It didn't matter.

When a winsome boy put his hand on the curve of my waist, I shoved him away. He fell.

People on the dance floor stared. I hid in a bathroom stall, covered in cold sweat.

Not good.

I needed back in with Black Iris. Another mission, another sexist shithead I could beat the stuffing out of. A male punching bag.

Yeah, I've got issues with men.

Got issues with women, too.

I've hooked up hundreds of times since I transitioned and had a grand total of zero relationships. It's not the sex—at least, once I figured out what the fuck I was doing. They came. I didn't. Fine with me. No way would I get vulnerable with a stranger. It played out in my head: closeness, intimacy, her inevitable dismay when I refused to receive pleasure. *Don't you want me to make you feel good?* she'd say, but I'd always hear, *What's wrong with you?* Then came sympathy, concern. Attempts to fix me.

What is it about broken men that's so fucking irresistible to women? Don't they realize they deserve better?

I kept things short and sweet. Satisfied the urge, moved on before it became longing. Lived with that constant low-level loneliness and thought: This is safe. If I don't get invested, I can't be hurt.

What's wrong with me? I'd asked Armin. *I'm becoming another male cliché. All I have is meaningless, emotionless sex. Is this really what guys are like?*

No, he said. *It's what you're like.*

Thanks, doc.

Years ago I'd made a mistake. I let someone in too far. Let her twist around my heart like barbed wire, and when I tried to pull free she ripped me to shreds. She loved that heart but not the body it was trapped inside, not the way that body was changing. Ingrid fucked me up pretty good. There was only one real way out of that pain, I decided. So I put a belt around my neck, just to see how it would feel. It felt good. It felt like a solution. So I tied the belt to a timber beam in my closet, to see how *that* would feel.

They strapped me to a stretcher, after. Pricked me with silver needles (later Inge would prick me, 0.5 cc of T every other week), kept me in Velcro cuffs in the ER. I couldn't stop throwing up. Compression of the vagus nerve. The vomit wire. For a while I was more in danger of dying from dehydration.

Why did you do it? the doctor asked, and I said, *Because this body is a cage.*

That got me referred to a gender therapist, finally.

My parents didn't visit. They told my sisters the suicide attempt succeeded. I almost expected a thank-you card. Ingrid sat at my bedside, stroking my hand. *I don't want to lose you, ~~Sofie~~,* she'd said.

And I thought, *But you already have.*

Laney told me how, in the hospital after her mother's suicide, she'd felt like a ghost. People looked through her. When she spoke, no one seemed to hear. As if she were the dead one. *It was like she killed us both*, Laney said. *Like she'd taken me with her.*

That was what being trans felt like. Dead to my family. To my sisters, to Ingrid. To the trophies and newspaper clippings and girls' basketball scholarship, to all I'd done as *her*. *I'm still me*, I said, *still the same person inside*. But no one heard or saw. They looked at old pictures, crying.

Sometimes I was so sure of who I was.

And sometimes, like tonight, I felt like a stranger standing in someone else's life. Not even knowing myself.

One thing always grounded me: human touch.

This girl, Norah, had tenacity. She'd propositioned me once and I turned her down because *Don't fuck fans*. But she kept coming back. One night she danced with Blythe and I couldn't take my eyes off her. The firm curve of her ass in her sheath dress. The velvety girl-down on her arms, glistening with peach-juice sweat. When she turned toward me, her dark hair curled in fingers of shadow at her throat. The animal in me roused. We spoke through glances, and Blythe bowed out as I stepped in. No conversation but body language: fingernails scraping stubble, hip bones colliding. Her softness molding to me like silk on stone. Norah ran her palm up the inside of my thigh and I grazed my rough cheek against her neck. Without words we left the dance floor, our fingers knotted loosely. I led her to a room under renovation, the walls half torn apart, wood like snapped bones and insulation frothing out, all the seams and guts showing, and in a darkness pierced by pins of streetlight I pressed her to a concrete pillar, my mouth on hers. Her thighs spread, lips parting. This. I could never get over this. How right it felt, a girl opening herself to me. How badly I wanted her to hold my whole body. How badly I wanted to be inside her. I slipped a hand beneath her dress and rubbed her panties till they clung wetly to her pussy. She clutched my dick, squeezing.

That's right. I have a dick.

And it was as hard as any man's would be.

"I'm going to fuck you," I growled, and nipped the ear I spoke into.

Her spine arched. She tugged my fly. "Fuck me with this."

I let her open it a little, then pushed her hand away. When she gripped my crotch again I shoved my weight into it, let her feel all the heft and hardness of my body on hers. Small hands grasped at the slab muscle of my back. Nothing gets a man off more than feeling how desperately someone wants his dick. And she wanted mine.

Not in me to deny a girl that.

Dress hiked to her hips. Knees up, around my waist. I unzipped, and she was kind enough not to look as I pulled myself out, adjusted the angle, made sure the harness was tight. The silicone cock was warm from my body and she gasped when I slid inside. Slow, controlled. Inch by inch. I withdrew slightly and went a bit deeper, over and over, until the whole length of me was slick and I brought my hips all the way to hers and fucked her against the pillar, rock steady. All I felt was the pressure of plastic on my real dick, but through it I could sense her softening, spreading to take me deeper as she clawed the nape of my neck. Our voices played against distant club music: the grit in mine, throaty and low, and hers high, breathy, all smoke. My hands cupped her ass. She was air, weightless. So light. It set off a strange alchemy inside me, converting every muscle to metal, my blood to hot oil. Making me into some monstrous machine. It took all my self-control not to hurt her—not because I wanted to but because I wanted to fuck as hard as I could, make her feel how possessed I was by need. Testosterone is liquid libido. The chemical link between sex and violence. The same hormone that fuels lust also ignites aggression. That chemistry plays out inside the dirty laboratories of our cells and sometimes the difference between sex and violence seems as small as a molecule, a safe word.

An image flashed into my head: a butterfly of blood spreading on Crito's wall.

It should have been *him*. The monster whose ear Crito whispered into. My Poseidon. My hand on the gun, his forehead taking that bullet.

Giving it to him as hard as he gave it to me.

"Baby, don't stop," Norah moaned.

I kept going, dutifully, mechanically. And she came, because I knew how to hit both her clit and G-spot on each stroke. But I was numb. With one hand she feathered my damp hair, the other tracing the ridges of my chest. She inhaled. Sweat and the musk of sex mixed into a virile cologne.

This was supposed to be the ultimate fantasy. Fucking a beautiful girl, making her come. The thrill of her basking in my masculinity. Of being 100 fucking percent man.

Yet all I could think of was the sound of that bullet. The one that found flesh.

When we left the room a shadow leaned at the end of the hall, watching us.

Cressida.

As I washed up in the bathroom I watched a familiar stranger in the mirror: his face all lean angles, contoured with dark scruff. His lips full and salmon red, his eyelashes a touch too thick, too long. In clothes he was pure male but beneath the fabric was a chimera. Thin pink crescents limned his pecs, still visible through the tats. His pubis was a smooth sexless arch, like a Ken doll's.

The rigid packer in his boxer briefs dug into my thigh.

God, my life was fucking weird.

I couldn't get off—tried jerking it in a stall but only got sore—so I wandered the club, through faceless silhouettes in throes of ecstasy and fervor, bodies distorted, mangled by bliss. Armin deejayed in the Cathedral and I watched him like I used to, trying to understand what made him different from me. He moved slowly, fluidly, almost as if drugged, but the drug was confidence. For every dozen movements I made, he made one. The right one.

Something was wrong with me. I hadn't been this moody and insecure since I was pre-T.

What was wrong with me was Cress.

I tried to catch her as she followed me around. Whenever I got close she was talking to someone, or dancing, or disappearing. Those leather pants looked painted on. Why the stare? Another girl who saw me as a circus freak, the Bearded Lady? I didn't have room in my life for that shit. If Laney thought she could replace me with some transphobe—

But she wouldn't. Laney was vehemently antiphobic.

My head whirled.

"Excuse me," a girl said. Fire-engine-red lips. Fuck. "You're Ren, right?"

I looked intently into her eyes till she lowered them. "Yes."

"Oh my god. Hi."

"Hi."

"I've seen all your videos. I've been watching since you started. You're my favorite YouTuber ever. I guess other people tell you that a lot, but I mean it. You're so, so brave. You're one of my heroes."

A hero. For existing. "Thank you. That's very kind."

"Could I—I'm sorry, but could I get a pic with you?"

Good girls always apologized for their desire. Only boys and sluts were permitted to show it openly.

This world is impossible for women.

"Don't be sorry. It's my pleasure."

In the pic she blushed and my dark eyes looked off into the distance. At Cress, who watched us.

Restlessly I wandered the Cathedral. Other girls touched my arms, my face. Smiled and held for a moment and let go. Their touches clung to me, tingling, a second skin spun from electric frustration and want. I found Blythe dancing alone, her hair ice blond in the frozen light. I watched her as I'd watched Armin. What made this girl so sure of herself, of her place in the world? Every day she took shit for being a woman, and queer, and bipolar, and faced it without apology or shame. Her whole personality was a middle finger to the universe. I'd seen her stand up to strapping frat boys, throw a drink in a jerk's face. Argue TERFs into the ground. Blythe was pure id, acting on every impulse, fierce and feminine at once.

A face floated through the crowd, eerily familiar: one eyebrow cocked, a knowing slant to his lips.

Was it real? Or was I just seeing *him* in every man?

"Are you babysitting me?" Blythe purred as I drew closer.

"No. You're an adult. Technically."

"Then let's dance."

Her fingertips glided against my neck, a smirk coiling the edges of her mouth. Her smell was dizzying, dark and sweet, blackberry wine, and for a moment I forgot my fears. It was hard not to fall in love with Blythe McKinley. I'd thought I'd fallen for her, once. But it was the T. Spend five minutes with any pretty girl and you'll fall in love.

Before transition, I had preconceptions about men. Thought they experienced emotion less acutely, with less range. That they felt only horniness and hunger and hate. *Fuck eat kill.* What I found once my T level hit cis male average was that emotions, for men, were single-minded, slavish. Intense to the point that they could not be processed mentally, only felt in the body.

Armin told me about emotion maps—images that showed where people physically experience emotions, where the actual blood flows and nerves fire. Sadness is primarily in the lungs. Anger is in the fists. Happiness permeates the whole frame. It struck me how certain feelings—pride and anger, for instance—looked almost identical.

Women are better at this, he'd said. *There's wholeness in the way they feel things. Their maps are diffuse, more evenly spread. For us, it's a light-ning strike. A discrete devastation.*

What stuck with me was the way he'd said, so casually: *for us.*

"What are you thinking about?" Blythe said.

"How you're more of a lightning strike than a thunderstorm."

She grinned. "Don't know what that means, but I like it."

We danced close, her slimness sliding against my muscle. I felt the weight of others watching. From afar we looked like two beautiful people, anointed with sweat and rainbow glitter, completely without care. Inside I was a depressed mess and Blythe was barely staving back bipolar disorder.

So much of a person lies beneath the skin. You never know what you're really seeing when you look at someone.

That familiar man's face drifted in the crowd again. When I looked at it, it turned.

"I need air," I told Blythe.

Outside, the pavement was still warm and sun-softened, like a body settling down to sleep. Wind wove ribbons of coolness down wide streets. You could never see stars in the city but the moon was clear, and the lights of cars and shops and lamps made a cosmos at ground level, as if I waded through spindrift full of stardust. People passed me, snippets of dialogue floating by like I was walking in and out of a hundred films.

For someone so haunted, I felt pretty fucking alone.

At the Adams Street Bridge I took the stairs down to the river. An oil painting of the city lay reflected in the water, gently melting into pure light. I stepped close to the edge and let my toes hang off. My center of gravity was still in my hips. When I was learning how to pass I practiced walking with my weight held high in my chest, which felt ridiculous, like some cartoon bodybuilder. Later I realized it wasn't just biomechanics that made men move differently—it was socio-logical. The way men took up space in the world was different from the way women did. They took it without permission or hesitation, took as much as they could get away with. I watched them manspread on trains, their legs in wide Vs, devouring extra seats while women folded themselves up like Swiss Army knives. I watched them play chicken and shoulder-check each other on the street, coldly refusing eye contact. If you didn't participate in these little violences it only made them keener to target you, dominate you. Put you in your place. So I took up more space than I needed. To avoid attention. To pass. And I thought: What a simpler, saner world this would be if men were socialized like women.

I balanced on the wharf's edge and walked along the river. In the damp darkness beneath the bridge, there were too many echoes. Someone else was there.

Cressida stepped out of the shadows at the far end.

I didn't stop, because men are too dumb to back down. We march headlong into confrontations we know we'll lose. Otherwise we're making a statement on our penis size or something.

I passed her and kept going.

"Ren," she called.

Dammit.

Beneath her jacket she wore a plain white tee. Her curls were pinned back. In the dimness her skin glowed a burnished umber, as if it still held the autumn sun, too.

"Look," I said, "stalking isn't okay just because you're a woman. It's still creepy and threatening."

She frowned. "Do I threaten you?"

"No. But that's not the point."

Pause. Then, "You're right. I'm sorry."

I shrugged and made to leave. She touched my arm, brief, light, but the imprint of her heat lingered on my skin.

"We've had a bad start," she said.

"Seemed pretty intentional on your behalf."

"You must understand I'm curious about you."

Internally I cringed. Another curious cis girl. "Google it. I'm not a spectacle."

"I'm curious about *Cane*. My new partner."

Wait, what? Laney hadn't said shit about this.

"We're not partners," I said. "I'm suspended."

"The Wolf sent me to tell you that you're officially unsuspended."

"Great. So now you've got my old position. Where does that leave me?"

"We're sharing this position, so I suppose it leaves us tangled up together."

My face went hot. I kept my mouth shut.

Cress leaned against the tunnel, her boots jingling faintly. Knee bent, arms crossed. Wry pout. Like a black girl version of James Dean. It was infuriatingly attractive.

"We haven't been properly introduced," she said. "I'm Tamsin Baylor."

Her name did something to me. Another little surge of heat.

"Renard Grant," I said.

"Pleasure to make your acquaintance, Mr. Grant."

That "Mr." made my belly tighten. I couldn't look away from her mouth. Lush lips, tinted dusty violet. "Likewise, Ms. Baylor."

"Forgive my aloofness, Renard. I've been wearing your bruises for weeks."

"You left your calling card all over me, too," I said, and lifted the hem of my tee to show a fading scar.

Her eyes went straight to my Adonis belt. Then climbed, slowly, up the ladder of my abs. I let the shirt fall.

"I see why the girls talk about you," Tamsin said. "You have a certain charm."

"I'm not trying to charm you."

"It's working anyway."

Our eyes held for a moment. The air seemed to tremble palpably on my skin. When I breathed I felt the fullness of my chest and shoulders, thick and tight. "You were wrong about me, Tamsin."

First time I'd said her name. Her lungs swelled, her breasts lifting. So I was getting to her, too. Good.

"You said I hold back too much. But that's something I only do with women."

"Don't think they can take it?"

"No. I know they can."

"Then why?"

I stepped out of the tunnel, into the purple dusk. "I don't hurt women," I said, "because I know how it feels."

———

Armin's condo complex had a nice gym, and he'd given me the door code. I found him on the rowing machine. Everything shone: sterling mirrors, chrome barbells, his skin polished with sweat like buffed copper. We nodded wordlessly to each other. I stripped my shirt off and hit the squat rack; he spotted. Despite his being a head taller and naturally V-tapered, I had more muscle. Broad shoulders, chiseled pecs, a six-pack even at rest. The tats across my chest rippled when I moved: Poseidon whipping the sea into furious foam, a centaur swinging a wicked ax. Reminders of what hadn't killed me. My sweat brought out the olive-gold of my skin. I was a pretty damn good-looking guy.

Until I stood side by side with Armin. Then I might as well wear a neon sign flashing FEELINGS OF GROSS INADEQUACY.

He caught my eye in the mirror. "Everything okay?"

"Fine." I dropped into a squat and stood with ease. My body was a well-oiled engine, my muscles pumping like pistons. I'd grown used to it over the years but sometimes I remembered, viscerally, how I'd once felt like I was inside a puppet, only partially in control. Tugging at strings and praying it would obey. Praying no one would notice it was actually a girl.

Armin bumped my elbow at the end of the set. "Want to talk about it?"

"About what?"

"Whatever's eating you."

Instead of answering I threw myself into the next set. And because I was overcompensating, I lost the rhythm and failed the third rep. The barbell clanged onto the safety hooks. Armin braced me as I stumbled.

"Ren."

I shrugged him off. "No, I don't want to talk about it. That's what I'm supposed to say, right? Bottle it up. That's what men do."

"That's what men-*children* do. You're not a child."

I stuck out my lower lip. He smiled, that male-model freeze-frame every time.

"Is it about what happened with Laney?"

"No. Yes. A little. I don't fucking know." I sighed.

"Something else happen?"

I dropped onto a weight bench. He got me to talk after all. "My anniversary is coming up."

Armin sat beside me. "Of your transition?"

"Yeah. Starting T."

"How many years will it be?"

"Five."

"Wow." He swept a hand through his hair. That body of his was insane. I like girls—at least, 99 percent of my attraction is to girls—but T ramped my libido so high that preference sometimes mattered less than a beautiful body in my immediate vicinity. I looked away. Armin went on, "I don't know if I have it in me to devote myself to something like you have."

"It's not devotion. Devotion is a choice."

He thought about that. "Getting tired of it?"

"I'm not sure." I raised my head, felt the tethers of muscle twining down my neck. "I sort of feel tired of everything."

"That sounds like depression. Still seeing your therapist?"

"Yep," I lied.

Not going to tell him I didn't have the cash.

Not going to fess up that exhibiting myself to a million viewers twice a week paid peanuts. That I needed a real job but had probably boxed myself out of ever having one. Google my name and you'll find Renard Grant's entire medical history. His surgeries. His scars. This TERF blogger actually put together a mock medical chart for me, full of words like *mental disorder* and *elective amputation*. So thoughtful of her.

People don't hire weirdos like me. Once you cash in on your weirdness, you're stuck milking it for a living.

I would always be seen as trans before anything else. I'd guaranteed it.

"Okay," Armin said. "But you don't have to save it all for him. We're your friends, Ren. Talk to us." He clapped my delt. Strong but gentle. "We'll shoulder your burdens with you. That's what friends do."

I looked away again, with a different sort of awkwardness.

Testosterone inhibits crying. It's a documented biological phenomenon: men don't cry less than women because we're uncaring assholes; we cry less because T jams it up. We still *feel* everything that makes women cry. We just can't express it as freely.

So I sat there with my throat closing around a tiny pearl of pain, unable to push it out.

Armin twisted a towel and said, "By the way, there's a job opening at that clinic you go to. Intake screening, no medical training required. I could drop your name."

I frowned. "You know people there?"

"I volunteered. After Laney's . . . exposure of my past, I wanted to serve other people. To offset what I'd taken."

Penitence.

Strange, how Laney was more forgiving of her demon than I was of mine.

"It's merely an offer," he said. "You don't have to—"

"Did she tell you I'm broke?"

He shrugged, noncommittal.

"Armin, I appreciate the gesture, but I don't want a handout."

"It's not a handout. You do the work, you get paid."

"I don't need your help." I totally did.

"Okay. Like I said, simply an offer."

"It's not okay." Here came hothead Ren again. "I'm sick of people treating me like I need special considerations. Like I'm weak and helpless. I'm a normal fucking guy with an unusual history. That's all."

"Maybe I phrased it badly. Of course you're a normal guy, Ren. You're not helpless, or weak. But you *are* marginalized, and I've treated people like you poorly in the past. And people like Laney, and Blythe."

"And Ellis."

"Lots of people." He shifted uncomfortably. "I can't change that. The world has always been harder for you than it is for me. But if I can tilt the balance in the right direction, I will. Using my privilege to correct imbalances is the right thing to do."

"Sorry. I appreciate it, man. I'm just—touchy, lately."

"Job offer stands. I'd rather it went to a friend."

Me at an LGBT health clinic. Counseling scared kids whose parents didn't know. Telling them it was going to be okay, the way I told millions of strangers online.

Way back, when I'd first googled all this stuff—*how do I know if I'm really trans?* and *should I transition?* and *transition regrets*—much of what I found was deliberate misinformation. It was planted by TERFs—trans-exclusionary radical feminists, an offshoot of feminism that wasn't actually feminism anymore, but a hate group. "XX = woman," they said, apparently having flunked Human Physiology 101. Two X chromosomes made you a woman no more than a vagina or breasts did. TERFs saw everything through a lens of hate and ignorance: they called trans men traitors to womanhood, and trans women rapists in dresses. It was a caricature of feminism, a veneer for misandry. It took months for me to sift through their bullshit and understand that vulnerable trans folks were prime prey for any nut with a chip on their shoulder.

Sometimes, I thought, Ingrid flirted with the fringes of TERFism. Her most vitriolic essays suggested that gender was socially constructed. That the differences between men and women were invented and performed, like roles in a play. Dress equals submission, pants equal dominance. An age-old system of social hierarchy that we'd confused for biological truth. All that made us different, she said, was what was between our legs, not our ears. "Masculinity" and "femininity" were made up.

Except that didn't explain people like me. People so miserable in our birth bodies that we must either change or destroy them.

If masculinity was made up, why did it feel so right to me? Why did femininity feel so wrong? Why did I feel an overpowering need to alter this body from the inside out, not just my name and clothes and hair, my superficial expressions?

Why did starting testosterone feel like waking up from a deep, two-decades-long sleep?

It's all in your head, Ingrid had said. *Patriarchy taught you to hate femaleness. That's what causes your gender dysphoria.*

Resentfully, I thought, *I don't hate femaleness. I hate that it was forced on me.*

But things were changing now. Whatever the origins of dysphoria, transgender rights won legal recognition. Trans people gained public visibility. Maybe I could use my voice to reach trans kids struggling with their identities, too. Shelter them from predators and liars. Show them what a self-made man looked like.

My phone rang, shrieking from the other side of the gym. I'd set it to priority. Only Ingrid.

And Ingrid never called.

When I answered she said, flatly, "Come home now."

"What's up?"

"Just come home. We need to talk."

"Inge." I cupped the phone closer. "What happened? Are Mina and—"

"They're fine."

The coldness in her voice unsettled me. What could be so wrong, so awful she couldn't say it over radio waves?

What else but the one thing I'd been dreading and seeing everywhere?

"On my way."

In the car Armin didn't speak, but our silence was brotherly, close. Sometimes I worried I'd grown to loathe men, like Ingrid. That I'd exiled myself into a gender I couldn't stand. We were the ones who did most of the hurting, the destroying. Men wrecked the world and women picked up the pieces. Armin was guilty, too. He'd hurt Laney and Blythe and Ellis. Hurt us all by extension. But beneath the baggage of gender he was simply human, like me. We fucked up. We tried to be better.

Progress wouldn't exist if we never fucked up.

At my apartment building, the windows were dark but the curtain twitched and fluttered like a ghost. Inge met me in the front hall.

"What's going on?" I said.

She shut the door and locked it. Knob, dead bolt, burglar lock.

"Ingrid?"

She gave me a stark blank look, unreadable. Then she took my hand.

"Let's sit," she said.

I let her lead me to the sofa. No lights. In the shadows her paleness was ethereal, almost glow-in-the-dark. All I saw was the shine of her eyes.

"You are creeping me the fuck out, Inge."

"Where's your gun?"

My spine hardened. "Why?"

"Just tell me where it is."

"Not in the apartment."

"Good." Her thumb moved over my knuckles. "You said if this ever happened, I should make sure you didn't have access to a gun."

Now I knew, for certain, what this was about.

I began to stand.

Ingrid tugged me back. Surprisingly strong, but I was stronger.

We rose together, entangled. She was taller than me, thinner, that lanky, boyish build I'd so envied. In high school, in the weird hours after midnight when she lay on the floor of my bedroom in her underwear and a faded tee, the graphic fragmented, indecipherable, my hand floated toward her as if someone else controlled it, traced the straight lines of her hips. *I'd kill to be you*, I had said. She'd rolled onto her back and stared up at me. *Why can't you see how pretty you are?* she said, and a wildness in me reared. I pinned her wrists to the floor, knees astride her waist. *I don't want to be a fucking pretty girl. I want to be myself.*

Ingrid lifted her chin, gave me that expressionless stare she was so good at. Empty beauty, untouchable.

"Let me go," I grated.

"No. I know what you're going to do."

"So let me do it."

"If you kill him, you'll go to jail, you idiot."

"I don't care."

"You do fucking care." She wrenched my arms, hard. "They'll put you in a men's prison. Do you realize that? You'll be everybody's bitch. Don't be stupid."

My muscles tensed, firm as stone, but I refused to use my strength to overpower her. "Let go of me, Ingrid."

"Not till you promise you won't go after him."

How could she ask that? For five years I'd been waiting for this. Convinced myself all too well I'd been seeing a ghost. But he was real, he was bone and skin and blood and *here*, and I was going to take those things from him, one by one.

"I can't make that promise."

"At least for tonight. God." Her face was an alabaster mask but I heard the crack in her voice. "How many fucking times am I going to lose you?"

Fury drained. I released, and her fingers trailed down my arms.

"Promise me," she whispered.

"Fine. I promise. For tonight."

She pushed me back onto the couch. Sat on the coffee table, took my hands in hers. There was something so familiar in this. Like that night, years ago: me, broken, and her picking up the pieces. Building a weapon out of them.

"So. Adam's back in town." Her fingers tightened on mine. "Now how are *we* going to kill him?"

−4−

Laney was alone when I arrived. We sat cross-legged on bare hardwood, her cat curled in her lap. Sun painted stripes of gilt over his orange coat, and the smell of smoke and soap blended into bittersweet perfume. Their energy mingled here—Blythe's fire, Laney's ice—resulting in something volatile but contained, a hurricane trapped under a glass. Blythe said their crazinesses balanced each other out. Armin called it codependence. It was just love, I thought, between two broken girls. Two forces of nature meeting, wrecking each other, spinning out the bright shards of their mutual destruction.

Maybe I had issues with love, too.

Orion, the cat, watched me through slitted eyes as I spoke.

"I get why you didn't tell me about Crito. I understand it very, very well. Because someone else from my past is back, and I need help before I do something crazy."

Laney nodded as she stroked Orion's head. "This is what I like about you."

"Emotional instability? A hair trigger for violence?"

"Total lack of bullshit." She set Orion on the floor. "Come on."

We stepped onto the balcony. Windy today, a whirl of invisible blades slashing at our hair, our skin. Laney huddled in her flannel, so small and frail-looking I felt an impulse to sling my arm around her—no matter that she was one of the most powerful people in town, the black hole center of our universe. That she could crook her finger and destroy a man's life. And had. Still, in all her willfulness there was something vulnerable. The wounded warrior, doomed, hell-bent on taking everyone else down with her. Or maybe I was projecting, like Armin. Seeing the person I used to be.

Below us the streets rushed with endless streams of light, electric veins twisting through the city's neon heart. Laney lit a cigarette and exhaled.

"What do you want to do to him?"

"Kill him. In the most painful way possible."

A ring of fire ate its way down her cig. "That's pretty crazy."

"I'm not going to sugarcoat it. I need this, Lane." I leaned on the railing, scraping my nails through thin frost. "I wouldn't ask if there was any reasonable alternative."

"Are you sure it's him?"

"Yes."

Months ago, when I first thought I saw him, I'd told her, *Either I'm losing my mind or he's back.* She didn't judge. She didn't try to convince me otherwise. She believed me.

Being believed feels almost as good as vengeance.

Laney ashed and the wind shredded it into a little blizzard. Her face was blank but I saw the war in her eyes. Finally she said, "I can't. I want to, but I can't."

"You owe me."

Her forehead creased, a fine fracture on a porcelain doll. "Black Iris is a house of cards. Threats leaning on threats, lies built on lies. He's connected to Crito, Ren. They're old friends. You know that. Messing with him right now could destroy everything I've been building up. Those cards could collapse on *us* instead of *them*."

"You owe me," I said again.

Her eyes closed. She sighed. "I know."

Inside the apartment she moved pensively, aimlessly. Out of character. Delaney Keating always had a goal and always poured every ounce of energy into that goal. Now she drifted, scattered. At last she grabbed her coat and keys.

"Where are we going?" I said.

"I want to show you something."

We took a bus east, got off in hipster wastelandia, thrift stores standing cheek to cheek with pricey bistros. Laney led me to a café that looked like a page from a Restoration Hardware catalog. This was Ingrid's milieu. A place where people who were marginalized—but not *too* marginalized—could meet and talk. Queer white kids with trust funds, like her. We used to argue about it endlessly. *My money doesn't matter*, she'd said. *You have male privilege* and *straight privilege. But I will always be a woman, and a lesbian.*

It's not the Oppression Olympics, I'd said. *Being a trans guy isn't easier than being a queer girl.*

She'd shaken her head. *Margaret Atwood said the difference between men and women is that men fear that women will laugh at them, while women fear that men will kill them. Do you get that? I'm on the side that laughs. You're switching to the side that kills.*

I swallowed, pushing down the memory.

"How are you not breaking out in hipster hives?" I muttered as we picked up our drinks.

"Blythe inoculates me."

"Ouch."

Laney gave me a small, mysterious smile. "It's what I like about her."

"That she's no bullshit and total bullshit at the same time?"

"Exactly."

We took a table and people-watched for a while. I kept my face low, shaded. Laney sipped serenely at her chai latte.

"Why are we here?"

"Following up on a case."

Black Iris maintained two sets of case files: actionable and closed.

Actionable cases were ones Laney deemed legit. They came from friends, friends of friends, an expanding network of people—mostly girls—who'd been wronged. Blythe tracked certain hashtags on social media. *If he hurt you*, girls said, *use this tag and* they'll *be in touch. My abusive ex lost his job. My cheating boyfriend got his Tinder account hacked. Use this tag; they'll take care of the rest.*

We vetted them thoroughly. Background checks, anonymous observation. Tests of resolve. We mocked up all the contingencies. *Your Honor, I've never heard of Black Iris. I have no knowledge of those events.* If a client seemed off we'd drop them flat. Sometimes Laney dropped them on gut feelings. *Not her*, she'd say, and close the file.

Didn't make much difference. There was always another girl who'd been hurt.

Closed cases included our successes, too.

My job was all on the front end. My fists in a man's face, my voice snarling in his ear. I'd never seen the aftermath—what happened to the girls we'd avenged.

Till today.

I knew her the moment I saw her. We hadn't met IRL, but I remembered that face—it had been in a hundred pics taped to candles in the shrine her stalker ex-boyfriend built. He burned one every night as he chanted words like "slut," "liar," "cunt." When he started following her to work and chanting those same words, she flashed our bat signal:

#HeWontLeaveMeAlone

So I taught him a lesson, in twenty-nine bruises.

She took a table in the corner so no one could get behind her.

Rail-thin torso swallowed in a chunky sweater, nervous bird hands fluttering, bony. Girl, deconstructed. When someone called out her name and waved, she jerked like she'd been stabbed. Then it was all smiles, hugs. The two friends sat and fell into conversation.

"How long has it been?" I murmured to Laney.

"Three months."

"Is she getting better?"

"Does it look like it?"

From this far I couldn't discern tone, but the girl's eyes held a dull, feverish luster. They kept slipping away from her friend, scanning the shop. They met mine and I stared back for a second.

I knew that look.

Five years ago I walked out of a police station without pressing charges. Got on a bus and rode it from one end of the line to the other. Too scared to go home till Ingrid was there. That night we sat on the couch with our biggest kitchen knife, a chair wedged against the front door. She listened to me cry and scream and held me when I curled up in her arms, exhausted. I woke to her stroking my hair in the darkness. Her eyes had that fever glaze. That dull luster, like being drunk, but on hate. When dawn came we huddled over my laptop, and Ingrid typed: *how to buy a gun in Illinois.*

I looked away from the girl. "There's something you're not telling me."

Laney dipped a fingertip into her scalding tea. No flinch. "She's pregnant."

So she was trapped in her body, too.

"He'll find out." Laney swirled the foam idly. "He'll fight for custody to stay near her. He'll warp that kid and drive her insane."

"Why doesn't she just . . . terminate?"

"It's part of her. She loves it."

Nausea fumed in my throat.

"This is what we do." Laney looked up at me intently. "We help those society fails. Girls who slip through the cracks."

"She can go to the police. She can fight him."

"She tried. It went about as well for her as it did for you."

I didn't flinch, either. "Then you know how important it is to me, making *him* disappear. There's no way to make it right—I just want him gone."

"That's how I used to think. An eye for an eye. I'd blind the whole world if I had to." She peered at her fingertip. "It doesn't work. The world makes monsters faster than I can dispose of them."

"But if there were more of us—"

"If we kill every monster we find, it won't be enough. Some will still get through. We can't win that way."

"So what's the point of vengeance?"

"It feels good." She wrapped both hands around the hot mug, her eyes gleaming. "But it doesn't help those girls. It doesn't make their fear stop. There's only one thing that can cure fear."

"What?"

"Power."

The girl's friend left the table to use the restroom. Across the coffee shop, a man folded his newspaper and stood. We watched him approach the girl. Watched her cringe at his greeting, muster a brittle smile. Watched him bend close, closer, begrudging her with body language. Taking up space so she had nowhere to go, nothing to do but share it with him.

Laney and I came up from behind. I clapped a hand on his back.

"Hitting on my sister, pal?"

"Excuse me?"

My fingers dug into his jacket. "You. Are hitting. On a woman. Who's not interested. And her big brother is *very* protective."

He went rigid. His eyes locked on empty air beside my face. "My mistake. Pardon me."

Laney and I watched him leave. The girl watched us.

"Who are—" she began.

The Little Wolf slid something across the tabletop: a postcard print of an O'Keeffe painting, luscious petals parting silkily against each other, ivory, violet, onyx. *Black Iris*. It was unabashedly feminine, unrepentantly sexual. A symbol of female power.

"We're looking out for you," Laney said softly. "Don't be afraid. You're not alone."

We were on the street before the girl's jaw finished dropping.

"I know what you're doing," I said as we walked. My fists furled in my hoodie. "I know why you brought me here, Lane."

"Then don't ask me to do something that would endanger us all."

"I don't need *you* to do it. I'll pull the trigger. I just need information."

"I know what you need. And I can't give it to you."

I snapped to a halt, hands trembling. "That's so goddamn selfish."

"What you're asking is selfish. You want me to make an exception for you when it would jeopardize everything."

"I want you to tell me where Adam is. Give me a place and time so I can do what I need to do. Is that asking so much?"

"You'll kill him. And that'll put all of us at risk. You want vengeance, but it won't satisfy you."

"It'll help me take my life back."

"You have a life, Ren. It's helping girls like her."

"What about girls like me?"

The words shot out heavy and dense as lead. Bizarre, in a man's voice. Laughable. Instantly I recoiled, distancing myself from them physically. Laney's mouth had fallen open. I'd never caught her off guard before.

And I'd never said something that fucked-up.

"That's not what I meant. I meant the past. The old me. Not— look, I spent eighteen years being called that. It's hard to unlearn."

"I get it." Laney touched my arm. "No need to defend yourself."

"But there is." I shook her off. "Because you're telling me we can help everybody else, except ourselves. Except me. The person who's been hurt the most. The person who *deserves* revenge the most. This will help others, Lane. I'm not the only one he's hurt, or will. He's a monster."

Again, something strange brewed in her eyes. Hesitation. Ambivalence. She was hiding something from me. And unlike the Laney I knew, she wasn't hiding it well.

"What is it?" I said. "What aren't you telling me?"

"I gave you my answer. Drop it."

"Or what?"

No reply. Laney didn't give ultimatums. She cut problems loose, regardless of whether those problems were people.

"I can't believe you," I said. "Ingrid is ready to do this with me. She's got nothing—no training, no connections, but she'll stick her neck out for me because she cares. You won't even lift a fucking finger."

Those bright blue eyes darkened. "I've done more for you than you know. Be a little less judgmental of your friends, and a little more careful who you trust."

"Ingrid *is* my friend. And she's a better friend to me right now than you are."

"I asked you to trust me once, remember? And I gave you collateral. A sword to hold over my head."

"I'd rather trust the girl who's willing to kill for me than the girl who made me kill *for* her."

It was insane, saying this on the street in broad daylight, but for all anyone knew we were filming some prank video to go viral. It was easier than ever to get away with this shit. So much of what we saw online was fake that people were skeptical of live reality.

"I have never asked you for anything before this. This is the only thing I need, Laney. You owe me."

"*I can't.*"

"Right," I said, backing into the flow of foot traffic. "*I* get it. You won't help me because of who I am."

"Ren—"

"Don't worry. Priorities understood. I should've known better. You only care about girls."

"Ren, wait."

But I was gone.

———

Run.

There was nothing else I could do. This fury needed a physical outlet. I needed to hurt someone, and the only person I could hurt was me.

I ran east, toward the water, into the long fingers of mist curling off the lake. Leaf shadows fluttered in the twilight, a collage of dark wings rippling over pavement. I was pure heat. A meteor hurtling through space, burning a trail through the cooling city.

Running reduces the world to its simplest forms. Muscle stretching, contracting. Oxygen saturating blood. An inescapable oneness with your body, no matter how ill-fitting it feels when it's still. Ellis hooked me on running when she said it helped with dysphoria—she stopped fixating so much on being stuck in a girl's body and instead became a nameless, wild animal, a skeleton in motion, a living machine fueled by air and water and light. Even if your body wasn't quite right, it could do amazing things. It could convert base elements into emotional release. Take you, for a moment, out of your own skin. If you ran fast enough, you could escape the very machinery of yourself.

But tonight I wasn't running for catharsis. I was outrunning the avalanche of rage bearing down. That infinite heaviness that had almost crushed me once, when I was wronged. When I was hurt.

By him by him by him.

I flew under a bridge and kept going. No rest. The oxygen in my lungs combusted into a million particles of flame. I didn't feel like myself anymore but some dragon, limbs heavy and graceless from long years of slumber, ready to crack my wings and take flight, roar fire, snap my jaws on the motherfucker who'd done this to me. Tear him in half.

Someone was sitting on the bench up ahead.

I staggered, slowed. Tamsin raised an eyebrow.

"Not in the fucking mood," I gasped.

"I know. Laney texted me."

"Great."

"I'm not here at her behest. I'm here on my own. Please, rest a moment."

I dropped to the bench, gulping air.

Tamsin watched awhile and said nothing. I wanted to scream. I wanted to run again until I couldn't breathe so I couldn't scream, because if I started, how could I stop?

Laney was not on my side. Didn't have my back when I needed her most. Didn't want to stop a monster, because his victim wasn't a girl and that didn't fit her feminist vigilante narrative.

She'd shown me time and again: In her world, only men hurt others. Only women deserved our help. Not once had she sent me to hurt a girl—not before Tamsin had I ever fought one.

Not once had she sent me to help a boy.

Now I saw why she chose me as her right hand. Because she knew my biases. Knew I'd be happy indulging my internalized misandry. Until it came time to help a man—to help *me*—and then it was "risky" and "jeopardizing" and "selfish."

Fucking hypocrite.

Wind rumpled the river, pulling folds of black satin over the reflections of skyscrapers, stirring strands of twinkling gold filigree. I shivered, sweat-soaked. The hot throb in my heel was probably blood.

Finally Tamsin said, "You want to hurt someone."

"Yes."

"A man."

"Yes."

"But the Little Wolf said no."

We regarded each other in a dusk tinted sepia with streetlight. "Did she tell you that?"

"I inferred." Tamsin crossed her ankles. "Who is he?"

"Someone who's lived too long."

Light flared in those hazel eyes. She mulled over this bit of info. Then, "I have one, too."

"What?"

"A vendetta."

Electricity zigzagged down my arm, to my fingertips, to the warm aura of her body beside mine. The space between us pulsed.

"Perhaps we can help each other, Renard."

"I don't trust you, Tamsin."

"So let me earn your trust."

She stood and so did I. Wind combed her curls, pulled at my hood. Steely edge of cold in it, running down my neck like a blade. Tamsin bent one knee, stretching.

"Earn it how?" I said.

She touched her toes, her tight little heart-shaped ass facing the sky. Fuck.

"Like this." Tamsin eyed me coolly. "I know where Adam is. If you want to know, catch me."

Then she was off, a blur of leather and oiled hair.

Unthinkingly, I chased.

She ran down the riverbank, leaped up the stairs to street level. Dashed headlong into the nightlife rush, the musk of cologne and suede and cigarettes. Cut her silhouette against the searing beams of headlights. When she veered out into traffic on Lake Street I almost stopped.

But she knew his name. How?

I chased her beneath the L tracks, a rusty spine throwing ribs of shadow over us. Above, a train screeched into the station. She hopped nimbly up the steps and I followed, exhausted, as she vaulted over a turnstile and disappeared into the crowd on the platform and I, like an idiot, hit the bar. That was an end to that. Maybe she didn't mind being busted, but I could not afford a police record. I fumbled my CTA pass out of my wallet, lurched against the turnstile and through the closing doors.

In the fluorescent light all the faces looked ghoulish. I felt sick. I felt like the girl who rode public transit all night because she was afraid to go home, to run into her "boyfriend."

Laney must have told her his name. Warned her not to help me.

This was nothing. Taunting. Trolling.

I staggered toward a vacant seat at the far end of the car. Sat down beside a familiar pair of shiny black pants.

"Well done," Tamsin said.

I never put my hands on a girl without her permission. But I was exceptionally close to breaking that rule right now.

"How?" I rasped.

"I told you. I need to understand who my partner is."

"Who told you that fucking name?"

Her head tilted. Her eyes were oddly soft, and her voice, too. "Laney did. Who is Adam, Ren? What has he done to you?"

I had half a mind to pry the doors open and jump out.

Instead I sank into my hoodie, beaten. No energy to fight. I tired easily these days. Maybe Armin was right—maybe I *was* depressed.

We rode the thundering train in silence, thrown into each other as the car bucked and braked. It barely registered. My head was full of poison. A memory: another train, a skeezy older man hitting on me while I squeezed my thighs together and prayed the bleeding would stop.

My body tightened reflexively. Made itself smaller. Too small to contain so much pain.

Tamsin rose at the next station, touched my shoulder. "Come on."

Too tired to say no.

Story of my life.

It was somewhere near the lakeshore, in the cold glamour of

money. Skyscraper lights twinkled far above like tossed coins. I let her
lead me into a vestibule lined in navy velvet and glowing brass. Some
glitzy tourist hotel. The doorman nodded at Tamsin.

"What is this?" I said as we entered the lobby.

"Home sweet home."

I stopped. "You live here?"

"For the moment."

"How can you afford this?"

"I can't. My sister can."

"Who's your sister?"

"So many questions. All in due time." Her hand rose, light glimmer-
ing on her dark skin like gold powder. We didn't quite connect but I felt
the charge arcing off her fingertips. "Let's talk. I'll tell you everything I
know about . . . him. Not much, but it's a start. Join me for a drink?"

In the warm tungsten glow of the lobby, everything seemed softened, faintly imbued with magic. My fear and anger washed away. I
wanted to stay, so badly. I wanted to fall into her spell.

"I'll pass."

"Why?"

"Because I don't know a thing about you, and you know too much
about me."

Now those fingers made contact, curled over mine.

"Come and learn," she said, stroking my palm. "I'll tell you everything."

I'm not made of stone. I'm made of the same stuff as other boys,
and it responds very, very willingly to throaty invitations from pretty
girls.

"Why did you run?" I whispered.

"To make you chase. To bring you here."

"Couldn't you have asked?"

"Would it have worked?"

I thought of her at Umbra, staring, stalking, and shook my head.
"You know what you are, Tamsin?"

"Tam."

"You're a female pickup artist, Tam. You play games. Push me, pull me. Jedi mind tricks."

"You know what you are, Renard?"

"Ren."

"You're a little boy who's intimidated by assertive women, Ren."

Conditioning finally kicked in. I flipped her hold, twisted her wrist as I stepped close. "Is this your new strategy? Couldn't win a fair fight, so now you're negging me? This is some seriously fucked-up seduction technique."

Her eyes went flat. "It isn't seduction."

"So what the hell is it?"

"It's me wrestling with infuriating feelings of attraction, you daft twat." She snapped her hand free but didn't back down. "Pardon me for presuming they're reciprocated."

"They're not," I growled, my face inching closer. "Not even a little."

"Good," she spat.

"Good."

"You're not even that handsome."

I laughed, not nicely. "You have a serious attitude problem."

"You're an arrogant bastard."

"You're trying too hard with the whole rebel-without-a-cause thing."

"You're trying too hard with the whole—" She glanced down at my torso. "Big. Muscles. Thing."

She glared at my chest for a moment, then my face.

And suddenly I laughed again, genuinely.

It was like a catch coming loose. I leaned against a marble pillar, shaking with laughter, and relief. Forgetting everything else for a blissful moment. Tam crossed her arms and donned a stoic look that didn't last long.

"You are irritatingly intriguing, Mr. Grant," she said.

"Likewise, Ms. Baylor."

"And annoyingly handsome."

"I thought you said 'not even.'"

"Yes, well, I lied."

"It's just a shell."

"A very fetching one."

"I'm not what you think, Tam."

"I'm not what you think, either. Now join me for a bloody drink. You've made me ask twice."

"I will." I gazed up at a chandelier dripping crystal and metal from the ceiling. That glitter was in Tamsin's eyes, too, and I was afraid to look because I was goddamn sure I wouldn't want to stop. "But not tonight."

She walked me back to the train. Something was unfolding in me, delicate and see-through thin, a rose made of rice paper. Trust. I wanted to let her in. Let the bars down, let these feelings loose. Instead I kept my mouth shut and crushed that fragile white bloom in the black soot of my heart. Nobody got in. No-fucking-body.

As I jogged down the subway steps, she caught my arm.

"There's something you should know. I told you Laney gave me . . . *his* name."

All the warmth was gone now. Just cold, tired. "But?"

"But I didn't tell you when."

I put my hand on her. I didn't have to ask.

She tried to read me, her eyes tracking back and forth rapidly. "It was summer. Near half a year ago."

Before Inge heard he was in town.

Before anyone had known.

Nearly half a year ago I'd told Laney, *Either I'm losing my mind or he's back*, and she'd said, *I believe you. I'll find him. When I do, you'll be the first to know.*

Little fucking liar.

"Thank you," I said, and took the stairs at a run.

———

"Ingrid?"

The apartment was smoky blue with midnight, and empty. Where the hell could she be this late? Off living a life I wasn't part of anymore. Laughing with some girl, leaning close. Dizzy from the alcohol and sweetness on each other's breath. I grabbed a beer from the fridge and guzzled, and when my head came down I saw something stuck between fridge and counter. Flicked my folding knife open to fish it out.

School photo. Mina's first-grade portrait. Dark eyes solemn, like mine.

I slid to the floor.

It felt as if a hundred years had passed since then, and I was old now, too old to understand anything. I stared blindly into the dark, remembering. Mina perched at the kitchen table, her pencil working furiously. Savaging her paper with the eraser when she messed up. *It has to be perfect*, she explained, as if I were the child. *Or they won't take me seriously.* I said, *Why not?* and she answered, matter-of-fact, *Because I'm a girl.* Kari looked at us both and said, *I'm a horse*, and galloped around the table. *I'm with her*, I said. *Giddyup.* Mina rolled her eyes. Later that night she'd come to my room and asked me to read her writing assignment. *The person I admire most is my big sister because inside she is a boy but can't tell anyone, which I think is very hard. I would be sad if I could not tell anyone I'm a girl.* I'd never told her anything. She figured it out herself. *You can't show this to anyone*, I said, my voice breaking. *Mom will kill me, Mina. Please don't tell.* Mina said, *I won't. I wrote a different one for class. This is for you.*

I tipped the bottle into my mouth, but it was only dry air.

The front door rattled. Bell, Inge's cat—named after her favorite feminist, of course—went bounding to say hello. I watched the tall shadow step through a portal of light. Watched her lock the door, go still, and turn to me, slowly. That sixth sense for each other. Always knowing exactly where I'd be.

"Hey," I said.

"What are you doing?"

"Waiting for you." To save me. Like always.

Languidly she unbuttoned her coat, not turning on a light. Scratched Bell's head. "Do we need to talk?"

"I need to tell you things, Inge."

"You never tell me anything anymore. Now you need to tell me *Things*. With a capital *T*."

"This is serious. It's about something I've been hiding for years."

"Oh god." She inhaled sharply. "Are you . . . are you trans?"

"You're fucking hilarious."

Ingrid kicked her shoes off. "Like you've ever successfully hidden anything from me, asshole."

"I hid this. And I can't anymore." Deep breath. "It endangers you. Both of us."

"If it's about Adam—"

"It's bigger than him."

She snorted. "What isn't."

I turned my head away.

She said, "Shit. Sorry. Insensitive."

"I'm not fucking around, Inge. We need to talk."

"So let's talk." She cocked her head. "In my room."

I hadn't been inside in a long, long time. I paused at the door, that habitual hesitation triggering. One night I'd walked in while she sat at the vanity in bra and panties, a hand on her heart and her hair curling over her shoulders like gold shavings on porcelain. I'd stood there staring till I realized she was watching me in her mirror. At the question in my eyes she answered, *Checking if it's still beating. Come here, ~~Softe~~. Touch it.* For all that I hated the world seeing me as a girl, I didn't hate it, always, when she did. It didn't even feel like we were girls. Just wild things, rough beasts wrapped in soft skin. Sometimes I thought I could hold on to androgyny for her. Live in some gender limbo to stay that close, that deep, caught under each other's nails.

It frightened me, that willingness. I'd joke and call her Svengali but it wasn't a joke, really, the same way it wasn't a joke when she said *Be a girl for me, just for tonight* and touched me till I couldn't say no. So when Adam Halverson kept asking me out, kept pushing his nice-guy act, I said *Yes*. I fucked him. Let him come between us, figuratively. Literally.

Let the whole disgusting narrative play out.

Like the weak little boy I am.

I drifted through Ingrid's room, fingers gliding over things. Brass-plated basketball trophies. Framed newspaper clippings. DOUBLE TROUBLE: SVENSSON AND KHOURY ARE UNSTOPPABLE TOGETHER. My stomach clenched as I looked at my seventeen-year-old body. So small, so delicate, all bone and glass, like something made purposefully to tempt the world into smashing it.

Ingrid watched me in silence. Different now: My body was strong, hard. Not that frail thing anymore.

"What's the big secret?" she said.

I touched the bottles arrayed around the mirror. Her smell was everywhere, cool and mysterious. White-blond hair knotted in a brush like a glistening spiderweb. These strange things I'd never understood: liquids and powders and creams, wands and sponges, the insane amount of work it took to be a girl, to put a mask on each day so the world wouldn't eat you alive. Beauty as battle armor.

There was an unmarked vial filled with something clear, viscous. I wondered what it was. Some chemical to correct a minor flaw.

Funny. In a way, that's what I was doing, too. Correcting myself from the inside out.

"You know my friend Laney? You've seen her in pics."

Promise me, she'd said, running the blade against my palm. Hot blood kissed cool steel. *Never tell anyone about us. Never betray us.*

"Creepster with the hot Aussie girlfriend?"

I promise, I'd said.

"And Armin, and Ellis."

"Your friends from that nightclub."

"We're not just friends, Inge."

She gave me a look. "Is this about to get X-rated?"

"I'm serious. It had to be this way, okay? I couldn't tell you before."

Ingrid flopped onto her bed. "Fucking spill it already."

There's a scene in every superhero movie where the mask comes off and the loved one reacts with shock. As if a scrap of polyester hides everything. As if you don't know someone you love by their eyes, the inner self that shines through.

My parents had been searching my room. I should've known. Ellis helped hide my tracks online, all the transition videos and before/after pics I fantasized over, but it didn't matter. They found Mina's assignment. *What am I, Clark Kent?* I'd said. *I put on a pair of glasses and suddenly you can't see what's so obvious to everyone? I'm a boy, Mom. I've always been a boy. Everyone else saw it but you.*

I crouched at Inge's feet. I'm no hero, and she's seen through every mask I've ever worn.

"Ingrid, I'm a member of a secret vigilante group that avenges women who've been wronged. We do very illegal stuff. Very bone-breaking, scar-making stuff. Laney, Armin, Ellis, Blythe—they're all part of it, too. We call ourselves Black Iris."

Blank stare. Then she started laughing.

"Ingrid—"

"You're good. You almost had me."

"I'm not kidding."

"So, what, you're a superhero, saving damsels in distress?"

"Not exactly. More like . . . balancing the scales of justice."

"Oh my god, you sound like a comic book. Is this for YouTube? Are you filming this?"

I frowned. "I'd never do that to you. I'm dead serious, Inge. I'm deep into some heavy shit."

Slowly, her smile faded. "With Black Iris?"

"Yes."

"I've heard of them. Of you, I guess. Why did you hide this?"

"Because it would have endangered you."

"Why are you telling me now?"

It had been so long since I'd touched her. When I grazed her bare shin I couldn't stop. Fingers wrapped around bone, skin, felt her calf flex, her muscle hot and firm. She gazed down at me, pitiless. Ever so slightly her legs parted.

God, Ingrid. You still do it to me.

"I'm telling you because I fucked up. I pissed off someone from our past. Someone who hunts down and harasses girls for kicks. Now Black Iris is on the run from *him*, and they don't have my back anymore. It's just a matter of time till he finds me. And hurts me. And the girls I love." My thumb pressed hard, pulse to pulse. "Including you."

THREE YEARS AGO

VLOG #104: MONSTER

REN: See this shit? [Touches his mouth.] It's not makeup, you guys. This is real. Real red American blood. All it took was one fuckup to remind me how fragile it is, this fucking illusion of gender we're all performing for each other.

Let me start at the beginning.

I got drunk tonight. Really, really drunk.

[Jump cut.]

Lately I've been feeling like garbage. Moody, insecure, self-loathing. Almost—I hate to say this, but it's true—like a girl. The girl I used to be, anyway. And I know exactly the reason why: my T level is low. I'm not properly absorbing the gel, or something. My endo's upping the dose. But until the prescription goes through, I'm self-medicating with everyone's favorite fix-you-upper: alcohol.

T and booze have similar effects. Overconfidence. Lust.

And, crucially, not fucking recognizing danger.

Tonight I got drunk at the club. Made a total slut of myself. And because I was in a shit mood, I was a jerk to my friends. Can't remember what I said, but now E won't return my texts.

I deserved this.

I'm a monster.

My roomie thinks it's because my T's too high, that it's making me aggressive, mean, but the bloodwork says the opposite. So what's the fucking answer? I'll tell you: I'm just an asshole. I'm a bad boy. Not in a sexy-leather-jacket, cigarette, pomade way—I mean I'm bad at *being* a boy. I overcompensate. Try too hard to be hard. It's all an act, covering up how fucking weak and fake I am inside. My body's so different now, so much stronger, but behind *this* [taps his chest] I'm a scared little kid who doesn't know what the fuck he's doing. No one knows I skipped all the formative lessons. It's like that nightmare where you show up for a big test at school, and you didn't study. That's every day of my fucking life. I'm not ready for this.

I'm a man who never had a boyhood.

[Jump cut.]

So I was drinking. And flirting my ass off with this girl. We danced, and touched, and for a minute I felt like everything could be okay. She wanted to hook up, and I wanted to be a normal guy who could give it to her.

I went to piss first, to check myself. Not myself, exactly— the *equipment*.

Trigger warning: anatomical talk.

One of the most common questions I get is: *How do trans men fuck?*

And like, okay. You could just google that. But it's one thing to read a dry—pun intended—explanation of how this stuff works, and another to hear it straight from a real live trans boy. To have that information *humanized*. The whole point of this—of me getting on camera and sharing my life with you—is to humanize a transgender life. To show you that I'm flesh and blood, just like you. Well, except for my plastic cock.

Let's learn together, kids.

One of the effects of being on T is growing a dick. It's my clit, technically. Testosterone enlarges it. When we're in the womb, we all start off with the same junk. Depending on which hormone we're exposed to, that junk turns male or female—or ambiguous, as the case may be. You know the little notch that runs down the underside of a penis? That's where the labia fused to form the scrotum. And when people with clits get aroused? Their clit gets stiff and erect. Literal lady boners.

Our junk has the same origin. And T blurs that line.

But a trans guy never gets to typical cis male size. We get a small dick that can't penetrate, not satisfyingly. But it gets hard. I get morning wood—after I take my daily T dose. I jerk off like a guy, except with two fingers, not my fist.

So, I compensate. I wear this thing that gives me a bulge, called a packer. Mine is the deluxe kind: it also lets me piss standing up, and if I slide a stiff rod inside of it, it lets me fuck. It's the all-in-one silicone wonder-cock.

I'm supposed to see this as an extension of my body. But to me, it's a constant reminder that I'm not the same kind of man as the average cis guy on the street. Sure, some of them know how this feels—take a dude with testicular cancer who gets his junk surgically removed. We're in the same boat. We were both supposed to have fully functioning original plumbing. We're never, ever going to be satisfied with some prosthetic. It's the most intimate part of your body, the most sensitive, the core physical component of your sexuality.

It's the one part of being a guy that I will never truly know.

Don't get me started on surgical options. Modern medicine can 3-D print a human heart, but it can't make a flesh-and-blood dick that gets hard the way a cis guy's does.

Do you know how a surgically constructed phallus becomes erect? They have to put a rod inside it.

Yeah.

I've already got something that does that, and I didn't have to go through years of painful and expensive surgeries. I didn't have to worry about loss of sensation or my body rejecting it. It cost fifty bucks online.

I want the real thing. And I can't have it. None of us can.

I picked the wrong century to be trans.

Look, I won't romanticize this shit. This is fucking hard to deal with. Being transgender is an endless compromise of half solutions and almost-like-the-real-things.

Sorry if that triggers you. Sorry if my definition of "real" makes you feel less real.

I'd like to not feel that way, too. I don't know how.

But tonight a girl wanted to ride this half solution in my pants, and for a second I was drunk enough to believe that made me a real boy.

So I stood at a urinal, pretending to piss while I put the rod in to make my plastic dick hard.

This is what I mean, by the way. Tell me that is *not* the weirdest fucking sentence you've heard today.

Well, I was so damn drunk I dropped it.

The rod, the dick, the whole shebang.

And it rolled right against the shoe of the guy next to me.

I was so utterly wasted that I could only laugh. The guy's face was priceless. He didn't know what he was looking at, and when I put the cock back in my pants he walked out, fast. I didn't care. Everyone knows me at this club. Not like I hide who I am.

Me and the girl hooked up, but I was too drunk to fuck like a man anyway, so I knelt between her legs and showed her what growing up identifying as lesbian can teach a guy.

Lust, check. Overconfidence, check.

Lack of situational awareness, check.

As I walked to the train on my way home, some guys followed me.

You probably know how this story goes.

It was late. Too late to run to the station for help. And I was still pretty damn drunk. So I turned into an alley and waited.

There were three of them. One was the guy who'd seen my dick. He said, "What the fuck are you?"

I said, "I'm the guy who's going to kick your ass."

A year ago this never would've left my mouth. But T is pure swagger. It makes you stupid.

They thought I was funny. They asked to see my dick. To pass it around.

Cute.

Bathroom Guy got in my face. He made various remarks implying I was a disease-carrying degenerate, then gave himself away by saying he'd "fuck that boy-pussy straight."

As you can imagine, that's when I hit him.

My body really is different. I've been lifting hard. It's one thing to see your muscle in a mirror and quite another to feel it galvanized by adrenaline, propelled by rage. Few things feel as good and primal as bone impacting bone. It was beautiful almost, the elegant cascade of nerves firing, muscle contracting, fist crushing jaw, a spark of violence tracing its way from my brain stem to his bloody mouth. And the hitting—the hitting felt like fucking. Violence is tangled up with sex, and when I slammed my knuckles into his cheek, his temple, I felt the same explosive jolt as when I jerk off. I beat the shit out of him and thought: I don't mind not having a real dick if I can get off like this.

Besides, violence is better than sex. You don't have to hold back.

Then his two buddies were on me, and this happened.

[Ren leans close to the camera. His face is mottled with bruises and cuts.]

I lost. But I lost clean.

Those fuckers just had to ruin it.

When they saw I couldn't get back up, they started talking. They kept saying "it." Obviously, "it" was me. Been a while since I've been a thing, not a person. And you can do almost anything to a thing.

Their voices were low, furtive. One of them said, "Let's see its pussy."

He moved closer and I drew the gun from my jacket.

I said, "Stay where you are."

He said, "That's not real, either."

I said, "If you take another step I'll shoot your dick off. Then we can compare holes."

So I won, in the end. But I had to cheat by scaring them with another fake phallus. That's all men care about—dicks, fucking dicks. They're obsessed. It's super homoerotic.

You know what hurts more than a busted face, and fractured ribs, and having to go to the ER and take your clothes off so strangers can ogle your chimera body?

Losing your pride.

On the plus side, I think I'm gonna look good with scars.

[Jump cut.]

My roomie's wrong. T didn't make me a monster—it gave me access to the monster that's always been inside me.

Tonight I found a piece of myself. I learned that I'm a man who enjoys beating the shit out of other men.

I can work with that.

———

All night, she asked questions.

How do they find you?

How do you know they're not lying?

How do you hurt the people who hurt them?

We brewed coffee, talked in low voices as the sky healed from the bruises of night. It'd been years since we'd stayed up together till dawn. Ingrid sat in the windowsill, one knee bent. A silver-blue thread of smoke unraveled from the cigarette in her hand. Legs bare, pale and iridescent as nacre in the breaking dawn. Her camisole barely covered her underwear.

I thought of all those high school nights we'd kept each other awake. Half-clothed, half-delirious, whispering about the future. The apartment we'd share, the entwined life. My sisters coming to visit when they were older.

Like a real family.

Black Iris, I told her, was my family now.

It was Laney and Blythe's mad brainchild. Back in college, Blythe cheated on Armin, and Armin lashed out at her and everyone she loved. He challenged an underling—an incoming Corgan freshman who aimed to join his secret society—with a task: ruin a random queer girl's life. That not-quite-random girl was Laney Keating. She was bullied, humiliated online, harassed mercilessly at school. When she tracked the trail of those who'd hurt her, it led to Armin. So she entangled him in her web and set about gradually ruining *his* life. Drugs in his drinks, sweet lies about love in his ear. A slow neuro-chemical dismantlement. The ultimate what-goes-around. And the whole time she was poisoning Armin, Laney was hooking up with both him *and* Blythe. One for love, one to make her final revenge sweeter. She was stone cold and stone hard. She fucked a man and made him fall in love just to hurt him more when she revealed how she'd been systematically destroying his sanity.

If Laney Keating ever met Ingrid Svensson, the universe would implode. The big bang in reverse.

Laney started Black Iris to organize what she was already doing—wreaking vengeance on those who'd wronged her. When she ran out of victims, she extended her services to others. Revenge for hire.

That's where the rest of us came in.

Laney and Blythe enlisted Armin as their first recruit. He'd been broken, subjugated. Tamed. He bankrolled their early projects, smoothed hairy situations, tapped his social connections. He used his psych training to profile their targets. Guilt drove him to be a good little lapdog. Laney kept him on a tight leash; Blythe did the dirty fieldwork.

When Ellis came home to announce her engagement, Laney seized the opportunity. Ellis was the drama that started everything—the girl Blythe had cheated on Armin with, the only girl to ever break Blythe's heart. Black Iris needed a tech to handle communications and make the group untraceable online. So Ellis stayed behind in Chicago while her fiancée went back to Maine. *It's just a temporary thing*, E said. *I won't get into hot water, I promise.*

I saw the way Ellis looked at Blythe. Not with longing—maybe a faint smolder—but mainly worry. It made me think of Inge, always watching over me. Disapproving but still caring.

Once you love someone that deeply, it never really stops. It just evolves into other forms.

Plus, Laney wanted Ellis here for a reason. A balance point within her twisted threesome. Someone to haunt Armin and keep him in line—and someone to look after Blythe, hold her back from the edge.

Once Ellis was officially on board, she recommended me.

I'd known them all for years now, but being in Black Iris brought us closer. We'd seen sides of each other we never had before. Our capacity for cruelty—and for kindness. Laney sheltering that girl at the coffeehouse. Armin pulling strings for me unasked.

There was good in us, beneath the righteous outrage.

It didn't surprise me when Ingrid said, "I want in."

I spun the ashtray between us. Cinders flaked off, sparkling darkly. "Not possible."

"Why not?"

"Because Laney will kill me for telling you, for one."

Inge nudged my hand with a toe. "For two?"

"For two," I said, cupping her foot without looking at her, "I don't want you to get hurt."

One of the most frightening and admirable things about Ingrid Svensson was her consummate self-control. An iceberg of a girl, all her cracks and jagged edges below the surface. Beneath that smooth façade she could rip you the fuck apart. And I was one of the few people on earth who knew. Who'd seen.

Who'd touched her there, and been torn.

Now she sat very still, expressionless, but I felt the churn of something cold and terrible inside her.

This time, she surprised me. "Bring her here."

"Who, Laney?"

"The British one."

I sat up straighter. "I don't know anything about Tamsin."

"You know she doesn't trust *them*. She told you they've known about Adam for months. That puts her on our side."

"Why are you us-versus-themming already? I've been friends with these people for years."

"That doesn't mean shit." Her foot slid across my lap, thrust between my thighs. Nerves lit with pain, and arousal. "Don't be naive. Laney is ruthless. She'll do anything to get what she wants."

"I'm familiar with the type."

Our eyes locked. Against the wan morning sky she was a statue carved from opal. Sun turned her cami translucent, traced the contour of the breasts inside. Her curves were blue shadow. For months—years, actually—I'd been too daunted to stare like this. *Don't look at me with that fucking male gaze*, she once said. The same gaze that had adored her before I boosted my T to cis male range. *Why is it different now?* I'd asked. When did it cross the line from adoration to objectification?

It's predatory, she said.

You always look at me that way.

But I'm a girl, she said.

So?

So girls can't be predators.

Wrong, I thought, but she'd ended the argument by pushing me onto the bed and unbuckling my belt.

"What are you doing?" I breathed now.

Her foot ran up the inside of my thigh. "I'm fucking horny."

"Ingrid."

"Talking about hurting men gets me off. You too. I can feel it."

Her voice made me shiver. It was vapor coming off a hot spring, a long-buried heat.

Halfheartedly I said, "Don't. Stop."

"Take that period out," she said, her foot kneading, "and the meaning changes completely."

I was hard as fuck. I'd been battling an erection all night, first over Tam, now Inge, and I couldn't fight it anymore. Embarrassingly, I was wet, too. It'd been so long since I got wet.

She always did it to me.

"This is fucked-up," I said.

"I know. That's what makes it hot."

"No, it's *fucked*. You're a fucking lesbian, Inge."

She leaned closer. "And you have a fucking pussy."

Something snapped in me, a spasm of furious eros, inseparable rage and lust. Denying and desiring me in the same breath. Fucking with my head, like she always did. I wanted her to feel how much that hurt. I could *make* her feel it. With this body's strength, its ability to focus on something so single-mindedly it would deafen me to her pleas until I was done. Like the men I destroyed. *How do you hurt them?* she'd asked, and this was the answer: my hands clamping her thighs, my body shifting over hers. Our limbs twisted, tangling.

Then I realized the wetness between my legs felt . . . wrong.

Wrong in a very familiar, very alarming way.

I shoved her off. Stumbled to my feet.

Warmth ran down my thigh.

Oh fuck. Oh, fuck.

I made it to the bathroom, slammed the door. Dry heaved over the tub. Peeled my jeans off and stared with my mouth hanging soundlessly open, like someone in a nightmare.

Blood. Soaking my boxer briefs.

Everything went fuzzy and dim. Reality on pause.

When I came back to myself Ingrid was banging on the door.

"Are you okay? Talk to me, dammit."

"I'm fine," I croaked, scrabbling in the toiletry cabinet.

Nothing but tampons. God, fuck. I could not. I *would* not.

"Please, just open the door. Let me see that you're okay."

Her tone was wild, high. I nearly screamed, then remembered: the belt, the closet, her finding me.

So I made myself presentable and unlocked the door.

Quickly she scanned the danger points: wrists, neck, pill bottles. Then she touched my cheek, tentatively.

"You look like you've seen a ghost."

"My own."

Ingrid frowned. I sat on the rim of the tub, and so did she.

"Something's wrong with me. All the symptoms add up."

"What symptoms?"

"Moodiness, fatigue. Depression. And now this." I couldn't quite look at her. "I got my period, Inge."

It sounded so wrong, so jarring. I half expected my old voice to squeak out. To look up at the mirror and see *her* sitting there, the skinny nervous wreck with a belt burn around her neck.

"What does it mean?"

"My hormones are messed-up again. If my period's back, then my body's running on estrogen."

She laid a hand on my knee. "Why does this keep happening?"

"Who knows. Because I'm fucking with nature? Playing God, like Mom says? Maybe my body really, really wants to be a girl."

"Or it's stressed. Maybe your body's telling you that you need a break."

"From living?"

"From T."

I detached myself from her, stood. "That's not going to happen."

"Okay, cool. Kill yourself in slow motion with hormones. I'll just stand here and watch."

"Don't be a drama whore."

"Don't be a sexist prick." She rose, loomed over me. "It's been what, five years? Five fucking *years*. You got the changes you wanted. The voice, the beard. Listen to your body. You're killing it."

No matter how impassioned, Ingrid never called me Ren. It was a compromise we'd come to: *I can't call you some man's name. You'll always be S͟o͟f͟ie to me.* She'd dropped the deadname, at least, but at times like this I could hear it echo in her pauses. I could see the pearl blade of teeth knifing her bottom lip, forming the sibilants. *S͟o͟fiya, S͟o͟fiya. Your name feels like a kiss.* Then she'd smile. *Or a bite.*

"I need some privacy," I said.

"To do what?"

"Not kill myself, okay? Just give me space."

Pointless moments of glaring, sighing. Finally I locked the door behind her. Pulled the box of testosterone gel from the med cabinet.

APPLY 1 PACKET TO UPPER ARM/SHOULDER DAILY.

The clear gel smelled sharply of alcohol. I rubbed it in vigorously. Then I opened another packet.

This time I smeared it over my pecs. My tats glistened, the colors bold and bright.

Then another.

It worked best in places with little hair, and close to a blood supply. This one I spread between my thighs. It looked obscene, like someone's come on my skin. I squeezed my lap shut and imagined Ingrid's foot there, and groaned.

Another.

Empathy is correlated with estrogen. Higher E means higher empathy, and empathy is the dampener between the spark of rage and the fuse of violence. It's not that men have lower empathy than women, per se—it's that testosterone raises the threshold for accessing compassion. It's harder to feel for someone. To flip the switch from selfish to selfless. If too much T could turn you into a brute, maybe too much E did the opposite. Made you too human. Too able to feel.

So I'd dope myself till the bleeding stopped. Till all feeling stopped.

Make myself hard, cold.

The perfect monster.

The kind who could kill.

-5-

Watching Tamsin dance was sheer torture. That leather ran over her body like ink, and she knew I was watching, so she ran her hands over it, too, till I felt light-headed. Somehow her ass always pointed in my direction, my dick pointing back like a fucking compass needle. I'd come to Umbra at Ingrid's urging. We were doing this: breaking away from Black Iris, seeking our own vengeance. Assuming Tam was game.

And I had a feeling Ms. Baylor was just as hooked as I was.

The lights painted her body, cyan and magenta scribbling over black leather, and people stared. Some frat fuckboy tried to get her to grind and she teased him with smiles, hip bops, the gleam in her eyes somewhere between invitation and scorn. Her sexuality was intimidating. While Blythe was seductive in a mad, unmoored way, Tamsin's allure was precise and controlled, calculated. Like Laney's mind in Blythe's body.

Almost too much girl for me. Too much of what I wanted, what turned me on.

I always fell for the girls with fangs and claws.

Must have a death wish.

In all honesty, tonight was as much about seeing Tam as avoiding Ingrid. Our apartment felt like a powder keg. Months passed with barely a word, then in one night everything ramped right back to full-tilt batshit. Armin said we all followed the same pattern: Laney and Blythe, Ellis and Vada, me and Ingrid. Toxic homoerotic friendships crossing the line from platonic to something more. Like some kind of book series or something. At first it was innocent: We'd change into basketball shorts and jerseys in the girls' locker room, our skin grazing carelessly. Inge played lookout while I squeezed into my binder every morning, helped me unmummify before going home each night. Lied to my parents (*She was studying at my house* when I saw an LGBT crisis counselor), kept me closeted, safe. Love crept over us like a stain. Not real love, but a delirious poison. Her fingers lingering on my skin, mine on hers, then that first time in a shower stall, her hands on my tits and her mouth hot and vampiric. *You're so pretty*, she said, and kissed me, and kissed me, and kissed me. Denial and desire in one breath. I thought, *She likes the parts of me I hate, but it feels so good.* So I didn't stop.

In the end, we broke Armin's mold. No HEA for us. Ingrid liked girls, and I was a boy, and that was that.

As I skulked around Umbra, I ran into Ellis in the Cathedral. Sweater and tie, red hair raked roguishly. She made a prettier guy than I had before T.

"You're dapper as fuck, dude."

She blushed. "Seriously?"

"You could give Armin a run for his money."

"But really, how do I look?"

"Like the cutest boy in the room."

Crooked smile. Pride radiated off her like heat.

It made me feel . . . strange.

Yes, men actually are shit at parsing emotions.

"What are you doing tonight?" she said.

"Meeting someone."

Ellis squinted at me, then at Tam. Without glasses her face was more angular, nymphish but male. For a moment I had a vivid image of her if she transitioned—a beautiful pixie boy, pretty enough to still make queer girls swoon—and it made me weirdly uneasy. Was I encouraging this in her? All my videos, groupies, the illusion of trans glamour—was I pushing it, like a drug? Take this pill for automatic male privilege and self-confidence. Rub this gel into your shoulders for instant muscle mass and internalized misogyny. Maybe she was experimenting for herself, or maybe she was trying to impress me. To feel like *one of the guys.*

Night after night in high school I'd watched transition videos, soft faces growing chiseled, soft voices hoarsening, and I'd felt a deep ache. Hunger for the body I didn't have, the life that wasn't mine. In Armin's emotion map, jealousy lives in the core. In the bile and acid and bacteria of the gut. I'd felt it burning there, bitter and vile, as I watched other trans guys get ahead of me, grow facial hair and Adam's apples and pass. I wanted to be like them.

When I told Ingrid, she said, *Have you thought about whether you're actually transgender, or just want to fit in?*

It crushed me.

I put off transition for the first year of college. Took classes to help me understand society's sexism better, and why it hurt so much to be seen as a woman. Examined my own internalized misogyny: Did I want to transition to escape being a girl, or did I *need* to do it because I was a boy? And why did it have to be one or the other? Was it so horrible if part of my identity was a revolt against the way I was treated for having tits and a vag? I never wanted them. Maybe I could have tolerated them, in a better world. But in *this* world I experienced my physical womanhood as a stigma. And why did everyone keep telling me I had to be *100 percent sure* I was male before I put the needle in my thigh? I was 100 percent sure I wasn't a girl. Wasn't that enough?

College showed me how deeply gendered everything is. How society would remind me, for the rest of my life, that I was assigned female at birth. A lifetime of the wrong name, wrong pronouns, wrong bathrooms. Of mammograms and Pap smears. Of *When are you having children?* and *Don't be so emotional* and *Stuck-up bitch.* When I died and was buried and my flesh dissolved to dust, the bones that remained would say to history, *This person was female.*

Inside it made me scream.

In one of those classes—Women and Technology—I met a boy. At first he reminded me of Ellis, geeky and shy, oblivious to his own hotness. *It's messed up, right?* he'd said. *Nobody believes you're a girl online unless you say something they don't like. Then you're a girl until proven guy.*

He seemed different. Clued in to the absurdity of gender.

I'm Adam, he said. *What's your name?*

And I thought: I don't know. Maybe Inge is right. Maybe Ren is just a manifestation of my internalized misogyny.

So I said, ~~Sofie~~.

Weeks later, lying with me in bed, he said, *You're not like other girls,* ~~Sofie~~.

What am I like?

One of the guys.

And my chest filled simultaneously with nausea and elation.

"You're having a deep thought," Ellis said. "Share."

It was too heavy, and I was still too tender from Laney's refusal to help. Instead I said, "I'm thinking about Tamsin Baylor's ass."

Her eyebrows rose. "Are you guys, like, a thing?"

"We're an It's Complicated. Mutually attracted against our better judgment."

"This is perfect. She's totally your type. And you're—well, she seems to really like you."

I laughed. "Thanks for the vote of confidence, old sport."

"Oh my god. I didn't mean—"

"Kidding. Hey, by the way." I cocked my head, feigned cavalierness. "What do you know about Tamsin, exactly? Give me some details."

"Age, place of birth?"

"More like psych profile."

Laney had commissioned Armin to profile us all, himself included. We'd done video interviews—Delaney too—confessing that we were members of Black Iris, as collateral. So no one would turn. Then we'd watched them together. Each of us talked about why we joined: Blythe's devil-may-care love for Laney, Armin's hopeless devotion to them both.

Tamsin must have done one, too.

I'd kill to see it.

Ellis fidgeted with her tie. "You should really ask Laney about that."

"Why, is it classified?"

"I don't want to step on her toes after we screwed up that last mission."

Ellis Carraway was too pure of heart to lie to my face. Or so I thought—but once upon a time, she'd catfished her best friend by posing online as a man named Blue. Blue was Vada's dream guy: nerdy, sensitive, sexy when he wanted to be, and completely obsessed with her. Blue had everything Vada loved about her female BFF, but with one key advantage: the all-important dick. When Ellis finally came out as genderfluid, Vada realized the body didn't matter—it was the person inside she loved.

If only Ingrid had been so understanding.

Now I looked at Ellis and said, "Did we really screw it up, old sport?"

"What do you mean?"

"I mean, what was Tamsin doing there? Was she there to take Crito out, or for another reason?" I punched her shoulder playfully. "And how about you? You seemed pretty damn reluctant to let me go after him. Why was that?"

It took effort for Ellis to meet my eyes and say, "Because I was worried you'd get hurt."

"By Crito?"

"By everything."

"What's 'everything,' E?"

She gave me a miserable look. "I really think you should talk to Laney."

After Ingrid, Ellis was my oldest friend. She'd always known me as Ren. Accepted me, unconditionally. Took care of me during top surgery when Inge refused to even look because *It breaks my heart to watch you ruin the body I loved.* Ellis brought me into the Umbra fold. Gave me a new family when mine disowned me, gave me somewhere to belong. When she'd left for Maine, I'd lost an actual piece of myself. My shoulder angel. My pure-hearted boy. And soon she'd leave again, go home to her girl.

Ellis knew something I didn't. Something about Laney's plans, something she desperately wanted to share. But if E had a good reason for keeping secrets, I had to trust her.

When it mattered most, she'd been there for me. The one time Inge wasn't.

"Forget I asked," I said, smiling. "Getting way ahead of myself. Tam's probably not even interested."

"'Tam'? You're on a monosyllabic-name basis?"

"She beat me up the first night we met. We're not big on formalities."

The seriousness lifted. Ellis grinned.

"What's so funny, Professor?"

"You always fall for girls like that. Glutton for punishment."

"Look who's talking. If you and Vada weren't joined at the hip, I would've hit her up." I puffed out my pecs. "She was into this."

"She just said you had good muscle definition."

"Then put her hands all over it. She was Swayze in *Ghost,* and I was the wet clay."

"She's an artist, Ren. It's part of her process."

"Her process sure is hands-on. But you'd know from experience."

Ellis turned an impressive shade of red. I laughed and threw an arm around her, brotherly. These moments were priceless. Worth preserving.

It was late and she was tired, so I walked her to a cab. She hugged me before she got in.

"What's that for?" I said.

"Calling me a boy."

I watched the car pull away. In my gut, that acidity sizzled.

Back in the club I zeroed in on the sleazebag rubbing himself against Tamsin's leg, and every muscle in me tensed. I threaded through the crowd, bodies parting around my broad shoulders. Tamsin held my eye as I drew near. The man beside her was nothing, a faceless bro, irrelevant. He tried to sound tough saying *blah blah this guy bothering you babe* and I cut in hard, elbowing him out.

"Bold," Tamsin said. Her lips made me think of my finger parting freesia petals.

I didn't speak. I let the beat pump in my veins, my blood drumming in sync. Tam moved with me. Oh, to touch her. Hips that could perfectly fit the cups of my palms. The smooth cut of her collarbone like carved wood. There was no one else—my peripheral awareness faded. Only this girl, and the music, and my body moving in response to both. We danced and the air between us teemed with lightning and salt, electrochemical. I slid closer; she mirrored me. We played with negative space, pushing into it, narrowing the gap, almost touching, almost, then pulling away. Her heat was thick and palpable against my skin. Every muscle in me coiled, biceps swelling, the V at my groin going taut. I hadn't felt this *present* inside myself in so very long. Not once did we touch.

"You're good," she said.

"Actually, I'm very bad."

"Much better at this than martial combat."

"I could show you other things my body does well."

That earned a laugh. "You talk a big game, Renard. But I'm faster. Harder. Meaner."

"If you knew what I've been through, you'd see me differently."

The track switched, the crowd spiraling around us. Her eyes searched mine.

"I didn't know," she said. "That first night, I didn't know about you."

That I'm trans, she meant. That's always what they mean.

"Weren't you stalking me?"

"I prefer to call it recreational reconnaissance."

"As long as you admit there's a double standard. If I'd done that to you, you'd have handled me like you did Crito."

Tam shrugged. Light crazed over her hair, a thousand little rainbow wires. "Fair point. I took you for a bloke, and I don't particularly give a fuck about boundaries and fairness with blokes."

Something caught in my throat. *Took you for a bloke.*

As in, didn't anymore.

Oh, hell.

"The thing is," she went on, "I don't see how my original assessment was wrong."

"What?"

"You're a bloke, mate. So, sorry-not-sorry, but you're not getting the kid-glove treatment from me."

I swallowed that sticky emotional unpleasantness. I could've kissed her then and there. "Thank you."

"For treating you like shite because you're a man?"

"Yes."

"Masochist."

"Totally."

Tamsin smiled. "Me too. I like it rough."

Her words dizzied me. All my blood was going to one place now. "I'm game for a rematch. Let me rough you up."

"I'd like to see you try."

Desire surged. I moved in, reached for her hips.

At the same moment she sidestepped and whispered, "Have you reconsidered my offer?"

"That's why I'm here."

"Then we should go somewhere *else* to talk."

Despite the fiery breath melting my ear, I froze.

By "else," she meant "safe."

"My place," I said. "There's someone there you should meet."

"We'll leave separately."

I texted her the address.

"How do you spell 'Renard?' " she said, then, "Never mind."

She'd input me as BAD BOY.

"Give me a good name," Tam said, and kissed my cheek, silk on stubble.

My heart got the memo a second late, after she'd gone. Still it shot straight up my throat, a bubble of pure happiness.

My dick had gotten the memo hours ago. When I moved it reminded me it was rock hard.

BAD GIRL, I typed into my phone.

The downside of being a well-built five-foot-seven guy is that you're still five foot fucking seven in the City of Big Shoulders. I waded through hulking Midwesterners, nodded at friendly faces. Someone called my name. Girls, clasping each other. Two kissed passionately as the others squealed. They wanted my approval, I guessed, as the local prince of queerness. I tried to watch impassively but all I could think of was teenage me, lesbian tomboy, making out with girls like that. How much easier it had been when I thought the worst thing in the world was homophobia. How it always felt slightly off, slightly sad, when a girl touched my face and called me pretty.

"I'm sorry," one girl said, "but could we get a pic?"

Smile, oblige.

Remember how hard it was growing up, Ren. How much it would've meant for someone older, someone seemingly strong and brave, to bestow their blessing.

I glued the smile on as they maneuvered me and jockeyed for position. Phone LEDs flashed, an endless pale dazzle. My vision went fuzzy. Someone grabbed my pec like a tit, squeezing, shrieking with laughter. Then my hands were jerked and shoved against something warm, soft. Flash flash flash. The girls convulsed, breathless. *He's so hot*, they said, *so strong, so well dressed. So* ours.

"Gotta go," I said, gently removing their hands. "Thanks for your support, ladies."

One girl, red-faced and giggly, blurted, "I love you, Ren!"

"I'm your biggest fan!" someone else screamed, and, "I *love* watching you!" and, "Can I have your babies?"

Raucous laughter.

"Thanks. Really, thank you, everyone. Have a great night."

On the street I leaned against the stone façade, shaking.

Just girls, I told myself. Just young girls. Not predators.

They didn't respect my physical boundaries because they saw me as safe—assigned female at birth, made of the same base parts. They fetishized gay cis men, too. Anyone who didn't want to put a penis in them, or didn't have a flesh-and-blood version. Nonthreatening male eroticism.

They needed that, the freedom to express sexuality without personal risk. In a world that both slut-shamed and objectified them from childhood, there was scant chance to feel normal. I could be that handsome, neutered boy they fawned over. That fetish.

My lot in the world now. Most days I coasted on male privilege. I could stand a little harmless manhandling.

If only I could stop fucking shaking.

I punched the wall and muttered sardonically, "Man the fuck up."

My hand didn't start hurting till I looked at it on the train. Skin shredded off the knuckles, exposing red pulp. In the sickly fluorescence it seemed an omen.

On my block, the shadow sitting on my front steps stood.

I slowed. Every nerve screamed: *It's him.*

No gun on me. It was back in a locker at Umbra, and I was—

Tamsin moved into a circle of streetlight. "Ren?"

I tried to respond. My vocal cords were a noose.

"You all right?" She closed the gap. "You're out of breath."

When I edged around her she grasped my hand.

"You've been hurt. What happened?"

"Accident. It's fine." I made my voice gruff. "Let's go inside."

Dust hung in the dark spaces of the stairwell, spinning stray fibers of moonlight into luminous fabric. The floorboards creaked. At the top landing we turned and saw it simultaneously:

A basket of flowers wrapped in cellophane, sitting on my welcome mat.

We moved in tandem, but while Tam drew her gun I pulled air. I fumbled, found my knife. Only sounds: wood groaning beneath our weight, the skeletal skittering of leaves clawing across sidewalks.

"Is there another way in?" Tam hissed.

I shook my head *no*.

She lowered her weapon. "I've been waiting downstairs nearly an hour. This must have—"

Metal and wood screeched. Our heads pivoted toward the apartment door.

Ingrid opened it and gasped, eyes wide.

"Get back inside," I said.

Inge stared at Tam's hands. Tam said, "It's a gun, love."

"No shit."

"Ingrid," I said, "please."

A minute later we all stood in the kitchen, anxiously peering at the bouquet. Bell sniffed it, then flicked her tail in dismissal and stalked off.

"Why are we treating this like a bomb?" Inge said.

Tamsin had holstered her weapon, but still she scanned the apartment. "Because it's dangerous."

"Flowers are dangerous?"

"Black irises are."

No mistaking it: inside the cellophane was a profusion of dark purple petals, rippling and sensuous.

So Crito had connected the dots: from Black Iris, to me, to Ingrid.

She was the real prize. An unapologetic feminist, a vocal critic of all that was wrong with modern masculinity. Jay and Inge had always loathed each other. *Don't ever let me catch you somewhere alone,* he'd told her once, smiling.

Or what, you fucking creep?

Or you'll see who's stronger, men or women.

I'd fed her right to him.

Ingrid reached for the wrapper and I caught her hand.

"We don't know what's in there," I said.

"You think some basement trolls have access to anthrax? Get real." The plastic sang eerily as she tore it. "There's a card."

Tam and I traded a look. Maybe it was better Ingrid learned this way: seeing her name, her details, printed on paper. A threat in cold ink.

Inge flipped the card open and read. Then frowned, and read again.

"I'm sorry," I said. "I never meant to endanger you, Ingrid. I promise we'll—"

"It's not for me."

As she passed it over, Tamsin moved to my side, too quick for me to hide it.

Men feel everything. We don't default to silence because we're emotionless. It's that the feelings translate to words in a way that would terrify others. It's not okay for me to scream right now, *I'll kill you, motherfucker, I'll kill you, hunt you down, tie you up, hurt you every way you've hurt me, in every hole you have and every hole I'll make.* It's not okay to let these words loose, even though my blood pressure is the highest in the room, my muscles the densest, the environment inside me the tightest, tensest, most unstable. So I hit something. Didn't see what. Didn't matter because it was only a thing, and it's better to break things than non-things, than skin and bone.

Violence is a slippery slope. If you break things too often, it grows less satisfying. Then you move on to breaking people.

The girls stepped back as I smashed the glasses on the counter.

Simple message. Five words, one name. The name I'd never wanted Tam to know.

I love watching you, Sofie.

————

Ingrid plotted the timeline. It was second nature to her—her mind worked in flowcharts and inescapable chains of logic.

TEN MONTHS AGO

- Adam's best friend, Jay, begins calling himself "Crito" and trolling women online. Doxxing, RL harassment, etc. Leaves flower bouquet w/cryptic message each time.

FIVE MONTHS AGO

- Adam returns to Chicago.
- Laney orders Tamsin to watch Adam.

Ingrid frowned as she regarded Tam. "Your face is familiar. Have we met before?"

"Doubt it, love."

"I know I've seen you somewhere."

"Perhaps you've confused me for another black girl."

Inge didn't reply. Instead she kept writing.

TWO MONTHS AGO

- Black Iris botches mission to intimidate Crito. Crito is wounded, goes silent online.

ONE WEEK AGO

- Ingrid learns Adam is back. Laney refuses to help take down Adam.

TODAY

- Bouquet of black irises is delivered. Deadname in card.

We stared at the whiteboard. Morning had sprung on us without warning, silvery light oozing through the blinds like mercury. My pulse hammered at the inside of my skull, iron on iron. My eyes felt like embers.

"He's after me," I said hoarsely.

Ingrid crossed her arms. "Maybe he's after me, and you just got caught in the cross fire."

"No. My deadname means it's personal."

Tam eyed the board strangely, then darted a querulous look at Inge.

The fact that Laney had known Adam was in town before any of us—and set Tam to watch him—turned over and over in my head.

My instincts were right.

I'd seen him. I *knew* I'd seen him. That face in the crowd, watching me.

"They know," I said. "Both of them. They recognized me, somehow."

Tam frowned. "You wore a mask that night with Crito. And Adam never saw you after you—after you transitioned, right?"

In that pause, she'd pictured me as a girl. It made me a little sick.

I'd cut all contact with Adam before starting T. Ingrid and I moved to a new place. Corgan was a big campus—I wore hoodies, took night classes. My YouTube channel didn't break a thousand subs till a year in. By then, people I'd known freshman year didn't recognize me anymore.

I'd made *her* disappear in plain sight.

"I don't know," I said. "But they found me. They know who I am, where I live. What I'm a part of."

Ingrid plucked an iris from the basket and tore its petals off, one by one.

Tam's gaze bounced between us. "What's Crito's motive to hurt you, Ren?"

"Aside from me existing? And breaking into his apartment, and letting you shoot him? He's Adam's best friend. In the past, Jay . . . encouraged Adam. Egged him on. To do things he didn't—" I raked my hair, wishing I could claw the spiderwebs out of my brain. I was *this* close to defending Adam as a victim of Jay's manipulation. "They're fucking bros. You hurt one, you hurt the other. For all I know Adam's told him some fucked-up version of our history, and now Crito wants my blood."

I grimaced, hearing myself articulate exactly what Laney had been trying to tell me: if I went after Adam, it would tip off Jay. And she wanted Crito to pay for his sins fully. I couldn't touch either of them till her whole plan came to fruition.

Whatever the fuck it was.

What was she waiting for, anyway? What more did we need to take him out? Tam could've killed him that first night, and the world would've instantly become a better place.

Ingrid crushed the nude stem in her fist. "How do we know these came from Jay?"

"It's his signature move," I said.

"Right. So if someone wanted to make you *think* he was after you . . ."

"What are you saying?"

"I'm saying there's only one person who knows your old name, *and* that you're part of Black Iris, *and* that you have a history with Adam and Jay, *and* who's gone behind your back to do God knows what with them."

The Little Wolf.

"No," I said automatically. "That's nuts. Laney wouldn't screw me over."

She couldn't. I had collateral.

"She already did. She fucked you over when you asked for her help."

"But now I think I know why. She's got some long-term plan. Something she hasn't told me yet."

"So? Couldn't she at least tell you that she found Adam, that you weren't crazy, instead of letting you doubt yourself? That's basically gaslighting."

The term made me stiffen. "That's a comforting way to look at it."

"I'm not trying to comfort you, asshole. Don't be stupid—consider all possibilities."

"He's just had a terrible fright," Tam snapped. "You might be kinder."

Inge unveiled her trademark frosty glare. Then she said, "I'll go for a coffee run. Be *kind* to each other while I'm gone."

The door slammed. I rubbed my hands over my face.

"I think she likes me," Tamsin said wryly.

"Inge hates every woman in my life. It's nothing personal."

"Ah, the jealous ex."

I turned the kitchen tap on. "What makes you think she's my ex?"

"The way she looks at you." Tam hopped onto the counter beside me. "Odd, though. Thought you said she was a lesbian."

"She is. It's—" Water spilled over my cupped hands.

"Complicated?"

I doused my face. "God, what isn't. I'd kill for some fucking simplicity."

"Here's something simple: Ingrid is lying to you."

Tap off. Pause. "About?"

"Adam, among other things. How does she know he's back?"

The night was a whirlwind of factoids and details, a jumbled dossier. "Some friend of hers saw him. Took a pic. She showed me."

"Saw him where?"

"Cubs game."

"Right. Now, I'm no American, thank God, but according to the Internet"—Tam scrolled her phone—"baseball season ended in September. More than a month ago."

My brain could not process numbers. "So?"

"So her timeline doesn't match up. She only told you last week."

"There could be a million reasons. Maybe she didn't know till then. Maybe it slipped her—"

Tamsin pushed off the counter, crossed swiftly to the whiteboard. Rapped it hard with a fist. The noise startled Bell out of the room.

"Does this look like the work of a careless mind?"

"Tam, you don't know her."

"That's why I can see her clearly. Your eyes are clouded by history."

"Believe me, they're not. There's a reason we're exes."

"Look at the board. Read it to me."

"Tamsin—"

"Read it."

I moved toward her, our shadows thrown long in the colorless dawn. Ingrid's scalpel-sharp handwriting slashed impeccably across the whiteboard. I recited the words.

"And what didn't she write once," Tam said softly, "in this massive plot against Renard Grant?"

My name.

"Tam, it's complicated."

"So you say. But I think it's rather simple, really."

"Let's not do this. The clichéd love triangle, the emotional tug-of-war. I trust both of you."

"How bloody presumptuous."

"Should I not trust you?"

"Trust the person who sees you as you are, not as you were. And don't presume to know my emotions."

I leaned closer. "Am I wrong? Am I the only one who feels this?"

Our breath mingled, tinged with the beer we'd drunk. The wash of metallic light darkened, and a whiff of wet stone and copper filtered through an open window. Rain coming.

Her reply was unexpected.

"Sorry I saw the name. The old one. It's not right, using it against you."

"It's okay."

"It's not okay. I know a bit about being stigmatized by your past."

"That sounds like a story." My hand rose, and I traced her chin with my thumb. "Tell me someday?"

Her mouth opened at the same time as the front door.

We stepped apart.

"Breakfast," Ingrid called.

In the kitchen she parceled out coffee and bagels with a weird, seemingly genuine cheer. Few things put my misanthropist BFF into a good mood like other people's misery.

When she pressed a paper cup into my palm, she said, "Hot, black, and bitter. That's what you like now, right?"

I sputtered.

But Tamsin merely smiled and said, "His taste is improving."

———

None of us had a car, and I needed time to think. So I rode with Tam on the bus back to her hotel. But even the caffeine couldn't kick my mind out of zombie mode. You, I thought. You didn't hurt me enough, did you? You came back for more.

Whatever those bastards wanted with me, they'd find more than they bargained for.

~~Sofie~~ was long gone. Ren was here now, and he broke men for fun.

Tamsin and I sat side by side, staring at the city, the gunmetal lake sliding beneath a steel sky. The warmth between us knit our bodies together and I thought of how good it would feel to put my arm around her, how dangerous that desire. At her stop she didn't move. Her head lay against the window, skylight starring her sooty lashes like bits of diamond forming in coal. I let her rest. Clouds swept in, then rain, clear buckshot bombarding the glass. Tam stirred and looked at me and neither of us spoke, but in her half sleep she touched my cheek, rubbed the stubble where she'd put her lips. Something in the center of my chest went soft.

"Tell me your story, Ms. Baylor."

Drowsy smile. "You'll think poorly of me, Mr. Grant."

"Let's make a deal. For every bad thing you've done, I'll tell you something bad I've done."

"You'll get the better end of that deal."

"I'm no angel."

"Your face says otherwise."

For the first time, she made me blush. "You must be very tired. That's grade-F pickup artistry, Tam."

"Why don't we stop this senseless flirting," she said, tipping her head toward mine, "and get to the bloody kissing."

The gravity between our bodies pulled us closer. My skin felt magnetized, drawn. Craving connection. Touch, pressure, heat. I wanted my mouth on those thick, luscious lips. I wanted to start this thing and not be able to stop it.

Instead I leaned away. "I want to know who you are first."

"Fear of intimacy."

"Really? That's like, item number one on my psych profile. You can dig deeper than that."

"Know what item number one is on mine?"

"Bet I can guess." I looked her over. "Fear of commitment."

"Am I that transparent?"

I ticked off my fingers. "Expatriate. Not employed in your field of study. And you're running from something."

"You've read my file."

"Actually, I haven't. Ellis didn't give me jack shit. I'm reading you."

Tamsin propped herself on one elbow, amused. "Let's dig deeper. Quid pro quo. Ready?"

"Ready."

"I dropped out of college. High school, in America."

"I lost a college scholarship. University, in England."

We eyed each other.

"How'd you lose it?" she said.

"It was a girls' basketball scholarship, and I stopped pretending to be a girl. Why'd you drop out?"

"Couldn't live up to my sister."

Rain pounded the glass, a hundred syncopated heartbeats.

"Round two," Tam said. "I use men for money."

"I use women for sex."

Saying it aloud was a shock. I knew, obviously. Joked about it with Armin, other men. But admitting it to a woman I was pursuing was like shooting myself in the foot.

"Well," Tamsin said, "aren't we the pair of walking clichés."

"This game is dangerous. Maybe we should stop."

"It's just getting interesting." She laced her fingers over her ribs. "Round three. I let a man use me. Beat me. For years. Let him put me in hospital."

It was as if some spell had fallen over us. My words came like an incantation. "I slept with a man who didn't know that . . . that I was a guy inside. I led him on. Made him think I was a girl."

"I ruined the man who hurt me."

"I let a violent criminal walk free."

"I'm a fugitive."

Horrified, I whispered, "I'm a killer."

She whispered back, "So am I."

In the glass behind her the world was liquid chrome, her face the only color in it, flushed, that deep brown richening with red undertones. Her eyes were a little manic. No one sat near. No one could have heard. But it felt like our words blazed in the air, scarlet letters branding us.

Tamsin said, "I was wrong about you."

"Wrong how?"

"I'm not harder."

We reached the L station at the end of the line. I stood and offered my hand, and she took it. Hers was slim as spun glass while mine had grown thick and rough, veins roping the skin. Her fingers twined through mine, tight.

Out in the rain we ran, immediately drenched but not letting go. In the station we broke through the commuter rush and found a place against a wall. I pushed her to the subway tile, lifted her face. Her skin was lacquered with rain. This close I saw that the hazel of her eyes was a fine weave of green and gold, a splash of sun on autumn grass. My mind knew I should stop but my body was its own creature.

Tamsin made a fist in my wet shirt. "Do you think less of me, Renard?"

"How could I? You hurt someone who deserved it."

"Not for the hurt I've caused. For the hurt I took, because I'm weak."

My hands framed her jaw, olive against umber. We'd both been hurt by men. I could never victim-blame someone else, but I could blame myself. And did. For letting it happen. For letting him get away with it.

For letting him walk free in the world, able to do it to others.

"Being hurt doesn't make you weak," I said.

"Oh, rubbish. Be real with me. You feel weak, too. It fuels you."

At the ridge of her jaw, her pulse fluttered against my palms like butterfly wings. "Maybe it does."

"Good. Gather it. Hoard it. Keep it close to your heart." Her body lifted off the wall, rising to mine. "We're going to use it to kill someone."

―――――

Tamsin took the photos, and Ingrid plotted his movements. Together they drew a map of Adam's life in the city, a dark web looping in on itself over and over. Old haunts and hangouts. The basketball court at Corgan, where Ingrid had played. A coffee shop all four of us had frequented till Inge deliberately knocked a scalding mug of tea into Jay's lap. A network of memories.

Adam was looking for me. The me I used to be.

A girl who no longer existed.

Tam reported dutifully to Laney. We didn't tell her about the flowers, the threat. That Ingrid was one of us now. This wasn't Black Iris business, anyway—this was personal. And I trusted Delaney Keating about as much as a feral wolf among sheep.

Laney knew things I didn't. Something made her keep an eye on Adam while she kept me in the dark. Something stayed her hand against Crito. She could've tracked him down, taken care of him.

But she waited.

Tamsin's reports revealed no clue as to why.

If I could trust them.

"She needs a code name," Tam said one night.

Ingrid gave that slow, glacial smile. "Like Cressida, betrayer of Troilus?"

"I liked the sound of it. It has no meaning."

"Caeneus has meaning. Figured it out yet? Or are you still deluding yourself that he'll tell you?"

"Ingrid," I said.

Tam shrugged. "I think Frigid Cunt would suit you, personally."

"*Tamsin*," I said.

They smiled at each other.

"I like her." Inge's eyes were hard, unblinking. "She's a tough little nut."

Later, I cornered Ingrid in a dark hall, out of earshot.

"Can you at least try to be human around Tam?"

"Am I supposed to be happy you're moving on?"

My teeth ground. "You moved on, too. Don't be a hypocrite."

"None of mine had potential." Ingrid leaned against the wall, sighing. "I'll be a good girl."

"Just be my fucking friend."

"I don't know how anymore. All I know is how to be the crazy ex."

The words jarred us both. Too real. I started to raise my hand, to speak. To reconnect.

Then Ingrid said, "Don't fuck her in the house. Or I'll watch."

She left me there in the shadows, unsettled.

Days passed, growing grayer, colder, and still we stalked him, watching.

Like Laney, we were waiting, too.

————

Nothing makes you feel quite so godlike as the bench press. Flat on your back, feet on the floor, pushing that barbell up like you've got the whole planet in the palms of your hands—the power is intoxicating.

I finished my set and gazed out the windows of Armin's gym. Redbrick warehouses stretched to the horizon, quaint ironwork clinging to walls like bits of fragmented typesetting. All the factories had converted to tech and media firms, crafting only bytes, information. A city of industry now a city of imaginary things. In the abandoned places, beneath pelts of dust and in shafts of light splitting through broken glass, there was an air of melancholy about the way things used to be.

I knew that feeling.

Chicago was me. It had been built for other things, torn down, burned, rebuilt. Beneath the cement skin and neon veins it hid blood-soaked slaughter yards, pipes made of poisonous lead. A secret history. Sometimes the old bones showed through, reminding you: I was made for other things. Design isn't destiny.

From an aluminum sky came the first November snowflakes.

I toweled the sweat from my chest and headed for the shower.

It took all my willpower not to jerk off. My libido was just stupid—when water hit the wrong way it felt like my dick was getting the electric chair. Four times your prescribed T dose will do that.

What exactly *was* the etiquette for jerking it at a friend's gym, anyway? I thought of Tamsin's mouth, Ingrid's thighs.

And twisted the tap to cold.

Downstairs, Armin sat in the lobby, dressed like a prince in cashmere and gabardine.

"Looking for me?" I said.

"Need your help with something. Can you spare a few hours?"

"Sure."

Once I would've asked a million questions before committing. T made it easier to roll with things. My curiosity about the world shifted from risk analysis (*worth my energy, sanity, personal safety?*) to simply asking myself: Do I want to do this or not? I lived less in my head, more in my body. Wasn't sure if it was primarily hormonal or social. The unknown was always less risky for men. I didn't have to tell a friend where I was meeting an Internet hookup, or walk with a buddy to public transit, or have the taxi drop me off a block from my actual apartment. I—

Okay, so not a complete change. Still spent a lot of time spinning my wheels inside this skull.

Out in the crisp autumn air salted with snow, I looked up and let the sky dust my face. A thousand cold needles pricked my shaved skin. Every muscle swelled, taut as steel cable.

God, I felt good. Like myself again.

Armin drove his Range Rover downtown. Chicago was glorious in the clutch of late fall: leaves pasted the windshield, plum and pomegranate and marigold, and the snowmelt left a shine on the world like pottery glaze. Miniature white stars hurtled against my window and dissolved.

"Mind walking a bit?" Armin said.

"Not at all."

We parked in a garage and strolled up the Mag Mile, taking in the pageantry: shimmering tinsel, twinkling lights, and a high pure note pinging the sky like struck glass, just above human hearing but turning the air musical, crystalline. A coffeehouse door swung open and a warm cinnamon breeze swirled out. I wanted to taste the snow with my tongue on the chance it was confectioner's sugar.

At our last meeting, the girls had noticed the change.

You're so spirited, Tam said, smiling. Inge said, *Have you been drinking?*

Armin stepped into a tailor's shop, the leathery musk reminding me of Tam. We crossed a buffed wooden floor and a man in a smart suit glided toward us.

"Mr. Farhoudi, always a pleasure."

They shook hands. The tailor greeted me. I shook, too, feeling like an asshole in my skinnies and jean jacket.

"Is this the gentleman we spoke of?" the tailor said.

My heart made a fist. "Armin, you didn't—"

"Sorry for the deceit, but I had to."

"Please," the tailor said, "make yourself at home."

He backed off, giving us privacy.

"What are you doing?" I demanded. "I can't afford this."

"It's taken care of."

"We talked about this, Armin. No handouts."

He shrugged, and the snow dotting his topcoat drifted to the floor. "It's not a handout. You have a job interview coming up, and every man needs a suit."

"This is nice of you. Everything you've done is really nice. But also really, really humiliating."

"You're a friend, Ren. I help my friends."

I pitched my voice quieter. "Can you honestly say you'd do this for your cis guy friends?"

His eyes narrowed thoughtfully beneath thick charcoal brows. He gestured toward a pair of brass-studded club chairs. I sat beside him, uneasy. Our voices stayed low.

"You may not believe it," he said, "but I'm not friends with any cis men."

"Seriously?"

"None. My social circle in college consisted of the . . . organization I was part of."

Eclipse, the precursor to Black Iris: they were essentially the bizarro version of us, a bunch of rich, privileged douchebags who acted like masters of the fucking universe and abused girls and minorities in the process.

Laney had destroyed Eclipse from the inside out. Including Armin.

"The men I associated with were toxic," he said. "That poison tainted everything. Their masculinity, their worldview. And I immersed myself in it for years. Became accustomed. You can't exist in a culture like that without some assimilation occurring."

"Have you been reading Ingrid's blog?" I muttered.

"What?"

"Nothing. Sorry, go on."

Armin smoothed his coat. "I comforted myself by thinking graduate life would be different. I'd meet some different breed of man there. And I did, but it became even clearer that my little club hadn't been an anomaly—it was the microcosm. The masculinity I saw around me was entitled, violent." He ran a hand through his hair, sighing. "I don't have any other male friends because most men I meet are accustomed to those things. It's how we're bred. We're raised in it and we repeat it to each other and we end up in an echo chamber. I'm in it, too, Ren."

My chest felt tight. "You're not. Not anymore."

"Does it matter? I've already put evil into the world. But to answer your question, no. I wouldn't do this for any man. I think you're different because you were raised differently, treated differently, and those experiences shaped you into someone better than me. Someone more deserving." His eyes gleamed, flecks of gilt and bronze catching the light. "I've been watching your early vlogs. There's one called 'Adrift,' about birthdays, and growing apart from old friends. It got to me."

"Why were you watching those?"

"Would you believe I was comparing myself to you?" He smiled, so casually, devastatingly handsome. Perfectly designed face, flawlessly engineered body. Everything I'd ever wanted. "I was trying to figure out how you did it. What it takes to make a good man. You say you're 'self-made,' and I realized how much I want that. How I've let others make me, instead of taking responsibility for my own masculinity."

My whole chest seized up. I choked the words out. "I'm ordinary, Armin. Nothing special."

"Maybe you can't see it, but I can. Being yourself in this world *is* what makes you special."

"God. We're two dudes misting up about masculinity in a tailor shop. Let's talk about a war, or a dog, or something."

Armin laughed. Didn't hide his face or feed me psychobabble. Just let me see his vulnerability, his fragility, unflinching. Owned it.

Being a man meant being strong enough to let your fragility show.

Somewhere, I imagined Ingrid rolling her eyes. *Baby's First Man-Tears. How quaint. You used to be more interesting.*

"Need some air?" Armin said.

"I'm good. Let's dapper me up."

"Just so you know, he'll need you to undress. That okay?"

"Does he know I'm trans?"

"I didn't mention it. That's your call."

As we stood, a jag of panic rose. I was packing like usual, but it's one thing to see a bulge from a distance and another to wag it in a man's face. That plus the surgery scars plus my bone structure—

Okay, I thought. These things I cannot change. I'm a guy with scars and wide hips and a prosthetic dick. I can still look good in a suit.

I can own my fragilities, too.

The tailor put me at ease. Brisk but gentle, he asked about my job as he measured. I told him I yakked on YouTube for a living but was trying to transition to youth outreach. "Transition" had been such a loaded word for years, but here it felt unremarkable. Ordinary. People transitioned all the time—between careers, homes, relationships. Even their bodies, in nongendered ways: gaining muscle, losing fat. Life was constant flux. In all these little ways, I'd been preparing for the biggest change of my whole life. It felt good to be getting back to the small stuff. When the tailor measured my inseam I impressed myself by not clenching my thighs.

It was the fully clothed part that freaked me out. He pulled a suit coat and pinned it against my body. My shoulders were broad and square, masculine. My hips curved like a bell.

That hard twist in the pit of my stomach: dysphoria.

Tactfully, the tailor said we could tweak the silhouette. Slim fit, or—he released some pins—traditional. Which did sir prefer?

Sir preferred not to look like a fucking girl.

"Traditional," I said.

Too boxy, too dadcore. Paradoxically, the more it hid my hips, the more I cringed, slouched. Diminished myself.

Even if no one else saw it, *I* knew I was hiding something.

"Can we try the slim fit again?"

As I stared into the mirrors, my mind split in two. One part saw a guy of below-average height, muscular, dusky, chiseled. His jaw could cut glass and his eyes could melt it. Wide legs, narrow waist. Instead of the typical male V shape, his body made an X.

The other half saw a girl pretending to be a guy. All the muscle, stubble, body hair were merely a costume. She'd nailed it save for the dead giveaway: those childbearing hips.

How could I still feel like this after nearly five years on T?

I love watching you, Sofie.

"I'm kinda dizzy," I said. "Stuffy in here. Can we take five?"

On the street in my own clothes I paced up and down the sidewalk, compulsively rubbing my neck. Armin followed, silent. People passed between us, a blur of wool and snow.

I headed for an empty plaza. Something was revving up in me, an awful engine of anxiety.

"Ren," Armin said.

I snapped as if midargument. "It doesn't end. It never fucking ends."

"What doesn't?"

"This." I gripped my spine through my skin, as if I could tear it out, show him. "There's something wrong inside me. Fundamentally wrong. It's a design flaw and I can build a grand illusion on top of it, but the core is still broken."

I squatted in the snow. Imagined smashing my body into the pavement, watching shattered pieces tumble out, one of them the faulty gender mechanism. It was in me somewhere, the wrongness that caused all of *this*. The fault. Armin knelt beside me, his coat flocked with snow.

He said the last thing I expected.

"Did you up your dosage?"

"What?"

"I spoke with Ellis. She thinks you're self-medicating depression with testosterone."

"Since when are you and Ellis speaking?"

"Since she needed a clinical opinion. And I think she's right. I've noticed an increase in your energy level. You're working out more, skipping rest days. More positive, upbeat. And quicker to anger." He spread his hands. "I'm not your doctor, but I am your friend. I'm worried about you, too."

I rubbed my knuckles in the snow. Still tender, pink. A little harder and the wound would reopen. "My levels were low, so I raised them."

"Under a doctor's care, or your own?"

"I can't afford a blood test every time I get sad, Armin. Besides, I have five years of experience with this stuff. I know what I'm doing."

"That's what worries me. I think you're trying to boost your levels as high as possible, beyond a healthy range."

"What's healthier: anger or depression?"

"They're not mutually exclusive," he began, and then his phone rang. "It's Laney. One moment."

His face transformed as he listened to her. A frown first, dubious. Then his forehead furrowed, deep worry settling in. When he hung up he paused, ruminating.

"What is it?" I said.

"Do you know someone named Norah?"

I'd never forget those nails scoring my back, that girlish voice gasping *Fuck me with this.* I flushed. "Yeah, from Umbra. Why?"

Armin grimaced. "It's better if we show you."

———

They were all there in his apartment, their faces hooded with shadow. On the horizon the last light strained through snow, a pale gold mist. Tamsin moved toward me and gripped my coat. Her scent suffused the space between us: almond oil, leather, girl. She gave me a strangely intent look.

"I don't believe it," she whispered.

"Believe what?"

Laney called her name. Tam stepped back obediently.

"Why does this look like a funeral?" I said, my voice cracking.

Ellis broke from the group and took my arm. "Let's sit down together, okay? All of us."

Everyone clustered around me at the dining table. In the center lay an iPad with a video loaded. The thumbnail showed a pretty face I knew, mascara streaking her skin like black watercolor paint. Dark hair hung over that face, disheveled. The video title read MESSAGE TO R'S FANS (TW: RAPE).

A hand fitted over my shoulder. I wasn't sure whose. My body was beginning to go numb.

Laney tapped PLAY.

———

NORAH: [Crying.] I hate this. I don't want to do it. I wish I could just disappear. But I have to make this video, I *have* to. Not for me. For other girls out there. Girls who might be hurt by . . . *him.*

[Blows her nose.]

I can't say his name, or he could sue me. But I can give you hints. He's popular. Like, one million subs popular. And he's smart, and attractive, and honestly, before this happened? I thought he was so brave. I mean, being transgender is really hard. People hate him just for existing. It's horrible, and maybe . . . I don't know, maybe that's what made him do this.

I hate him now, too. But not because of who he is. Because of what he did to me.

He lives in the same city I do. Hangs out at this club all the time, and his fans go there to meet him. He's a local celeb. I was one of his biggest fangirls. I thought it was really cool of him to be there for us. Talk to fans, give us advice, all that.

But here's the part no one mentions: He *uses* us. It's all a front. He pretends to be this guru helping others, but the whole time he's sweet-talking girls, seducing them. If you want his attention you have to be pretty. And you have to be willing to do whatever. He. Wants.

Don't believe me? Just look.

[Images flash on-screen: Ren, his face blurred out, photographed with various girls at Umbra. In several pics, he appears to be groping their bodies.]

I have the originals, if anyone doubts me. With his face.

But like I said, I looked up to him. Admired him. I didn't mind that he's kind of a manwhore. Or that he's trans. To me, he's the same as any other guy. *Exactly* the same. Brain chemistry, personality, everything. He *is* a guy.

It's important you understand that, because I didn't. Not

really. Because I thought he was also . . . different. Special. That being raised as a girl meant he wouldn't hurt me.

[Cries.]

I'm sorry. This is—this is so hard.

[Looks off camera, composes herself.]

I kept trying to get his attention. He always talked to the prettier girls, but finally, one night, it was my turn. We danced, and he was so sweet at first. So charming. He gave me compliments, made me feel amazing. Like we had an actual connection. I was so fucking naive. Then he wanted to talk somewhere quieter, so I said yes, and he took me to this broken-down place that was under construction. Nobody else was around. He pushed me against a wall, started kissing me. I told him to stop. I just wanted to talk. But he's so much stronger than I am, and I couldn't get away.

[Cries.]

I—oh, God, I can't say it. He—he forced me. He just did it while I cried and begged him to stop. And the most fucked-up part is there's no DNA. Because of what he used. This—this *thing*. Not his own—because he's—God, I can't say this. I want to die. I want to fucking die.

I'm scared. So scared, so lost. I can't prove anything. All he left behind were bruises. But something is wrong inside me, something is *broken*. Because of *him*.

I'm speaking out for others. Not myself.

There's nothing I can do now but warn you.

He did it to me.

He'll do it to you, too.

[Reaches to turn the camera off.]

———

The room was utterly still. All that moved was the slow sequence of city lights blinking on and off, a glowing code printed on the floor.

I pushed my chair back. The others parted.

I looked at their faces but didn't see them.

Ren was not here anymore. *She* was.

She saw Adam (kill him), Adam (kill him), over and over.

Square chin. Broad shoulders. Cock in hand as he said, *I'm gonna fuck you with this.*

Sometimes an emotion is so intense, so much bigger than what a human brain can hold, that it no longer registers as feeling. It's just the way your hands are shaking, uncontrollably. The way your lungs are crushing your heart. The way your skin writhes so hard you would tear it off if you could open your fists.

People said things to me, things I didn't hear because I was walking away. A hand touched me. I kept going. Trotted down granite steps, hurtled against a fire door and slipped in the snow and threw myself into a flat-out run. As hard as I'd ever run, completely desynced from myself. All body, no mind.

If I stopped, the thought would put itself into words.

No. Feel this, instead. Raw rage. Let it rise and burn off like gasoline. Let it evaporate in a trail of fire.

Let me run until I stop wanting to get my gun, and an address.

If I stopped, the words would come back. And now they were slightly different.

Now they went:

Kill her. Kill her.

—6—

THREE YEARS AGO

VLOG #131: ADRIFT

REN: I probably won't even post this. Melodramatic wallowing, she'd call it.

What's the word for subtweeting when you're doing it on YouTube? Subtubing?

Whatever.

This is about her. I don't care if she knows.

It's four a.m., and I'm talking to my webcam instead of getting drunk with my BFF on her birthday. Because she hates me. Or at least everything I've become.

Friday was my two-year anniversary on T. My friends at Umbra wanted to celebrate, but I said no because it was Best Friend's birthday. I didn't pick my start date on purpose—I didn't pick it at all. The clinic assigned it, and when I saw it was her birthday, I thought it'd bring us closer. Something else we could share.

I'm an idiot.

We've spent every birthday together since we were eleven. The past decade. Half my life. Twenty-one is a big one, and lately birthdays are the only time we act like real friends.

She walked in on me while I was getting dressed. I haven't gotten top yet, and . . . it's weird. It's weird when someone looks at a part of you that you can't stand and says, "You turn me on." Like they don't care how much that part hurts you. Or how scared you are of losing it, because maybe it means losing them, too.

But she didn't put two and two together, because she said, "Hot date?"

I thought she was joking, so I said, "Yeah, with an older woman."

We bantered until she realized I meant *her*. Then she said, "I'm going out with people you don't like. You'll hate it."

Idiot me kept joking around. She kept rebuffing.

Finally it clicked.

I said, "You don't actually want me there."

"You invited yourself," she said. "I was trying to be polite and give you an out."

I said, "Didn't know I needed an invitation. This is our *thing*."

And she said, "It *was* our thing. But you're not you anymore."

[Jump cut.]

My first birthday in college, my natal birthday, was rough. I didn't want to celebrate but you can't just turn those feelings off after eighteen years. Each time the day came around I felt this stupid surge of hope, this sense that magic could happen. For twenty-four hours everything was possible and nothing was absurd. Secretly, I hoped I'd wake up as a boy. As a kid I thought if I had all boy things they'd *have* to let me actually be one. So

I asked for a bike, and got a robin's-egg-blue girl's bike. Asked for a suit, got a girl's pantsuit. As a concession to my mother, one year I asked for a Ken doll. I can still see her face crinkling, the way she looked at me like I was some ten-year-old stranger standing in her house, in the place where her eldest daughter should be. She got me the doll, and a Barbie to go with, and Barbie sat unopened in her box while I dressed Ken in the suit I couldn't have.

Without the faintest inkling of what "transgender" meant, I thought:

This is what I'll look like someday. If I'm good, I'll grow up to be him.

But I got older, and wiser, and stopped asking for boy stuff. I let Mom buy what made her happy, and gave it to my little sisters.

This is how the world beats you. It wears you down. It wins through attrition.

That first college birthday I hadn't started T yet, but I was transitioning socially. I was Ren to most people. He/him/his. When strangers said "sir" I could've kissed them. They saw *me*. Not the girl mask I'd been forced to wear.

But part of me felt this weird grief. The struggle was ending—no more girl bikes, no more girl clothes, no more constant battle to prove myself. Even though I hated it, that struggle shaped me. My whole life I'd waged a war against being seen as female. I'd put my back to a brick wall I never thought I'd topple. When it collapsed, I didn't know who I was without that not-me-ness to push against.

People tried to label me. They said, "Are you a man?" And all I could say for sure was "I'm not a girl." I was masculine, but what the hell did "being a man" really mean? If it meant renouncing my past, fuck that, because my past, for better or worse, made me who I am. Surviving in the wrong body made me strong. Staying true to myself despite my parents taking away everything I loved—that made me strong. I'd been tested, tempered. My body would always be an alloy, and that was its strength.

But I wasn't totally sure yet. Before I took T, I took a hard look at myself, and I felt . . . grief.

I was going to lose things I loved. My singing voice, the softness of my skin. My queerness. My visibility, period, if I ended up passing well. I'd look like any other cis straight guy. No one would look at me and see my history, the battles I'd fought. The sexism I'd endured, the homophobia, transphobia. Someday all I'd have left would be the scars on my chest.

And I'd lose her. My best friend. Who loved me, as a girl.

I knew I'd lose you. I knew I would.

Anyway, that first birthday night she found me curled up in the tub, crying. She said, "Be right back," and a minute later climbed in with pillows and blankets and ice cream. We talked till dawn. I told her how scared I was of transition, of loss. How it felt like starting over in the world. She said, "We start over all the time. Every seven years, our bodies replace every cell except our neurons." I thought that was beautiful—I'd already lived through three bodies, and now my fourth body, my male one, was taking shape. I hadn't lost myself the first three times, and I wouldn't now.

You were there for me that night. I will always love you for that.

[Jump cut.]

But tonight she told me I'm a stranger. That she doesn't know me anymore.

It was pathetic. I did exactly what every rejected loser does: demand explanations.

I asked if her friends hated me. No, she said. Was she dating someone, would they be there, would it be awkward? No. Then why couldn't I go to her party?

Finally she said, "Because I can't look at you like this. This gross half guy, with fucking tits, and a beard."

Just shoot me in the motherfucking heart.

She started crying. Said it was like watching me die. Seeing the girl in me wither and fade, and this rough, loud stranger take her place.

I said, "I'm the same person inside. Neurons don't change, remember?"

The look she gave me was just like Mom's. As if I was a stranger standing in someone else's shoes.

She said, "You *are* different. T changed you. You let it happen."

I told her what the brochures say: It's a second puberty. What every teenage boy goes through. It wasn't as bad, for me—I was a feminist, I was socialized female, I wasn't born into the world with a silver spoon of male privilege in my mouth. Men had hurt me, I reminded her.

And I wasn't like them. I *wasn't*.

That's the advantage I had over cis men: I fought for this. Put my body through hell to get here. I cherished and respected every moment of it: every needle plunging into a vein, every pimple, every razor nick, every unwanted hard-on, every crack in my new voice.

I was a self-made man.

And I would live and die a better man than the assholes who tried to unmake me.

But all she said was "You're not the person I knew."

Then she left. And I've been here, alone, wishing us both a happy birthday. Her twenty-first. My second.

The first one we've spent apart.

[Jump cut.]

I've lost the map to myself. I don't know where I am, if I've really wandered that far from the path and am stumbling blindly into a dark, thorned wood, or if I'm okay and she's the one off course. There's nothing to gauge it by. She's the only person who ever really knew me, pre-transition. No one else can tell me if I'm straying, if I should turn back.

She's my north star. The shining light I look to when I don't know where I am.

And I'm losing her.

I'm losing you, and I don't know how to let you go.

———

Tamsin found me at the train yard. I'd climbed off the bridge onto a Metra car, kicked the snow clear, sat on the roof. No coat, but I couldn't tell if my shivering was cold or emotion. All I felt inside was charred. Burned out.

I watched her hop the rail and trace my footsteps. Her scarf snapped, rich carmine, a thread of blood spilling stainlessly into the air. A messenger bag jutted from her hip.

Tam sat beside me, boots propped up next to mine. We stared east toward the Sears Tower. No real Chicagoan called it the new name. Clouds tore themselves apart on the needle antennae, fraying into shreds of fog.

"How'd you find me?" I said.

"Expert tracking skills. Katniss level."

Despite the numbness in my chest, I felt a glimmer of warmth. "No, but really."

"Cheated." She opened the messenger bag. "Ellis told me you come here sometimes. Something about your Instagram, urban fashion photos . . ."

"That traitor."

"She's worried. They're all worried. They—"

"Don't."

Tamsin shrugged. "Shan't."

Inside the bag were two paper coffee cups, lids securely shut. She passed me one.

For a while we sipped peppermint lattes and watched the trains come and go. My thoughts had the substance of dust bunnies. Caffeine only made them skitter.

"It's not true," I said. "That video. I didn't . . . do those things."

"I know."

"How?"

"Because I know you. I've tried to bait you into hurting me, taking advantage of me. Not once have you faltered. Not in the slightest."

A knit hat crushed her curls, but one had sprung free and hung jauntily. I fought the urge to tuck it behind her ear. To touch. Human contact seemed impossibly precious right now, and impossibly faraway.

She might be sure I was innocent, but when it really came down to it . . .

Was I?

Over and over I'd replayed that night. Norah's nails gouging into my back, pulling me closer. *Baby, don't stop.* But I had never asked her point-blank, *Is this okay?* Before transition, consent was mostly nonverbal—kissing a girl and feeling her mouth melt against mine, her hands undoing my fly. We didn't ask each other explicitly because we mutually assumed that we would never force it. That we *couldn't.* Because we were female. Our anatomy, our sex drive, our socialization were all so different from boys'. We knew about rape culture. We weren't seething with the hormone that fueled sex and violence.

But maybe that was the very thing that blinded me: my female history.

Had Norah at any point told me *no*, in some implicit, pleading way? Had I ignored it? Like Ingrid said, if you shifted the period, the whole meaning changed: *Baby, don't stop. Baby, don't. Stop.*

Had I heard what she said, or what I *wanted* to hear?

"Even without that," Tamsin said, interrupting my thoughts, "I'd still know."

"How?"

She cradled the cup in her lap. "Forgive me if this comes across the wrong way, but you're different. You touch me differently than other men do. There's an underlying presumption when they put their hands on me. As if I'm a possession, an object. As if permission to use is assumed until I say *no*. But when you touch me, I sense you asking how I feel. What I want. When you touch me it feels like a conversation."

Wind hurled little meteors of ice at our faces.

"No one has ever touched me like you have," she said. "No other boy is like you."

Heat shimmered through me, collecting in my fingertips, my lips. She reversed it. Made me the paragon, the standard to measure other boys by.

I thought of Armin saying, *I was comparing myself to you.*

How could these things coexist in the world:

A girl who said I touched her with respect.

A girl who said I raped her.

I took a scalding gulp of coffee.

"Perhaps," Tamsin said, sketching crosses in the snow, "it's time we tell them everything."

"Everything about what?"

"Adam, Ingrid, the flowers—"

"No." The cup trembled in my hand. "Don't you see? It's him. This is *his* doing."

"You think *Adam* is behind this? Convincing girls to shag you, then accuse you?"

"That's exactly what I think. He's flipping the table on me."

Tamsin frowned. "What do you mean, flipping it?"

Shit.

"Just trust me on this, Tam. It fits too well. Adam and Jay are behind all of this. They have to be." I shook my head, dazed. "This is surreal, being on the other side. The accused. I can't believe him. It's almost brilliant. The perfect irony."

"Renard." She laid a hand over mine. "Listen to yourself."

"Why?"

"You sound very paranoid."

"Yeah, well. A girl just fucking accused me of forcing her to—"

My voice fractured, crumbled. I looked away. Tried to pull free, but Tam held on.

"You didn't force Norah," she said. "But . . . someone hurt you, didn't they?"

"No."

"Ren."

"Not me. A girl I knew."

Her thumb ran across my knuckles. "What's her name?"

"Don't do this right now. Please."

Years ago, I'd put that belt around my neck and stepped off the chair for two reasons.

The first was the girl who broke my heart.

The second was the boy who broke my body.

Mom said you were gone, Sofie. Mina was shaking as I hugged her on the school playground. A teacher watched, phone to ear. Soon there'd be sirens and flashing lights, because Mom had convinced a judge that her *self-destructive daughter* was a harmful influence and must stay fifty feet away at all times. To my mother, transition was "self-destructive" because I was tearing down my female identity. But to me, it was self-*constructive*. Not that it mattered—all my princesses knew was that I'd vanished. *They wouldn't let me see you in the hospital,* Mina said. *I thought you died.* Kari, fearless, said excitedly, *Are you a ghost?*

Now Tamsin searched my face. But she didn't push further. Instead she drew my hand into her coat, against her heart. That fist-sized ember where anger and love burned brightest.

"I'm so fucked-up, Tam," I whispered.

"Not yet you're not." She squeezed my hand. "Let me get you wasted."

————

It snowed all the way to her hotel, covering the city in pearl dust, here and there a glittering fragment of gem. The ruby brooch of a stoplight, the diamond studs of a passing car's xenons. Evening fell, but without true darkness I lost sense of time. Before we went inside—before what I knew would happen tonight—I held her hand and walked along the river. No footprints but ours. Just us alone in this timeless, colorless limbo. Ice hung from a bench, a silver bracelet frozen midfall. Light shattered on the water in topaz shards. As if unbearably beautiful things had been hurled from a great height, smashed into the world to scatter their beauty.

Our breath steamed against the sky, white on white, lost. Our hands tightened.

The hotel bar was cozily dim, strewn with handsome calfskin couches, candles in hurricane lamps. The bartender gave a friendly nod. Tamsin sprawled on a sectional, hooked an arm over the back. Legs crossed, boots cocked. I imagined her in a classic Porsche the color of a shark, with a cigarette between her lips.

I sat a body's width away. I could count every inch.

The bartender brought rum, and Tam raised her lowball. Melted amber dripped down the inside of the glass.

"What shall we toast to?"

Candlelight flickered over her face, kindling the gold fibers in her irises like tiny wicks. I raised my glass.

To you, bad girl. To the things I want to do with you.

But I said, "To vengeance."

"To vengeance."

Clink.

Fire rolled down my throat, a slow burn crawling through my

veins. I watched her hand fall to the leather seat. Unconsciously, her fingertips rubbed a circle.

Look away, Ren.

"Tell me your story," I said.

"Which?"

"The one where you kill a man."

We sipped in sync. Without touching we held the same rhythm, instinctively aware of each other's bodies. I could dance with her with my eyes closed.

"It's an ugly story."

"I need to hear about someone getting what they deserve."

"He hurt me, Ren. Do you want to hear about that?"

Softly, I said, "Yes."

"You're fucked-up. Just like me." She smiled. "You want to get angry. To get off on it."

"I want to get you off."

I touched her hand. Ran my fingers through hers one by one. Traced an oval in the pale heart of her palm. Her lips parted, eyelids lowering.

All these months and I still hadn't kissed her. Not once.

Because I knew how this played out.

Same as it always did.

"Come upstairs," she breathed.

I leaned across the couch and her body softened, slackened against me. Not in surrender but in need. I cupped her face, not kissing that mouth I wanted so badly, but the sweltering breath we shared was close.

"What if this happens," I whispered, my words palpable on her lips, "and it changes things, and we don't like each other anymore?"

"I don't even like you now, you egotistic brute."

"I think you're lying."

"I think I actually hate you."

"If you already hate me, we should probably just let this happen."

"Agreed."

She moved to kiss me. With an excruciating burst of willpower, I pulled back. "Tamsin," I said. Her lovely name. The feel of her in my mouth.

"Arsehole. You won't, will you?"

"No."

"I do hate you. Truly."

"I know."

Her gaze tore away. "Be a gentleman and walk me home."

We stood, both woozy from alcohol and arousal. Sauntered toward the elevators, prolonging this.

My head said, *Be smart. Let it go.*

My body said, *You fucking idiot.*

The marble floor glared brilliantly. In the brass elevator doors, our reflections: the curve of her waist in that clinging jacket, the cut of my clenched jaw.

Ding. Our reflections pulled apart.

I stepped into the elevator with her.

Tamsin flashed a devilish smirk and said, "Going up."

Doggedly, I watched the numbers tick.

Every step down the hall to her room was a battle. When her key card clicked in the lock I felt faint. Torture. The door stood ajar, a seam of shadow beckoning.

With the last tenuous strands of my self-control, I said, "Good night, Tam."

"Bollocks to you."

Slam.

I leaned against the cool metal and slid to the carpet, hands raking into my hair.

Fuck this. All of this.

I'd spent five years piecing myself together from shards. Growing stronger, bigger, harder. Now, when I'd finally built a body and a life I felt safe in, he came back. To show me just how flimsy it all was. A little boy stomping on my sand castles.

There's only one thing that can cure fear.

What made me flit from girl to girl? *Fear of intimacy*, Tamsin said. So painfully obvious. Like a page from the fucking textbook. *Survivors of sexual assault often find intimacy difficult. Sex may be accompanied by feelings of guilt, anxiety, and fear.*

Norah and her crocodile tears. I could show that bitch how it's done. How to really sell it.

Fuck her. Fuck him.

They thought they could take this from me.

They were wrong.

"Tam?" I said quietly.

"What."

My heart leaped. Her voice was right on the other side.

"Open the door."

I sensed her standing at the same time as I did. Her hand on the lock, the flick. Her silhouette against the pale drapes.

I stepped inside, took her face in my hands, and kissed her.

First it was just heat, all over me. A wave of it breaking on our mouths and spilling down my body. Her top lip between mine, my tongue gliding across, tasting burnt caramel. Tamsin let out a little breath that felt like the word "finally." Then her arms circled my neck and I pressed her to the wall. The door swung shut, enclosing us in an indigo dark. Too much heat inside me—I meant to tease this out, but the slow-burning rum was lava now and it wanted to ignite and dissolve us both. My mouth on hers was animal, crude. My stubble dragged over her skin. She clawed the back of my head but her lips were supple, receiving me softly. Wild, her willingness to be roughed up. Her trust. This was where it got dangerous, I thought, my body against hers, my strength overpowering. This was where the lines blurred. Where consent could shift in a heartbeat. I pulled back to look at her.

Cool blue lit one side of her face. In noir monochrome her features were striking, lips swollen, nostrils flared. I ran my thumb across her mouth and it opened, revealing a moon-white arc of teeth. Those teeth closed sharply on the pad of my thumb. My core pulled tight, hips bucking against hers.

Tamsin laughed.

She shoved a palm into my chest and pushed. The mattress touched my calves; we toppled onto the bed. She climbed atop me but I wrestled her onto her back. So beautiful beneath me on the silvery sheet, dark and slender, her hair a black halo.

She touched the top button of my shirt, looking to me for permission.

I nodded.

Slowly she unfastened. It felt like my body coming undone, rib by rib until everything unraveled into my belly. Tamsin tugged my shirt off and stared up at me.

What will she think, what will she think.

Fingers touched my face tenderly. Sculpted cheek and jaw, traced the cords of my neck, moved without break over my pecs, my abs, coming to rest on my hips.

I didn't move. Barely breathed.

I'd faced this moment so many times. So many times they tried to be nice, and gutted me. *You look just like a boy. Not like you used to be a girl.* I'd smile and take it on the chin and in my head I'd scream, *I was never a girl. There was the way my body looked before, and the way it looks now. But I was always a boy inside.*

Tamsin gazed at me for a long moment.

And pulled my body to hers, kissing me.

I kissed back, so relieved I almost laughed, then her bare hot skin glided against mine and I forgot all else. Other girls had seen me shirt-less, touched me, but this was different. No curiosity or carelessness in her touch—it was raw need. She clutched at me so hard it hurt. Bruised me like she had before, lacing her marks across my ribs, my spine, so every time I breathed I'd feel her there. Roughed me up. I gave it back in kind, bit her lithe neck, scratched that perfect collarbone. Slid my hands inside her tee, and she arched against me and we clawed harder, harder, till blood bloomed beneath our skin. Our own black irises. I took her shirt off and crushed my body to hers. In a moment like this it was impossible to feel like anything but the man I was. No weak thoughts about shape and illusions, only her heat, her smell all over me. My mouth nipping at her throat. The taste of almond and salt. A kiss that trailed lower and lower to the dip between her breasts as I opened her bra. Tamsin let her head fall back, moaning, and I took her breast in my mouth, my hand playing down her belly.

It was too much, suddenly. Too fast, too overwhelming.

I kissed the hollow between her breasts. Paused there, heart wild, panting like an animal.

She grabbed a fistful of my hair and said, "Don't you dare bloody stop."

Huskily, I laughed.

I moved over her, kissed her lips, and after a fit of annoyance she went soft, sweet. Our legs tangled and the kiss turned openmouthed and intense, eclipsing everything. I wrapped my arms around her, marveling at how small she felt inside them. How pliant she was when I slid my tongue into her mouth. Absently, fingers twirled in my hair.

When we stopped for breath she said, "Fuck me, Renard."

Everything below my waist went white-hot. "Let's take this slow."

"We've taken it slow for months. Let's fuck."

I groaned. Her leg was moving between mine.

"Tam, this is hard, okay?"

"Yes, it certainly is."

I shoved a hand between us, blocking. "I'm not ready."

All at once her body stilled. "Okay," she said, cradling my cheek. "It's okay. God, I just want you so much."

You're so pretty, ~~Sofie~~. I just want you so much.

I closed my eyes and breathed. Stay in this moment, Ren. Don't slip.

Tamsin's touch turned gentle, reverent. We curled up face-to-face, limbs linked, tracing the lines of each other's bodies.

"Don't be afraid, beautiful boy." Her lips brushed my forehead, and I felt that coming-apart inside my chest again. "I want you when you're ready. And just as you are."

———

Not a word, Laney said. *Don't react to Norah's accusation publicly. Don't even acknowledge it.*

Pretend it never happened.

Anything I said or did would be picked apart, read into, distorted. So would silence. But at least silence wasn't something you could quote, meme-ify, make viral.

Trust me, Laney said. *I know how this shit works.*

The outrage machine will eat anything you feed it. If you want to shut it down, starve it.

Make it as unviral, unshareable as possible.

Pretend it never happened. Just like someone who's actually been violated pretends it never happened. To get through one more day. Then one more.

It surprised me, how much I missed vlogging. How much of an outlet it'd been. I missed sending those messages in bottles out into the universe, seeing them returned to me ten times over. The comments, the arguments, the support. Even the trolls, in some perverse way. Trolls were a sign you were saying something important. Something others wanted to silence.

It didn't surprise me when I got lonely, logged into YouTube, and saw:

This account has been suspended.

Laney told me my only power now was silence.

But how could it be a power when my voice had been taken from me?

———

I have something to show you, Ingrid texted.

Give me good news, I replied. I can't take more bad.

This will make you happy. Promise.

She sat me on the couch, phone on her knees. That witch-pale blond hair spun around her head in a loose chignon, elegantly mussed. Winter bleached all color but her eyes, a blue deep as blood in a vein, and for a moment I could remember the way they used to warm, looking at me.

"Another video?" I said wearily.

"Just watch."

It started with her facing the camera, smiling. So pretty it felt like a gut punch. She was a woman now, but sometimes the girl in her bled through, too—the one I'd met before high school, the one who'd pulled a knife on the boys who'd mocked my short hair, who'd drilled me on layups and passes in her driveway, sunset sweeping over us in fiery phoenix wings. Once, irked by her bossiness, I threw the basketball at her as hard as I could. Her middle finger made a sound like a stick snapping. In the ER later I cried, apologizing my ass off, but she waited till the adults left and said, *Stop saying sorry. You made me stronger.* There was something almost childlike about her relentlessness, something eerily pure. I loved that in her. And feared it.

Hello, princesses, she said, and swung the camera. Mina and Kari sat beside her on a park bench, bundled in duffel coats and rubber galoshes. My heart yanked toward my ribs. *I bring you a message from your exiled prince.*

Inge showed them a video of me on her iPad, recording their reactions. Kari, sunny-spirited, the youngest, laughed and smiled and soon grew bored, wandering off to the swings. Mina watched the screen fixedly. At the end she turned to the camera and said, *Is he going to see this?*

Yes. Do you want to send a message?

I miss you. One clear liquid thread ran down her face. Eyes like mine. Someday she'd look like the girl I once was, the woman I'd never become. *Will you ever come back home?*

There were other scenes—Ingrid buying them cookies, some YA books about trans kids I'd wanted them to read, finally dropping them off with my dad—but over it all I saw Mina's face in afterimage.

"Turn it off," I said.

Ingrid turned it off.

I took her phone and placed it on the table. I took her hands in mine.

And I started crying.

"Oh boy." She squeezed. "This was not the plan. I thought you'd be happy."

"I am."

It was true. I felt it all over—a diffuse, euphoric tingling, a sense of oneness with my sisters, with her. Somehow I wrapped my arms around her and she hugged back, fiercely. All these years, she'd kept visiting them for me. Bringing gifts and messages. Chipping away at my parents. Dad was okay with me coming home, but Mom would never be. Not as her son. So Ingrid kept playing courier, even when we weren't speaking to each other. She adored my sisters as much as I did.

I didn't know how to say thank you. Instead it came out as "I love you."

Inge stiffened. In the fading light the sapphire of her eyes turned dark, opaque.

"I love you, too," she said.

It needed more than that. More than words. I pulled her face to mine, cheek to cheek. It felt like this should be the way to fix everything—to pull her back into my life. If I just held tightly enough. If I just tilted my face, let my mouth graze hers. If we just kissed like this, like we used to, our lips fitting together so familiarly, the nip of her teeth lighting every nerve in my spine.

I pushed myself away.

"Fuck." Couldn't look at her. "Sorry. I'm so sorry."

"Stop saying sorry."

The taste of her was in my mouth, cool smoke and spearmint. Below my belt everything was electrified. Her hand lay on my thigh, slid higher.

"I'm sorry," I said again, meeting her eyes. "This was a mistake."

And stood before I let this happen. This thing I wanted so badly.

We'd been together before Adam, before any of this. Established an intimacy. She knew my body as it had been before *and* as it was now. No surprises or embarrassments. It was so easy with her. So safe.

Ingrid settled back on the sofa, unfazed.

Knowing me.

Knowing I'd come back.

"I can't," I said, even as I knelt at her feet. "I can't do this again, Inge."

One hand raked through my hair, rough. She twisted, made me peer up at her.

"There's a reason we keep doing this," she said.

"It's not romance. It's codependence."

"Whatever." She pulled me closer, between her knees. Into her heat. "You want it, too."

"Of course I do. But it's sick, Inge. You don't really want me, you want the girl version of me. She's gone."

Ingrid put her mouth to my ear. "When my eyes are closed," she said, "you're still her."

For the very first time since I started T, I hurt her.

I grabbed the hand I'd smashed years ago. She writhed but I held on, stronger. I pushed that weak middle finger back, farther, farther, till she gasped. Then I held it there.

Ingrid smiled. In a tight voice she said, "'I don't hurt girls.' Liar."

"You're not a girl." I pushed harder. "You're a predator."

"You're acting exactly the way people expect you to now."

"How is that?"

"Violent. Out of control. Like a typical guy."

I released.

Bitch, I thought. Pushing my buttons.

But I'd kissed her first. Crawled back, missing this intimacy. I didn't want it with her—I wanted it with Tamsin, with a girl who saw me as the boy I really am. But maybe this was all I'd ever have. Because I was broken, my heart's compass cracked, the needle pointing to this person, forever.

Get out. Get air.

Before I grabbed my coat, the buzzer rang.

"That's Tam," Inge said.

My eyes narrowed. "You asked her to come over?"

"We have a new development."

"Adam?" I said, strangling the name.

Ingrid didn't respond. She opened the door, smiling.

Tamsin sensed my sullenness and clasped my hands, but I slipped free, guiltily. I couldn't touch her when my dick was hard from Ingrid. Such a fuckup.

"What's this development?" I said.

Inge pulled up the map of Adam's movements on her iPad. We already knew that he'd been sniffing around Corgan U, coffee shops, even, once, my parents' house.

Trying to run into me.

Odd, because Crito knew where we lived. Wouldn't he have told Adam? Weren't they best bros? Hadn't they already gotten Norah to drag me through the mud?

Something didn't add up.

Ingrid zoomed in on downtown. To Umbra.

And pinned a marker on the map.

"When?" I said.

"Last night." Tam frowned at her phone. "Couldn't get a good pic."

"What was he doing there? They've already driven me out. I can't show my face at Umbra anymore."

Just a week ago it was the face of a "hero." A survivor.

Now it was a monster's face.

Inge shrugged. "Maybe he's meeting with someone."

"Who?"

"Who, indeed."

Tam touched me and again I withdrew. This time I got my coat.

"Where are you going?" both girls said, then eyed each other, shrewdly.

"Where do you think? Tam, stay here with Inge."

"Like hell I will. I'm coming with you."

"So am I," Ingrid said.

"No." My voice boomed through the apartment, startling them both. "This is my fight. My responsibility."

"Don't be a tool," Inge said. "He's dangerous, and Black Iris doesn't have your back."

Quieter, Tam said, "You don't have to do this. Why don't we wait and see what he does?"

"Wait for what, Tam? Another false accusation, another nail in my coffin?" My teeth gritted. "He's taken enough of my life. But I'm not dead yet. He won't take all of me."

"We're going with," Inge said. I opened my mouth and she preempted, "Don't argue. Two versus one. You lose."

Again they exchanged glances. These girls.

"Nice full-court press," I said. "Let's go, princesses."

———

First bad sign: the bouncers carded me.

Armin had beefed up security after the accusation vid, both as a gesture to clubgoers that we took their safety seriously and to cover our own asses. CC cams everywhere. Floodlights. No more dark hallways, no cloak of shadows and fog. No comfort of being half-seen, fashioning yourself from ambiguity and suggestion. It had helped once, before my beard and muscle filled in—Umbra's ambiance had been a soft-focus filter blurring away the parts of myself that T was slowly blurring away from the inside. At Umbra I was seen the way I wanted to be seen. I learned to be myself in the shadows until I was ready to step into the light. But things were different now. We didn't want anyone to feel unsafe.

Not that it mattered. The damage was done.

Second bad sign: When I sat at the bar, Sox cap shading my eyes, two slices of beefcake in button-downs joined me, towering at six foot fuck-off. I knew them vaguely: gay guys from some frat. There was a hierarchy of privilege in the queer community, and this sort sat at the very top: white, cis, moneyed, male. Cocky, but harmless.

So I thought.

I lifted my drink. Something bashed my shoulder. Rum slopped onto my thighs.

The man on my left said, "Sorry, miss."

From my right: "Need some help, little girl? Looks like you wet yourself."

I set the glass down. Thick honey beads rolled between my fingers.

Behind me a crowd gathered. At first I saw them only as pitchforks and torches, icons of hate, but when I looked harder they were faces I knew: boys I'd danced with, girls I'd kissed, all of them looking to see what the fuss was. To see the villain come home to roost.

Me. The rapist.

Instinctively my back flexed, feeling for the gun that wasn't there. It was down in my locker in Black Iris HQ.

I thought of an alley, the asphalt slick with rain, and my blood.

All I said was "Excuse me, please."

Walking through that gauntlet of my so-called peers was one of the most terrifying moments of my life. I could've called Armin, asked him to oust them, but then Black Iris would know I was here, up to something.

And if Adam was around, I didn't want to draw any further attention.

So I was on my own.

The guys from the bar followed me.

I wove across the dance floor, glancing back: stark white light seared all the faces, carved shadows sharply, a horde of grinning skulls. They could've been anyone. Any of these people I'd once trusted, felt safe among. Who *I'd* made feel welcome and safe. Now they saw me as a predator, hunted me like prey. Used my own identity against me, this masculinity I'd fought so hard for. While I was here hunting the man who'd actually done what they accused me of.

This was so colossally fucked-up.

I knew Umbra like a lover and I looped through halls and crossed catwalks till I shook them, like Tam shook me that first night. Then down into the catacombs, where the walls were soft and crumbling like bone, the air that of an opened grave. I meant to get my weapon—no intentions, just in case—but someone stood in the hall outside BI HQ. Someone short, raven-haired, brimming with dark energy.

Shit.

I did a one-eighty, ducked into a bathroom. Both Inge and Tam should've arrived by now, to triangulate Adam.

I texted Tam.

REN: I'm drawing too much attention
REN: And Laney's here

TAM: What a perfect shitstorm
TAM: I'll be your cover. Where are you?

I gave her my location. Then took a deep, calming breath and began blotting my pants with paper towels.

When Tam walked into the bathroom two girls trailed her. Makeup-counter queens, collarbones popping. Hips and elbows cocked like guns. Dangerous girls. The type I used to hook up with.

They saw my face and gawked.

"Let's go," I said.

The girls blocked the door.

"What are you *doing* here," said one.

The other's finger poised over her phone as if she could make me vanish with a button tap.

Tam said, "Pardon?"

"He shouldn't be here," said Phone Girl.

"It's a unisex bathroom," I said tiredly.

"It's not a *rapist* bathroom."

Tam lunged. I caught her arm.

"Please," I said. "Let's just go."

For a nauseating moment it seemed Tamsin meant to Take a Stand. To defend me. Start an argument where people would discuss my body parts like slabs of meat, my identity like a disorder. As much as I was grateful she cared, confrontation was the last thing I wanted. Especially with these girls. Their bravada was a revolt against years of sexist social programming, being told they either weren't virgin enough or whore enough, being shamed and scrutinized and on dis-play 24/7. They were sick of it. Sick of feeling like meat, too. They believed I was a predator, so they seized this opportunity to wield the small scrap of power they possessed.

I couldn't begrudge them that. No matter how much I wanted to scream in their faces, *I'm the fucking victim.*

Tamsin looked at my face and saw something there. "Move," she snapped at the girls.

We walked out together, her arm around my waist.

Ingrid intercepted us as we drifted through the empty halls of the Oubliette.

"What happened?" she said.

"Hate brigade spotted him. Tried to run him off."

Inge scowled. "I told you this was a bad idea. I'll take you home."

Tam tried to transfer custody but I stood my ground. "I get a fuck-ing say here, too. I'm not leaving."

"You'll compromise us," Ingrid said.

"Go with her," Tam urged. "I'll handle this. I've been watching Adam unseen for months."

"I hate that you two are teaming up against me."

Inge made a noise of disgust. "We're teaming up *for* you, asshole. You're fucking welcome."

Tam's fingers curled around mine for a moment, those pale eyes arresting. A glimmer flitted through them, reminding me of the coded patterns in city lights. She squeezed and I remembered, suddenly, *When you touch me it feels like a conversation.* She was telling me something.

And I was too freaked out and beat down to hear it.

I let Ingrid sweep me under her arm.

Tamsin murmured, "Be careful," and I wondered, *Of whom?*

Halfway up the marble steps to the Cathedral, I froze. Wisps of light flickered around our feet, ghost fingers pulling at us. Ingrid curved her body around me protectively.

"Did you see—?"

"I forgot something."

Her face was close, eyes glassy. "Your gun?"

"I need it, Inge. I feel so fucking . . . powerless." Grimace. "Don't make a dick joke, okay? It's not about compensation. I literally do not feel safe, anywhere."

"Hey." She touched my cheek. "I understand. Let's go get it."

We descended back into the chill depths. I nuzzled into her neck, hiding my face, but strangely I also felt succor. This was how it used to be: Me and her versus the world. So tight on the court no one could break through.

So tight nothing could ever break us.

I wondered what Tam would think, if she saw.

Now the hall to Black Iris HQ was empty. I stepped apart from Inge.

"Stay out of sight," I said. "I'll be right back."

She ducked into an adjacent corridor and I hauled at the heavy steel door. Before it budged an inch, it stuck.

From inside, Laney said, "Ren?"

Shit. "Yeah. Let me in."

"Hold on."

Pause, and the door screeched open. She looked up at me with that small elfin face. Thick eyeliner and ashen eye shadow, a little smutty, Lolita-ish. A girl caught between innocence and ruin. Other people's ruin.

"What's up?" she said.

"Need to get something."

"What do you need?"

Of course. This was Laney. She'd wring out every detail. "My gun."

No expression, but a thought spun in her eyes, a spiderweb woven from light. "I'll get it."

Against all instincts my hand shot out, catching her as she turned.

I had never laid a hand on Delaney Keating. And she had never looked at me with apprehension.

I said, "Let me."

"Why?"

"Because you clearly don't want me in that room. And now I need to see what's in there."

"Ren—"

My friends truly believed I'd never touch a girl with force, never make her do something against her will. Even Laney believed it. So when she blocked the doorway and I picked her up, she didn't fight. Just stared.

"Do *not* go in there," she said as I set her down.

Too late.

A man sprawled in the armchair where I'd sat months ago, scheming to tackle Crito. Without seeing him in full I could rattle off his stats: six feet, one-seventy, brown hair, brown eyes. Tattoo on left shoulder: the Lannister lion crest from *Game of Thrones*. For his favorite character, Tyrion Lannister, which should have told me something—a dwarf smarter than all others around him, but tragically seen as a "half man."

Someone life constantly deprived and fucked over. Someone who deserved more. We'd both related to Tyrion, but I'd never told him the reason I did. At the commotion behind him he stood.

Here's the face of a rapist:

He looks just like any other man. Nothing distinguishes him from men who don't hurt women.

Evil, we're taught—by cartoons, fairy tales—marks you. Drags its claws down your skin, inscribes you with your sins. The visibility of evil is so convincing even monsters believe it about themselves.

I could have anyone. I've got money, brains. I don't need to force girls.

That's sick, ~~Softe~~. It was just rough sex.

Stop crying.

Please stop crying.

He looked at me. He looked at Laney. In an ordinary man's voice, he said, "Who's this?"

Ingrid and I had scoured the Internet till we found someone equally desperate. We drove out to a house in the woods, drove back into the city with the Beretta. Sleek black, woodgrain grip. Lighter than I expected and still the heaviest thing in the world. I kept touching it the whole ride home, and Inge said, *That is one big surrogate dick. Can't wait to watch you fuck him with it.*

The Beretta lay in a locker across the room, behind the monster.

In my fantasies I savaged him. Turned his body into meat, same as he'd done with mine. Beat him till no inch of skin was visible, only blood and mucus, human smears. Smashed him as small as I could. As small as he'd made me.

In reality I just stood there, my hands shaking, my body hollow, vacant. I was not inside of it but tethered loosely to the spinal cord, receiving faint neural impulses.

I couldn't move.

"Ren," Laney said, touching me.

The monster and I stared at each other. A shadow scudded through his eyes.

His mouth opened.

"If you talk," I rasped, "I will rip your throat out."

The shadow in his eyes flared, caught fire. "Oh my god. It can't be."

Now I was moving. "I'm going to kill you. I'm going to fucking kill you."

Hands on me, holding. Laney then Ingrid then Tamsin, too, all of them calling my name, my living name, not the dead one, but all I really heard was Adam saying, "Sofiya, is that you?"

Something guttural and canine echoed in the stone chamber. A roar, so raw the air seemed to seep like a wound after. I didn't recognize my own scream—never heard myself scream like this in my new voice.

Reality got glitchy then.

One second I saw my hand clawing, raking his face, then I was on my knees in the hall outside, retching. Crimson curled under my fingernails. I smiled, tasting acid. In the background Tam screamed—I'd never heard her scream either—*I'm done. I won't be your lapdog anymore. Can't you see how much it's hurting him?* Seemingly in the next heartbeat I sat on a bench with a cup of water, the night air a cool balm on my fevered skin. Then the city blurred across the windows of a train, red and white lights streaking past, ribbons of blood and bone. Then I was home, bent over the bathroom sink, scrubbing my nails till the red ran pink and still scrubbing harder, harder, till fresh red ran in the basin. Getting all traces of *him* out of me. Just like before. At some point I stopped seeing the *now* and only saw the *then*. Blood dripping between my thighs into toilet water, spreading like a poisoned rose. It kept bleeding. Just kept fucking bleeding out every last bit of girl that was left in me.

–7–

TWO YEARS AGO

VLOG #203: TOP SURGERY

REN: Holy. Shit. You guys.

This is it. This is *the* big fucking day.

I'm here with my gracious caretaker, the world's cutest redhead, the ridiculously smart, charming—look, she's already blushing. Say hi, Ellis.

ELLIS: Hi, Ellis.

REN: What a nerd. You guys, Ellis is one of my favorite humans on the entire planet. And she agreed to vlog with me today, because—

[Video turns black-and-white. Maudlin violin plays.]

REN: Actually, there's something I need to get off my chest. It's . . . it's my tits.

ELLIS: [Groans.]

[Music stops. Color returns.]

REN: You totally laughed this time.

ELLIS: I did not!

REN: You made a noise.

ELLIS: Of *dismay*.

REN: Still counts.

Anyway, bad puns aside, I'm psyched. Today is Top Surgery Eve. My last day with these stupid water balloons stuck to my chest.

ELLIS: This is a huge milestone. I'm really proud of you, Ren.

REN: Want to touch them one last time?

ELLIS: [Blushes.] What?

REN: Do you?

ELLIS: I've never—

REN: I'm just saying. This is your last chance.

ELLIS: No, but . . . thank you.

REN: She's so cute when she squirms.

ELLIS: Shut *up*.

REN: God, Ellis. I've been waiting for this day since . . . well, when I was twelve and running through the park, thinking, "What are these things, and most importantly, *why*?"

ELLIS: Puberty is the worst.

REN: It is. It's like, "Hey, we heard you refused to pick a binary gender, so we picked one for you. Do these boobies fit? No? Well, enjoy your future mastectomy."

ELLIS: It's so wrong that it happens that early. Puberty should happen in, like, your thirties.

REN: Oh god. Can you imagine that world? Raging hormones and acne when you're supposed to have your shit together.

ELLIS: Some people transition in their thirties.

REN: Poor souls. We salute you.

[Jump cut.]

REN: So, Ellis here is driving me to the clinic tomorrow

Your Receipt

Regina Public Library

Customer ID: **********1652

Items that you checked out

Title: Bad boy : a novel
ID: 39085700269539
Due: Feb-26-2018 23:59

Title: The baby and the cowboy SEAL
ID: 39085600504043
Due: Feb-26-2018 23:59

Total items: 2
Feb-05-2018 11:05
Overdue: 0

www.reginalibrary.ca

morning. They're going to knock me out and when I wake up I'll be flat-chested again. Like I always should've been. I'm getting a double incision, which means he'll cut along here. [Draws a line beneath his pecs.] Recovery is brutal. I have to wear a compression vest with tubes hanging out to drain blood and pus and whatnot. Plus I won't be able to raise my arms for a week.

I have never been so excited to feel like absolute shit.

ELLIS: This is seriously brave of you.

REN: No, it's brave of *you*. You're the one who's gonna have to clean that shit up.

ELLIS: [Frowns.]

REN: This is a two-man ordeal, so Ellis is taking care of me during recovery. Because she's the fucking best.

ELLIS: It's the least I could do, since you wouldn't let me pay for it.

REN: Oh, stop.

ELLIS: And *someone* has to be there for you.

REN: Right. Someone who cares.

ELLIS: Someone who understands this is a lifesaving operation. Not a cosmetic one.

REN: [Eyes Ellis for a moment.] I owe you, E. Big-time. This is going to be one of the defining moments of my life. I'm glad you'll be here for it.

ELLIS: Me too.

REN: If you weren't so gay, I'd kiss you.

ELLIS: [Blushes.] You can. Like, platonically. On the cheek.

REN: I'll platonic the fuck out of you.

[Ren tackle-hugs Ellis.]

[Jump cut.]

[Their hair is mussed.]

REN: Once I'm in recovery, E's in charge of filming. If I say wacky shit while I'm high on codeine, edit it out, okay?

ELLIS: You're no fun.

REN: You want to fuck with me while my former boobs are bleeding? Monster.

Anyway, we've got a long day ahead tomorrow. Wish me luck, Internet.

I'll see you guys on the flip side.

————

[Caption: *Day One*]

[Ren is lying in a hospital bed, his chest bound with bandages.]

REN: [Moans.] Fucking . . . fuck.

ELLIS: How do you feel?

REN: [Slurs.] Like they shot me. Twice. Then stabbed the bullets. Then . . . set me on fire.

ELLIS: You're on enough codeine to knock out a unicorn.

REN: What? Wait . . . there's a unicorn?

ELLIS: You are *so* high. [Laughs.] Are you okay?

REN: Is it me? Am I the unicorn? What the hell. Ellis. Why did you make me a unicorn?

ELLIS: I'm sorry.

REN: Ellis. Ellllissss. [Laughs.] Words are *weird*. Do I have a horn?

ELLIS: Don't laugh, you dork. You'll pull the stitches out.

SURGEON: Ah, he's awake. How are you feeling, young man?

REN: You fucking sadist.

SURGEON: [Laughs.]

————

[Caption: *Day Two*]

[Ren and Ellis are in a hotel bathroom. She shaves his face while he stares at himself in the mirror. His eyes are wide, filled with wonder.]

[Caption: *Day Three*]

[McDonald's drive-through. Ren leans across Ellis to order several different Happy Meals. Ellis stares through the windshield with a long-suffering look.]

_____

[Caption: *Day Four*]

[Ren films Ellis frantically spritzing the hotel room with air freshener.]

REN: Stop being polite. Spray that shit directly on me, dude.

ELLIS: [Spritzes the camera.]

_____

[Caption: *Day Five*]

[Examining room at the clinic. The surgeon unwraps the final bandage from Ren's chest in front of a mirror.]

REN: Oh my god. [Touches his chest tentatively.] Oh my *god*.

ELLIS: How do you feel?

REN: I don't even know how to describe it. I feel like . . . a kid. Like I used to before all of this happened, all of this . . . wrongness. This wrong life. That's *me*, Ellis. In the mirror. That's who I've seen in my head all these years. It's—are you crying?

ELLIS: [Sniffs.] No.

_____

[Caption: *Day Six*]

REN: Back home. Still sore as hell. Just a quick update about—

[Distantly, a door slams.]

About that.

That's Best Friend, and she's pissed. Can't blame her—I can't take care of myself right now, our apartment is a wreck, the chores aren't done, and I'm late on bills because I put every penny into this surgery.

The surgery she calls "cosmetic."

And "an exercise in internalized misogyny."

And "trying to fit in with the people you hate."

I can blame her for making me feel like shit, at least.

[Jump cut.]

It's really hard to transition when the people you love are fighting it. When it feels like you're nonstop dropping burdens on them: the burden of understanding, the burden of caring, the burden of being happy for you. My therapist told me the trans people who are happiest are the ones who have solid social support.

The ones who don't? Well, someone has to fill up those post-transition suicide statistics.

I never expected her to be thrilled about this, but I did expect some recognition of how good it's been for me. How energized and optimistic I am on T, how much more *myself*. How miserable and depressed I am when my hormones slip back into girl mode.

When you love somebody—selflessly, unconditionally love them—their happiness is more important than your own. Even if what makes them happy hurts you.

My mother made it clear that her love is conditional. She said, "If you butcher yourself, you are no longer my daughter."

Funny thing is, she still doesn't get that I never *was* her daughter.

But my dear Best Friend—she's never said it in those terms. She's always been here at my side, catching me when I stumble, cleaning my wounds. She makes me feel strong and weak at the same time. Because through it all I sense her disapproval, her judgment. How ecstatic she'd be if I turned around tomorrow and said, "I was wrong. I'm a girl after all."

Sometimes I think she's fucking toxic. That she'd rather destroy us both than let me be happy without her.

And sometimes, part of me wants to let it happen. To self-destruct with her.

What a couple of fuckups.

––––––––

[Caption: *Day Thirty*]

[Ren stands in a friend's apartment, shirtless. His surgery scars have faded to thin red lines. Vada sketches tattoo plans on his chest with a marker while Blythe and Ellis watch. Ellis scowls.]

REN: Is all of this touching necessary?

VADA: Oh, I'm sorry. Am I making you uncomfortable?

REN: I'm enjoying the hell out of it, actually. But I don't think Ellis is.

ELLIS: It's fine. Vada's a professional artist. This is—

VADA: [Under her breath.] *Part of her process.*

ELLIS: —part of her process.

REN: [Laughs.]

ELLIS: What?

VADA: Nothing, nerd. Don't be jealous. I only have eyes for you.

ELLIS: And Ren's torso.

REN: Hey, male torsos need love, too.

BLYTHE: Bloody hell they do. They could put yours on a romance novel cover as the main character.

REN: That's the dream.

ELLIS: How *are* you that buff?

REN: Girls give me a good workout.

BLYTHE: Sex is cardio, you manwhore.

REN: Not when you're lifting them against a wall.

VADA: [Laughs.]

BLYTHE: Don't encourage him, V. We're trying to mold him into a decent bloke.

VADA: I thought you said there were no decent men.

BLYTHE: Yes, but he needs *something* to aspire to.

REN: Ladies, you realize I can hear you, right?

BLYTHE: Be quiet and flex.

REN: [Flexes his chest.]

VADA: Whoa.

BLYTHE: Be still my bloody heart.

ELLIS: I don't get it. It's just muscle. What's the big deal?

BLYTHE: You're a lesbian, love. It's like giving a fish a bicycle.

ELLIS: [Narrows her eyes.]

VADA: What about here? [Taps the center of Ren's chest.] This one should be special.

ELLIS: Aren't all tattoos special? They're permanent.

VADA: I mean extra-special, *pajarito*. Like the one I gave you.

ELLIS: [Blushes.]

BLYTHE: Oh, there's a story there.

ELLIS: No there isn't. And don't you dare tell them, Vada.

VADA: [Grins.]

REN: Blythe doesn't have a tat there yet.

VADA: Wait, has *everyone* seen Blythe with her shirt off?

BLYTHE: Yep.

REN: Yep.

ELLIS: [Bites her lip.]

BLYTHE: And yep. Anyway, I'm saving my heart.

REN: For what?

BLYTHE: For *whom*.

REN: Some poor girl who'll never know what hit her?

BLYTHE: [Shrugs.] Or someone as fucked-up as me.

REN: Sounds like a really healthy relationship goal. So should I save mine for Future Wife?

VADA: I always say lovers' tats are a bad idea. You don't need to prove your love with ink.

REN: Then what would you get?

VADA: A memory. My most important ones are memories. Things I want to hold on to, no matter what else I lose.

[Vada and Ellis trade glances. Blythe lights a cigarette. Ren thinks for a while.]

REN: That painting you did for me, of the boy holding back the sea?

VADA: Yeah?

REN: That's what I want here.

———

In the morning, I was calm.

"Black Iris betrayed me," I said. "They're the enemy."

Frail light fell over the three of us, laid a delicate silver foil atop our skin. Tamsin's hair shone darkly, and when she tipped her head against the window, snow spangled her reflection like stars.

"Speculation," she said with a sigh.

"Laney made her loyalties clear. She's working with Adam."

"Conjecture."

"He was sitting right there. Unharmed. In *my* world."

"We've had this conversation a dozen times." Tamsin stood. "All we know is he was there last night. Not why. Maybe she was working out some way to protect you."

"She didn't want me in that room. She was protecting *him*."

"Going in bloody circles again." Tam stalked toward the bathroom.

Ingrid watched her leave, only her eyes moving. Smoke spun a blue wreath around her temples. "Do you trust her?"

"Yes."

"Why?"

Because she's gentle with me, I thought. Because she sees the boy I am, not the girl I was. "Gut feeling."

"You sure it's not a few inches lower?"

I gave her a look.

"She's one of them," Inge said. "She's with Laney. She knows more than she's telling us. But you refuse to see it. You're thinking with your dick."

"I think about you with it, too, so . . ."

Ingrid stared at me, expressionless. Ever so slightly, the corner of her mouth curled.

When Tam returned, I said, "You're right. We're going in circles. It's time to take action." I stretched, cracked my neck. Felt the power of my body, this self-built pretty little hate machine. A man made to unmake other men. "I need to know what Black Iris knows. About Adam, Crito, Norah, all of it. Everything ties together, somehow, with me in the middle." I moved toward Tamsin. "You need to pick a side."

"I'm here, aren't I?"

"I need to hear you say it. You're either with me or against me."

Her brow furrowed, eyes momentarily skittering toward Ingrid. But she said, in clear, chiming tones, "I'm with you, Renard. I'm with you."

Each time she weighted the words differently. First they meant "I'm on your side," and then "We're together." Slight but meaningful difference.

Our hands clasped. Conscious of Inge's stare, I let go sooner than I wanted.

"So what's the plan?" Ingrid said coolly.

"Crito." I drummed my fingers against my leg. "Everything went wrong that night. Laney wanted you to handle him discreetly, Tam. Don't think she ever wanted me to see him, period."

"What's her motive? Why would she hurt you?"

"For being a man. That's all the reason she's ever needed to hurt someone. And all I needed."

"That's absurd," Tam said.

"It's not. All those men she sent me after—I never once questioned their guilt. Why? *Because* they're men." My knuckles cracked. I didn't remember making fists. "I saw them as inherently guilty, and so did she. Simply because of their gender. Laney's known about Adam for years. She preyed on my history, my distrust of men. She knew I'd attack any male target she gave me like a trained dog. And she was fucking right."

"But why not let you take vengeance on a man, then?"

"Because it's not just about hurting men—it's also refusing to help them. When I asked her, she balked. It didn't fit her view of the world. Her radical feminist fairy tale where masculinity is the root of all evil."

Ingrid's eyes narrowed, but she said nothing.

"You're attributing to malice what can be explained by other means," Tamsin said.

"So explain it, Tam. Tell me why Laney would deny me my right. Why she'd shelter someone who hurt me."

Her turn to fall silent.

"You don't see it," I went on. "You can't. Because you're a woman, Laney would never look at you the way she does at me. Only women are worthy to her, and only women are safe from her. It's some twisted chivalry. I had the balls to test it, so now I pay the price."

Neither of them argued. Smoke painted watercolor shadows on the floor.

I said, "We need info. Blythe's out—too close to Laney. Armin's a sycophant. That leaves one option: Ellis."

Inge's eyebrow twitched at the name. That's right, I thought. The girl who was there for me during one of the scariest, most exhilarating moments of my life.

The moment you should've been there for.

"We're tight," I continued, "and she has a strong conscience. I think she's been hinting to me about Laney's true motives. She'll help."

"Too risky," Ingrid said.

"Why?"

"Ellis is weak. If Laney bends her, she'll snap."

"Gentleness isn't weakness. Ellis is stronger than you think. You got a better idea?"

"Skip the foreplay. Put a bullet in the bastard who hurt you. In anyone who hurt you."

Then, with sheer brazenness, Inge looked straight at Tam.

My phone pinged. Thank God. Time for my daily T.

I left the girls to glare-fuck each other and headed for the bathroom. Nearly out of testosterone gel—I was burning through it four times too fast. I needed cash, quick. Needed to see a doc, get my bloodwork done, figure out why the fuck my T level kept bouncing around. And with my YouTube channel suspended and no sponsors returning my messages, my current income totaled a big fat zero.

I needed that job Armin offered. And he was Laney's lackey.

Always at her mercy, no matter what I did.

The door opened sans knock. "Ingrid," I began irascibly.

But it was Tamsin. She shut the door as softly as she could. Her voice was hushed, intent.

"Listen to me closely. You need to hear this. Truly hear it, Ren." She took my face in her hands. "An abuser separates you from your friends. Makes you believe they're the only person you can trust."

"Tam—"

"I know this intimately. I let a man do it to me for years. Let him isolate me, render me dependent upon him. Let him hurt me, because I believed it was love."

I gripped her wrists. "That's not what Ingrid's doing."

"I'm telling you what I see. I'm afraid for you, Renard." She leaned closer and whispered fiercely, "*You can't trust her.*"

"She said the same about you."

"Believe your instincts. Something feels right, and something feels wrong. Trust those feelings."

Such a cisgender way of thinking. When her body told her *danger*, she believed it. She wasn't subject to the whims of hormones and dysphoria the way I was. Didn't spend half her life battling her body's distress signals, trying to figure out which were real threats and which self-loathing distortions.

That was the tragedy: Being trans taught you not to trust yourself. To doubt everything, even your own heart.

"Answer me." My grip firmed. "Do you know what Laney's really doing? What haven't you told me, Tam?"

That coded sparkle in her eyes again. "The Wolf never does anything by accident. There's always a design within her chaos."

Tell me your story, I'd said. *The one where you kill a man.*

"Listen." Urgency in my voice, throaty and hot. "There's something me and Laney did together. Something damning. If it ever comes to light, she'll take the fall, not me. It was collateral, to make me trust her. Maybe that's her real motive. I tried to use it as leverage to make her take out Adam, and she—"

Footsteps in the hallway.

Tamsin laid a finger against my lips. *Not now*, she mouthed. *Meet me later.*

Then she flung the door open and breezed out.

Ingrid waited till I'd walked past, too, before saying, "You should change your code name, Cane."

"What? Why?"

"To fit her. Cressida." In the dark, her smile was a curved bone knife. "Because now you're her Troilus."

———

My sleep was fitful, restless. In the dream—it was always the same anxiety dream—I ran from something I couldn't see, chasing me through the tintype haze and mirror façades of the city. But I was too slow. My legs moved sluggishly through air thick as water, churning. I'd throw myself onto hands and knees and run like a wolf, nails clawing pavement, till my brain sensed the lack of biofeedback and slowed me down again. While you sleep, the body enters temporary paralysis. Without feedback from your limbs the brain can't maintain the dream fiction of running. That's why you're always slower than what's chasing you. Why you always stumble, fall, feel the humid breath snorting against your neck.

I woke sweating and cold. The apartment was empty.

On my phone, an address.

We met at a bar on the North Side, all weathered brick and raw pine, smelling of the wet salted street. Tamsin rose from a booth and headed for the back hall. When I caught up she wrapped me in a suffocating hug, and I hugged back just as hard.

"I'm so sorry," she murmured against my cheek.

"About what?"

"All of this. All the pain you're suffering."

"It's not your fault."

Her expression was sorrowful, sober.

"We must talk," she said. "Candidly. No more games."

We ordered two pints of beer, foam glittering as it dissolved. Her hands danced across the tabletop while she told me all the things she'd been holding back.

Six months ago, Laney Keating came to her. *A friend of mine knows your sister.* Half sister, technically. Frankie Baylor, friend of Ellis and Vada. Former webcam girl turned entrepreneur. Every year Tam and Frankie visited each other, in Maine snow or English rain. Frankie doted on Tam, beseeched her to move to America, to live like real sisters. But Tam's mom was sick, stuck in limbo on NHS waiting lists. Without Tamsin she'd never get to her doctor's appointments. She'd give up, wither.

"It's not an excuse," Tam said. "I'd have done something fucked-up one way or another. It's in my blood. But at least my fucking up in England served another purpose."

Frankie excelled in school and fast-tracked herself into college; Tam dropped out of sixth form and robbed the posh boys she slept with. They bought her designer handbags, heels in snakeskin and gold lamé, perfumes she never even sniffed before hawking them on eBay. She'd fuck a boy till he shared his bank card codes. The last day he ever saw her, she'd say, *Meeting a friend. Be a good lad and I'll suck your cock when I'm back.*

She cleaned out his account. He never got that blowjob.

"I didn't give it all to Mum," Tamsin said. "I wasn't bloody Robin Hood. I was selfish, young, stupid."

And overconfident.

Which was how she got caught.

She messed with the wrong wealthy white boy. He told his dad, who pulled some strings. The policeman who came to her flat was tall, handsome, smiling. In a svelte voice he explained how it would be.

You're going to shag me, he said, *or you're going to jail.*

From the corner of the room, Mum, her eyes clouded with dementia, said, *Stupid cow. What've you done?*

"Tamsin," I breathed.

"It's not what you think. He never forced me, physically."

"It's coercion. It's still—"

The word I could not say.

"You have to understand," she said, leaning toward me, "that my life *improved* with him. He earned a steady paycheck. Took care of us. It wasn't force—he paid for sex. I sold it willingly."

"If he held something against you, you didn't have full agency. You were a captive. A captive can't give consent."

Tam shrugged. "We're all trapped by something. Freedom is an illusion. It's the wind in your hair as you plummet off the cliff's edge."

"How could you love someone who hurt you?"

"How could you?"

"Hurt" was such a small, insufficient word for these things.

"Tell me," she said. "Tell me what he did to you, Ren."

If she hadn't used my name, I don't think I could have answered. But she validated my identity, let it supersede the past.

Made it the slightest bit easier for me to reclaim.

Once upon a time, I told her, there were two girls, two friends who were more than friends. One of them wasn't really a girl, and the other could never accept that. They hurt each other. Fought incessantly. Tried to cut each other loose, move on, but some awful unbreakable thread would not sever. Bound together and miserable, they stewed in their own toxicity. One of them—the one who wasn't really a girl— wanted to hurt the other in a permanent way. A way that would free her from their entanglement, forever. Let her become the person she was meant to be. So she found a boy who was willing, and gave her body to him. Not completely—there were certain things she would never do. But she put her mouth on him, tasted him, let him taste her.

The other girl raged. *I hate you*, she said. *You'll give yourself to anyone but me.*

I don't know who you are anymore.

I hope it makes you sick. I hope you choke on his fucking come.

I hope he destroys you.

And he did.

Because this boy had a friend who whispered poisons in his ear. A friend who would one day name himself Crito. Crito said a girl's "yes" had no expiration date, and if she took it in the mouth, she was a slut and she'd take it anywhere. The boy had tried before, pressed his hips against hers, and she shoved him away. *What's the problem?* he said. *It's less work for you.* She said, *Just don't.*

One night, drunk on Crito's venom and his manifest destiny as a male, the boy told the girl who wasn't a girl, *Lie back.*

Her instincts were frazzled, unreliable. She thought he wanted to suck her off. It felt good, sometimes, when she closed her eyes, thought of it in a queer way. Just one boy sucking another boy off.

But she could never tell him that. He'd hurt her.

If she knew he could hurt her, didn't she know this could happen?

Didn't she *let* it happen?

She lay back.

When he put his whole weight atop her she realized her dreadful mistake. *Don't*, she said, and, *Please, Adam. Please.*

Bewildered, he said, *You're a virgin.*

Because of the blood.

Please stop, she said, and he said, *But you're so wet.*

The printouts they gave her at the hospital read *The body may react to unwanted sexual contact with arousal, including vaginal wetness and orgasm. This does not indicate consent.*

But in the moment she'd thought, horrified, *If my body is acting this way, isn't that saying yes?*

How could she trust mind over body when her mind had told her terrible things? That her body looked wrong, completely wrong, every time she glanced into a mirror? That she should destroy it. That she should unravel and unstitch it with scalpels and needles.

She closed her eyes and thought, *Be quick.*

It was after, on the bus, that she cried. Couldn't stop crying. Then she understood: This was her body's way of speaking to her. Inarticulate and raw, a primal howl of pain. She should have trusted it. Should have listened. The dysphoria she'd felt was real—she wasn't a girl after all, but a boy. And this agony wasn't from rough sex. It was from rape.

There.

I said the word. In real time, to a real person.

Oh, fuck.

Tamsin braced me as I stumbled to the bathroom. For a ridiculous moment I hesitated between the doors, staring at the signs—pants, dress, meaningless fucking gender binary—till she pushed me bodily into the men's. I sank to my knees, face in my hands. Sobbing like a child.

Tam knelt beside me and simply held on.

Nothing in me but that map of blood and nerve lighting up my lungs. The place where sorrow dwelled.

Later, drained, I stood at the sink splashing icy water on my face. My skin had an ill pallor. The strange thing, the thing I didn't expect:

I didn't see Sofiya peering through.

Just me. Renard.

"It was him, wasn't it?" I said. "The man you killed. That cop."

Tamsin watched me in the mirror. "He disappeared under mysterious circumstances. I heard his body washed up near Gravesend. Death by misadventure."

"That's why you're here, living in hotels, getting paid under the table. You're still running from it."

"Perhaps."

"Your sister sent you to Laney for protection."

"Turned out I had some useful skills, and a powerful boredom, and a shite opinion of men. Frankie knew Laney'd have a use for me. So she hired me on."

"And told you to watch Adam."

"Yes." She slid between me and the mirror. "What's the collateral you have on her?"

In the early days of Black Iris, before Ellis upgraded our tech, we ran ops old school: me, a gun, and a name and address.

No one to watch what I did.

No one to judge.

Teach him a lesson, Laney would say. *Make sure he never does it again.*

At first, I thought rage would frighten them most. I tossed them around like rag dolls, let them feel how flimsy and frail they were in my hands. Relieved them of a few teeth, a fingernail, the joint of a toe. It was usually enough.

But not always. Some took a beating and came back stronger. I knew this process well. Some wounds are forever, and the scars harden inside you like diamonds, a sparkling, razor-sharp lace surrounding your heart. It can't be removed but also can't be broken. Diamond is the hardest naturally occurring substance on earth.

The most dangerous people out there? They're made of scar tissue.

It was time to adjust my strategy. Think long term.

I smacked them around, but before any serious damage was done I drew my knife and said, *I'm giving you a gift. I'm letting you go.*

Snick. Bonds cut. Gushing gratitude till I added:

I'll be watching.

Any moment, any day, if I see something I don't like—bothering a girl who wants to be left alone, pressuring her, hell, even bitching to a bro about being friend-zoned again—I'll strike. Take a finger, an eye, maybe a ball, depending on my mood. (Here I'd trace the named body part with the tip of the knife, for dramatic effect.) *So keep that in mind, bud, when you're out living your shitty little life.*

I'm watching you.

Laney said, *Whatever you're doing differently, it's working.*

One night I got a call.

Some kind of accident. She needed my help. When I got to the warehouse Laney stood over a man lying in a pool of blood thick and dark as tar. Paralyzed, but alive. One side of his face twitched, short-circuiting. Laney told me what he'd done—drugged girls, violated them, scared them into silence with threats of revenge porn—and she'd decided that for once, vengeance was too kind. She wanted him wiped from the face of the earth.

Why am I here? I said breathlessly.

So I can give you this. She passed me her phone. On it, a video of her pulling the trigger. *I've put blood on your hands. Now you have something on me.*

Why? I'd said.

She tapped SEND, forwarding me the video. *Because a day will come when I'll ask something of you that you don't want to do. This is your collateral. This is how you'll know I won't betray you.*

Tamsin gazed up at me, calculating. "What happened then?"

How light it had felt, that trigger pull. The frighteningly soft force required to end someone. "She turned off the camera, and I finished him. He was dying. There wasn't enough brain left for him to appreciate that fact anymore."

"You're not a killer, Ren."

"I ended someone's life."

"That was mercy, not murder."

"But it felt good," I whispered. "It felt *right*."

All I'd thought, when I saw the body still, was:

I wish it were *him*. My Poseidon.

Tamsin's arms were around me then, both of us trembling. "Mine felt good, too. We're both a little broken."

"I don't think I can be fixed, Tam."

"I don't intend to try, if that's your worry."

I cupped her cheek but couldn't quite meet her eye. "You're the first I've told, after Ingrid. About Adam. No one else knows."

"Did you think I'd see you differently?"

"Yes." I swallowed. "As . . . lesser. Less of a man."

Because what kind of man let another do this to him? Hurt him so deeply. Break something buried so far inside.

Not a real one.

Tam turned my face to hers. "What happened to you doesn't change what you are. You are every bit the man I've been falling for."

All at once, a heaviness lifted. I felt untethered, buoyant. The way I'd feel when I lined up a sure shot on the court and everything seemed to click: clear space, the hoop a red bull's-eye, the perfect arc of my wrist. Letting the ball go as lightly as dandelion fluff. The sense that I could turn around, let it sink without watching, because I could already feel the swish in my core.

Fingers touched my face, brushed the water away. Then her mouth was on mine, soft. I kissed her and tasted my own salt. Pushed her onto the sink counter, against the mirror, kissing harder. Our hands slipped into each other's coats. It was rough, suddenly, our bad blood stirring, raising a dark sediment: the things that had been done to us, the things we'd done. I bit her lip and she gasped into my mouth. "Did I hurt you?" I said, and she said, "Yes. Do it again." So I took her lip between my teeth, tighter and tighter till she cried out. Then I kissed her gently, sucking at that sweet coppery warmth.

"Hurt me back," I said.

Her fingertips skimmed my throat. My nerves sizzled. "I can't, lovely boy."

But that fire would not cool.

In the taxi, as snow gusted at the windows, my hand moved over her thigh. Then to the inside, her muscle tightening but her legs parting. Snowflakes melted into liquid confetti, dappled the glass with colored lights. Her heat filled my palm. She put her hand on my leg, and I stiffened, and she looked at me. That conversation without words. *Is it okay? Is this what you want?*

When we reached her hotel I told the driver to circle it.

Tamsin held my gaze as her hand moved. Every fiber in me tensed, tugged toward my center. I moved as she did, higher. To that densest heat, her hand cupping the bulge in my jeans as I slid two fingers into the hollow between her legs. We both gasped without sound. That we did this here, with a stranger, without being able to fully react, made it crazy. Wild. Broken. She rocked her hand against my cock. I'd gone so hard my skin felt like it was coming apart. A man's arousal is more than the erection—it's every muscle flexing, every artery swelling, a terrible intensity that needs to be released, received. In that softness between her thighs, her jeans damp against my hand.

I took my hand away. She removed hers.

Our breath fogged the windows.

"You drive me mad," she said.

I watched her walk through the snow to the brass doors, not turn-ing. Knowing my eyes were on her. Knowing I wanted nothing more than to tear through the lobby, throw her on the hotel bed, unleash myself. Knowing that someday I would.

And maybe let her do the same to me.

———

"I'm sorry to put you in this position," I said. "But you're the only one I can trust, old sport."

Ellis frowned at the papers in her hands. No question she'd turn them over, but first she needed to process this.

"I feel like I'm the rope in a tug-of-war," she said. "You and Laney are pulling me back and forth."

"You don't have to do this."

"But I want to. I want to help you, Ren." Her face rose, her eyes sanguine, earnest. "You know we're part of something bigger than ourselves, right? Nobody really understands what Black Iris is doing at any particular moment except Laney."

"And that's dangerous, E. We've concentrated all our power in one person's hands."

"She's never given us reason to doubt her intentions."

"She gave me reason." I nodded at the documents. Crito's current location, movement patterns, everything. "That's my cause for doubt. She's been hiding things from me. It's time to bring them to light."

Ellis sighed and passed me the papers. "Are you going to . . . hurt him?"

"Crito? You fucking bet I am."

"I mean—the other man."

We locked eyes.

"When I'm done with him," I said, "there won't be anything left worth calling a man."

———

Tamsin and I stood in a gold disc of streetlight at the bus stop, our breath knitting the air into gossamer scarves. Snow fell slowly, heathering our wool coats, and when Tam threw her head back and exhaled, her teeth shone as brightly as the tumbling sky. We were breathless because we'd ditched the cab a block away and run to the stop. Down the street through the haze of powder, the bus headlights burned hot.

"This is it," I said. "No screwing it up this time."

Tam raised an eyebrow, those violet lips curved. Snow sugared the lower one and I imagined licking it.

"I promise I won't pull a gun on you," she said.

"Likewise."

"Or knee you in the cock."

"I'd very much appreciate not reliving that."

"You know," she said, "you still owe me a rematch."

The bus huffed up, shedding steam like an animal laboring in the cold. We waved our wallets at the fare machine and fell in a heap of legs and arms on a side-facing bench. Tamsin laid her head in the crook of my shoulder.

"Got an eye on him?" I said.

"Yeah." Her knee linked with mine. "Nuzzle into me."

My heart broke into fluttering pieces, like the stuff sloughing off the windows. I pressed my face into her hair. Warm almond. Her scent drugged me, and despite the consummate fucked-upness of everything, I wanted her. T works no matter how fucked-up you are, how frightened, anxious, unsure. The wildest thing is how a body continues to function no matter how battered its mind. I imagined my mouth on hers again, our limbs tangling. That smooth belly pressing against the hard rack of my abs. It took every iota of restraint to not go too far. Instead I watched snow melt into liquid glass in her hair, and wondered if I could let her touch me the way I wanted to touch her.

"He's moving." Her eyes flashed like flicked pennies. She pecked my cheek, hopped out at the next stop with our target. I waited one more, pulled my hood up, and followed.

Snow fell in its haunting way, a million silent impacts per second. Crito was a shadow drifting through the quiet downfall. We tailed him at a distance. He walked head down, unaware. Something I could never do. Tam either. Owning a female body in this world, even temporarily, changed you. You could never go back to that male ease, that ignorance. A female body was a raw nerve. It reacted to everything—it had to, if it wanted to survive.

Crito trotted up the brick steps of a bungalow. Windows glowed creamy gold in the snow-bright darkness.

In the alley behind the house, Tam brushed her gloved hand against my stubble, dusting off frost. She leaned up to breathe into my ear, "You look like an old man."

It made me shiver. That breath traced my skin as if it were a fingertip.

Cressida, the girl who betrayed Troilus, her lover.

We watched the silhouette move against lit glass.

Our plan: second-floor breach. Tam made a stirrup with her hands and boosted me to the roof. I hauled her up, her body nimble, light. We wedged the window open. The attic bedroom was dark.

Below us he moved, oblivious. I counted footsteps, the creak of things opening and closing.

He's alone, I mouthed.

My knife blended seamlessly into the darkness. We padded downstairs, two menacing bodies clad all in black. Shadows come to life.

Crito stood peering at the backyard.

At our footsteps in the snow.

I was on him in a heartbeat, my arm snaking around his neck. Hard flex, blade to throat.

"Don't speak," I said.

Tamsin switched the lights off.

I sat him on a chair, the knife skimming his Adam's apple. His eyes were glassy in that way most men's are, filmed with dull light. You saw it in trans men's timelines. Ingrid saw it in mine. In the before pics my eyes held something tremulous and soft, a watery uncertainty. In the after pics they were hooded, hard, that animal glaze of confidence. Or uncaring.

It's not the T, I'd said. *It's what I've been through.*

You've been through T, she said.

"Stay quiet." I took the knife away.

Tamsin began strapping him to the chair with duct tape.

"You," Crito said, breathing fast. "You're the ones who—"

My elbow smashed into the center of his face. Something crackled, wetly.

"Told you to stay quiet," I said.

When Tam finished with the tape she pulled a hood over his head. He screamed through it, muffled.

"Shut up," I said calmly, "or I'll gag you."

Ragged, heavy breaths.

"Relax, Jay. Don't hyperventilate."

His body stilled.

Tamsin frisked him for weapons, found a 9 mm. Smirked and tucked it in her belt.

Concrete stairs led to a basement. I dragged him down, letting the chair screech and crash on each step. Startled cries emitted from the hood. The air was damp, dewy. I positioned the chair beneath a lightbulb and plucked the hood off while Tam yanked the cord.

Blood painted frantic wings across his face, as if he'd bitten a live animal. He cowered.

"Hello, Jay," I said. "How's that shoulder?"

"You may speak," Tam said. "Say hello."

"Please. I'm out of the game. I stopped that night, like you said."

"Good boy." I squatted at his feet, testing his bonds. "We're not here about that."

His eyes rolled from me to her and back.

"We're here," Tamsin said, leaning on the shoulder she'd shot, making him wince, "to talk about the past."

I fished the phone from his hoodie. Locked, of course.

"Tell me the password now," I said, "or tell me after I've broken all of your fingers."

He told me now.

I scrolled through his contacts. "It's been a while, Jay. How's it feel to be the victim again?"

Crito frowned. "Do I know you?"

I glanced up at him through my mask. His gaze ricocheted between my mouth, my eyes, the only features visible.

"You seem very familiar," he said.

"Are you shitting me?"

His frown became confused.

Impulsively, I tore the mask off. Not like it mattered—he knew full fucking well who I was. "Surprise, motherfucker."

Still no recognition, only suspicion.

Bizarre, but who knew what game Jay would play to get out of this. Back to his phone.

Tamsin said, "What made you like this, Crito?"

"Huh?"

"What made you a bottom-feeding misogynistic piece of shite?"

He shrugged. "I'm not a misogynist. I'm a humanist."

"And I'm the bloody Queen. What do you call the way you treat women?"

"Equality."

Tam snorted. "Your head's so far up your arse you could lick your tonsils. What do you know about equality?"

His eyes darted to me, then away. "I know it already exists."

"Right. That's the height of male privilege, mate."

"You women always talk about male privilege. But you have female privilege, and you never admit it."

"What, pray tell, does 'female privilege' entail?"

"Being a victim. A martyr. Having people automatically believe whatever you say if you cry."

My jaw tightened.

"Sure," Tam scoffed. "Like they believed the bruises on my body. Like they've believed all the girls who were beaten and raped, whose abusers walked free."

Blood pounded in my head. I focused on the phone.

The contact names were familiar: guys Black Iris had gone after.

All aliases, Greek philosophers and founding fathers. Typical. To these fuckwits masculinity was a white savior jerking off atop the world.

I kept scrolling.

"Your kind," Tam said, "will never know how easy you have it. The only way you could understand is if you'd been born female." She grasped Crito's jaw, made a fish face of his mouth. "Or maybe if *you* were transgender. If you had to enter into a world of misogyny just to be yourself. Give up your male privilege, feel what it's like to be seen as a girl. If life were fair, you would've been. You would've suffered with a body you couldn't stand. You would've felt the anguish and hatred that you bring women."

The phone screen shivered. I didn't argue, but I thought, *You're wrong, Tam. If life were fair, nobody would suffer. Regardless of gender.*

I said, "She came to see you, didn't she?"

Tamsin frowned. Crito's demeanor changed: no longer self-righteous, but wary.

"Answer me."

"There were two," he said edgily.

"Who were they, Jay?"

His gaze refocused, and I saw the moment it happened: when past and present aligned. He stuttered, then said, "Sofie?"

My hand shot out of its own accord. The phone glass cracked on his jawbone. Blood spattered the concrete.

"That name is fucking dead," I said, my voice still soft.

He coughed red, cringed. Tongued a loose tooth. "I can't believe it's you."

Tamsin smacked his cheek, and he moaned. "Answer the question. Who came to see you?"

But he was looking at me now.

"Two girls," he said.

"What did they look like?"

"They wore masks, like you. One was tall, blond. Other was short with dark hair."

Tam and I locked eyes.

A tall blonde and a short brunette.

What a coincidence. Just like Blythe McKinley and Laney Keating.

"Did the blonde have tattoos?" I said. "An accent?"

"I don't know. The other one did the talking."

"What did they want?"

He spat a glob of blood on the floor. "To deliver some flowers to your place."

The bouquet, with my deadname on the card. "Which you did."

"Nah. I'm out of the game."

"Lie to me again and I'll knock the rest of your teeth down your throat."

"I'm not lying, man. I'm retired." Crito shrugged uneasily in his bonds. "This shit isn't worth my life. You ever had a bullet in you?"

I didn't answer. Instead I stood, half turned. "They asked you to deliver flowers. The way you used to do, to threaten girls."

"Those weren't threats."

"What were they?"

"Reality checks."

Tamsin cracked her knuckles. "He could still chew with a few less teeth, don't you think?"

Some catastrophe was happening inside me, a feeling of bones snapping, collapsing inward. This conversation was leading to a place I'd hoped it never would.

"Why did you pretend not to recognize me, Jay? You know who I am."

"I didn't know you were . . . her."

"Liar. You and Adam have been after me since he came back."

"Huh?"

"Don't play dumb, you human garbage fire. Are you working with the Wolf to ruin my life?"

"The hell you talking about, man?"

"Those girls who came to see you. Why did they ask you to do this? To use my deadname, to threaten me?"

Crito looked me in the eye. "Because that's how women are. They hate us."

A part of me remained there while another part went back to a memory. The morning after *it* happened, my body both tight as wire and unraveled like frayed thread, while Ingrid paced in the dawn light, silvering the sunbeams with her smoke. Only once did I voice the question screaming inside me:

Why? Why did this happen, Inge?

She stopped pacing. Her face was cold wrath. *Because that's how men are. They hate us.*

All these years, it sat inside me. That othering. There were men, hateful, violent, and on the other side, us. Girls.

But she was wrong. I was never really either, was I? Not a girl, not a real boy. Just this other. This defective, fucked-up thing.

"Why did they come to you, Jay?"

"They've been after me for months. Picked off my officers one by one. It was just a matter of time till they got to me. So I preempted them—I made a deal."

"Let me shut his lying mouth," Tamsin said.

I waved her quiet. "What kind of deal?"

"You know Adam's back?"

"No fucking shit."

"Well, I asked him to help me out. To get those bitches off my dick."

I frowned. "You sent him to . . . meet with her? With the Little Wolf?"

"Yeah."

My thoughts raced. "Why would she make a deal with you? You have nothing to offer except going away."

Crito shook his head. "She didn't. The deal's with Adam."

Adam, sitting there in Black Iris HQ. As a guest.

A partner.

"What was the deal?"

"Don't know. You'd have to ask him."

"What did you get out of this?" I pressed.

"She let me go."

"After everything you've done, all the people you've hurt—she just let you go?"

Crito smiled. For a moment I saw the old Jay, that sly, knowing grin he'd shoot at me when I was *her*. As if he could see right through me. All the conflict inside me, the boy's name I hid from my boyfriend, the longing to start T. One night when we were alone together for a moment at a restaurant, Jay leaned obscenely close and said, *So, are you a tranny?* His tone was faux friendly. My heart spiked into my throat. *What are you talking about?* I'd said, stammering, so obvious, and he said, still cheerful, *Did you have the surgery? You know, cut your dick off, make a slit?* It had taken every ounce of restraint in me to not show my relief. He was calling me a trans girl—interweaving homophobia and transphobia, implying I wanted to trick straight men. In the most insane way, his awfulness was a blessing. It was so maliciously ignorant that it hid the truth. *Shut up, you creep*, I'd said, and Jay laughed. *If it's real*, he said, sliding a hand between my thighs before I could stop him, *why don't you like dick in it the way you like it in your mouth?* Before I could react, Adam returned to the table.

This person was the abomination who Adam had let indoctrinate him. Let into his head, his heart. He'd let Jay turn him inside out till his monster parts showed, too.

They're both dangerous, Inge had warned me. *Your boyfriend's "bestie" is poisoning him.*

I know the feeling, I'd said.

And I'd paid the price for that. For not trusting the one person who really loved me.

"Why?" I said now. "Why would they make a deal with either of you?"

Crito lifted his good shoulder. "We're not the biggest fish in the pond. They don't want us as bad as they want someone else."

"Who?" I said.

He merely shrugged that shoulder higher. He didn't know.

But I had a pretty good feeling I did.

———

Tamsin and Ingrid and I stared at the whiteboard in my apartment. At the diagram of my ruin.

There was a reason Laney Keating had taken me under her wing. She'd sensed it in me: that festering resentment, an eager willingness to believe the worst about men. To punish them. Our misandry fueled each other. *I know how it makes you feel,* she'd said. *It's the same for me. Catharsis.* As long as I'd been her consenting cat's-paw, she'd tolerated the fact that I was one of them, too.

Until now.

Until I pushed too far, showed myself too aware of her motives.

When I told her I'd seen Adam in town, tried to guilt-trip her to get what I wanted, to satisfy my own agenda—then she decided I'd grown too bold.

Laney was no different from Norah. Both girls who'd accuse a man of the worst crime. Foment loathing and indignation against him. Because who wouldn't believe a guy would do the worst thing? Of course he would. Rape culture, patriarchy, misogyny: these words had leaped from academic discourse into the common vernacular. Norah's accusation needed no proof. Just her tears, and the whole history of men hurting women behind it.

"You're not seeing this clearly," Tamsin said. "Why would Laney do this to you?"

"Because I'm a loose end. And I threatened to use my leverage against her."

"But she *gave* you that leverage as insurance. As a token of trust."

Ingrid sniffed. "And she broke it. Surprise, surprise, the diabolical mastermind is diabolical."

"Paranoia," Tamsin said dismissively. "Ren, the point of that leverage was so you'd trust Laney someday when you wouldn't want to. *This* is that time."

"How do you know?"

"Because your faith in her is being bloody tested. When else could it be?"

"No. Don't you see, Tam? I'm the biggest threat to Laney now. I have real shit on her, and I planned to kill someone without her permission. She wants to silence me more than she wants vengeance on a shitbag like Crito."

"That's wild speculation—"

"Did she tell you to get me drunk that first night?"

Tamsin bit her lip.

"Did she, Tam?"

"Does it matter now? I'm on your side. You know that."

"That's a yes." When Tam didn't refute it, I went on, "Laney kept me in the dark about Jay being Crito. She's smart—she doesn't throw away an opportunity before she uses it. And she doesn't reveal anything until she's forced to. When Adam came back, she knew I'd want him dead. So she kept him and Jay on a leash, to sic them on me if I demanded vengeance, used my leverage. Which I did. Now here we are."

"She's not after *you*. You're complicating things."

Ingrid sighed out a blue cloud of cigarette smoke. She would not quit smoking indoors. I had half a mind to toss her cigs in the trash, for her own good.

"It's not complicated," I said. "It all adds up. Laney must've been planning to dispose of me for a while. You know her—she sets up the dominoes long in advance."

"This is designed to look like something it's not. Someone is playing you."

Inge raised an eyebrow. "Have you checked your bloodwork recently?"

The interruption was so random I snapped, "How the hell could I afford to?"

Both girls stared at me.

"Sorry. Touchy. I'm not sleeping well." I ran a hand through my hair. "Why do you ask, Ingrid?"

"Because paranoid thinking is a symptom of androgen overexposure."

Testosterone has all sorts of bizarre, unexpected psychological effects, one of which influences trust. Higher T lowers your trust in others. In a clinical study, some women volunteered to increase their T tenfold, to average male level. Then they were shown photos of faces and asked to rate their trustworthiness. The more trusting a woman was before T, the more profound her loss of trust after. Her eyes changed, hardening. Losing empathy.

Trust interleaves with vigilance and suspicion. Vigilance taken too far becomes paranoia. All of these things correlate with testosterone levels.

We really do see the world differently depending on what hormones are circulating in our bodies.

"I'm not fucking paranoid," I said. "And I don't have the luxury of seeing a doctor right now."

Ingrid looked at me a long moment, as if giving me a chance to confess. Then she sighed again and said, "I didn't want to do this."

She left the room. Tam and I frowned at each other.

Inge returned with a handful of something shiny, crumpled. Tossed it at my feet. Empty T packets.

"You're overdosing," she said.

"What the hell." I dropped to a squat, frantically gathering them. "You dug these out of the trash."

"So?"

"So that's creepy as fuck. What is wrong with you?"

Her eyebrows rose, slightly.

You. You are what's wrong with me, ~~Sofie~~.

"I care what you're doing to your body," she said.

"You only cared when it stopped looking the way you liked."

Ingrid looked at Tamsin. "I can't get through. You deal with this. You tell him he's killing himself. I can't fucking watch him self-destruct again."

"Ren," Tam said worriedly.

"Don't. Do not gang up." I crushed the foil packets in my fist. "Everyone else has turned against me. I can't lose you both, too."

"It's okay," Tam said, kneeling. "We're on your side. Aren't we, Ingrid?"

"Of course."

"It's okay, love." Gently she pried my fist open, emptied it. "Let's take a step back from this. We all need some time to think."

Tamsin thought it too dangerous for me to stay in the apartment now that we'd antagonized Crito again. I thought it too dangerous for Inge to stay here alone—*Come with us*, I said, but she refused.

Clothes stuffed into a duffel bag. Laptop, phone, my dwindling supply of T. The bare bones of my life.

Tamsin pulled the suit bag from the closet. "You'll need this, too."

"Leave it."

She draped it over her arm. "Don't be petulant."

"I can't trust Armin, or anything that comes from him. Not clothes, not a job."

"You're turning down the interview?"

"My priorities have shifted a little fucking bit lately, Tam."

She got in my face, fearless. "If someone is trying to ruin your life, why help them? Why throw your future away?"

"What fucking future is that?" *Lower your volume, hothead.* "It's over. They've ruined my name. They've ruined my reputation. I can't work with teenagers, with kids—they wouldn't hire me in a million years."

"Armin can talk to them. He can—"

"What, use his privilege to get me in the door? That'll look great. Headline: *Rich asshole gets rapist bro a job at LGBT clinic.*"

"We'll clear your name. We'll suss out who's behind this."

"It doesn't fucking matter, Tam. The damage is done. That stigma is permanent."

Her jaw set. "I'm bringing the bloody suit."

Ingrid hovered in the hall, listening. That always-smooth face was troubled. Before we left, she drew me aside.

"You're not totally out of options. You can still have a future."

Wearily I stretched my neck. This weight on my shoulders never let up. "What's my option, Inge?"

"If they ruined your reputation, let it go." Her gaze was charged, electric. Relentless Ingrid, who never capitulated. Never backed down. "Start over."

"And how do I do that?"

"Girls can't be predators. So stop being *him.*"

—8—

ONE YEAR AGO

VLOG #300: DETRANSITION

REN: Today we're going to talk about the Big D.

No, not that D, children. Get your minds out of the gutter.

Before I started testosterone, I googled the shit out of two search terms:

"Transition regret" and "detransition."

I wanted to know my options. If this didn't work out, if the changes didn't make me happier, I needed an escape route. Last thing I wanted was to be trapped in a body even less bearable than the one given to me at birth.

When you contemplate something this drastic and life altering, you want to know the worst-case scenarios. You want to prepare yourself for disappointment, even regret.

I knew this wouldn't all go perfectly. I wouldn't become a male model—my face would always be my face, just a little squarer, leaner. I wouldn't grow any taller. I wouldn't wake up with a seven-inch dick.

But I definitely didn't want to wake up one day and think, "This was a huge mistake."

Transition is a set of trade-offs. You turn in an unmodified, unbearable body for one that will feel more comfortable, more yours. You give up cis privilege—the privilege of moving safely through a world designed around you—for transphobia, discrimination, violence, hate. You lose friends and family, people you love, but you gain a community who loves you unconditionally. Well, some of them. Some of the time.

Each person has to weigh these things themselves. Figure out if it's worth it. If there will be any regrets.

And I wasn't entirely sure I wouldn't regret it.

[Jump cut.]

Most of the physical changes T causes are permanent: hair growth, hair loss, the voice, the dick—those never change back. Muscle mass and fat patterns do. You won't stay ripped. Your booty will return.

And the brain changes, the mental and emotional shifts: all of those will change back, too.

In the end, I discovered it was those changes I needed most.

I told myself I could live with the permanent effects, if I had to stop T. I could deal with being a gender chimera the rest of my life. Anything was better than this inertia, this certain doom.

I had to at least try.

If you google the terms I did, you'll find a lot of scary shit. TERFs telling stories about women who temporarily thought they were men, who "ruined" their bodies with testosterone. Pics of receding hairlines and botched mastectomies.

Like any of that shit is scarier than the inevitability of suicide.

Before T, it *did* scare me. TERF propaganda is highly effective. I didn't want to become more of a freak.

But when that first dose hit my bloodstream and I felt the spreading calm, the sense of self-possession suffusing my body, I knew how wrong they were.

Self-possession—that's a strange term to a transgender person. We go years without understanding what it means, viscerally. How it feels to truly embody yourself. To love the feeling of your own skin, the breath in your lungs, the blood pumping through your heart.

Self-possession is mental, too. It's the confidence and assertiveness you've always felt should be yours. It's the sense of rightness when someone says "sir." It's seeing yourself reflected accurately in the eyes of others, as the person you really are.

I could never give these things up. This is what it means to be human.

[Jump cut.]

So many of you have asked me if I know anyone who's detransitioned, and why. I do know some, and each had their own reason: family rejection, medical costs, lost their job, feared for their life.

Not one detransitioned because they were wrong about the whole gender thing. It was society, family, and friends who failed them.

The world failed them.

If you ask what I think about all of this, I'll tell you:

Transition isn't a trap.

It's not a life sentence. It's a process that you can start and stop as much as you want.

You may find, down the line, that it doesn't work for you. You can stop taking hormones. Grow your hair out or cut it short. Shave or stop shaving. All the million little ways we signify gender to each other, to ourselves.

But there's one thing you can't know until you try it, and that's how hormones will affect you on the inside. In all the ways that you think, feel, perceive the world.

Before T, I thought I could detransition if I had to.

Now I know I could never do it willingly.

I'm myself on T, in a way I've never been. I'm happy. I'm confident. I'm *alive*.

There's no going back for me.

————

Sun streamed through the windows, soaking into the wood floor like honey. I pulled at my cuffs, cleared my throat, watched a galaxy of dust revolve in a sunbeam. This was probably hopeless, but once upon a time I'd thought transition was hopeless, too. Till I reached the point where I told myself: I will undoubtedly fail, but I have to at least try. I have to earn that failure.

"Renard Grant?"

I stood.

A woman in a business suit smiled at me.

"We're ready for you now."

————

Meet me in the bar, I texted.

This late, the hotel was dead. My wing tips glided silently over the plush carpet. The melodic ding of the elevator was a musical heartbeat. All the bright lights seemed to shimmer in time with my own pulse. Everything, everything orchestrated itself for this night, for us.

She sat in the bar, overlooking the lake. Candles spilled shivering gold pools on the floor. Tamsin gazed into the snowy night, and when I saw her my body slowed, my heart accelerating.

I had never seen her in a dress.

Her slender arms splayed across the linen tablecloth, legs tucked elegantly beneath the chair, so poised and perfect. The black dress cut off at her shoulders, leaving her brown skin bare. At her ears, two small pearls, liquid drops of moonlight.

She felt me looking, turned.

Neither of us spoke. Her eyes ran over me, lingering on my shoulders, hands. The gold stromata in her irises burned like fuses.

I unbuttoned my suit coat and sat.

Tam raised a hand and the bartender brought our usual rum. Candlelight refracted in the rich amber, marbling it with fire.

"You're wearing the suit," she finally said, excitement rising in her voice.

"You're wearing a dress."

"Where have you been all day?"

"You know where." I raised my glass. "Toast?"

She lifted.

"To being yourself," I said. "No matter how hard the world tries to stop you."

Clink. We drank without taking our eyes off each other.

"You're killing me, Mr. Grant. How did it go?"

"They offered me the job."

She broke into a smile. "I bloody knew it."

"I haven't accepted yet. If Armin's involved—"

"Your friends haven't turned against you." Her fingers brushed mine on the tumbler. "They want you to be happy, too. We all do. Don't you see that?" She pressed harder. "Don't you see who really wants your happiness, Renard?"

Quietly, I said, "We're all trapped by something, right? Love is my cage."

Her expression turned savvy, guarded. She released.

We drank.

"What do you think of the dress?" she said.

"It's stunning. Almost a shame I'm going to tear it off."

"I was thinking the same about your suit."

The moon hanging over the lake painted one side of her body

silver; the other was coppery from the candles. It was enough for the moment merely to look, to feel my lungs fill, my blood rush from sheer beauty. To feel alive when she looked at me.

She smiled, the faintest curve of lips and dimples. That was the moment. I felt it happen, a catch coming undone in my chest, something unbearably light tumbling out.

I want to let you in, I thought.

Please, God, don't hurt me.

Tam stood and glided toward the windows, and I followed. In her wake trailed ribbons of her scent, curling, wrapping my head in a veil of her. I stopped without touching, but close enough that our body heat merged. Her spine arched toward me.

Lake Michigan had begun to freeze, jagged ice lining the shore, jutting in wild formations like rock candy. Moonlight shattered on it, spraying metallic shards into the night. And the snow came down, relentlessly soft, over it all.

"Touch me," Tamsin whispered.

I didn't use my hands. I pressed my lips to her naked shoulder blade.

Her head craned back.

I laid my palms on the icy glass, bracketing her. Rubbed my rough cheek over the curve of her shoulder, touching her as softly as snow touched the city.

Her skin was so sheer, so smooth. If I touched it too much I would not be able to stop.

"I think of you." Her hand slid down my thigh. "When I get myself off, I think of you. I've wanted you since that first night."

The strangest feeling: apprehension and desire, braiding together.

"What if I don't live up to your fantasies?" I said.

"What if I don't live up to yours?"

I ran a finger along her throat. "That's ridiculous. You are everything I want."

She turned around and said, "Likewise."

The walk to her room was a dance.

We circled each other in a slow orbit as we moved through the candlelit bar to the chandeliered lobby. Never broke eye contact till our bodies were close. In the elevator, her toe dragged up my trouser leg. I ran a thumb down her spine. When the doors opened she darted out and twirled once, raising her dress. Showing me the dark sheen of her thighs. I didn't rush. Steady stalk as she waited at her room, tapping the key card against her chin. By the time I caught up she was already inside.

The door clicked shut behind me. Dark save for the bathroom light, a bright gap separating us.

"Nowhere left to run, Ms. Baylor."

Tamsin kicked her heels off. I caught one, slid a finger inside along the warm leather insole.

"Get over here," she said, "and do that to me."

I crossed the room.

For a moment we danced again, turning circles. Then I grasped her jaw in both hands. Her mouth half opened, eyes falling half-shut. That beautiful surrender when a girl gives herself to you. I brought my lips close and she breathed faster, faster, her body trembling toward me as I held her in place, drank in the burnt-sugar whiff of rum, and lifted her chin at last and kissed her.

We'd done this before, but this time, behind the momentum was a wild abandon, a letting-go. This time we weren't going to stop.

The kiss was fierce, a discharge of tension, the electricity between us grounding itself in our skin. We craved more friction. Tamsin raked her teeth over my lip. Pressed her cheek against my stubble. Her hands were all over me, raising static from the wool suit, then touching my face in pops of little blue sparks. I put my tongue inside her mouth, slow and hard. Thrust into that softness like melting silk. The slower I went the more she softened, letting me fuck her mouth. My hand trailed down her dress to the hem, to see if she was wet there, too.

Tam tilted her mouth away and said, "Can I touch you?"

"Yes."

"Where?"

"Anywhere you want."

She mirrored my movement, ran a hand over my chest to my fly. My teeth clicked together. She looked into my face. Touched it with one hand while the other moved between my legs.

I wasn't packing. Not for this, the first time. Nothing there but my own body.

Either that body was enough for her, or not.

Either I could bear someone touching me that way again, or not.

Tamsin didn't hesitate. She cupped my dick, squeezed. A deep moan escaped through my teeth.

"Is this okay?" she said, but her expression was pure mischief.

In response I slid my palm against her panties. "Is this?"

"Oh, bloody—" she started, and I covered her mouth with mine.

Our rhythm changed now, slowing. Savoring. Her panties were instantly slick, and as I ran a finger against them she lost her breath, broke the kiss. I kept my mouth close and said, "You're so fucking wet. I want to taste you."

Her thighs spread for me. I left her dress on, and her underwear. Knelt between her legs as she combed her hands through my hair. With one finger I pulled her panties lower. Exhaled, my breath hot on her wetness. Too dark to see clearly but that only made it more sensual. All scent, heat, damp, my tongue delving in to touch her clit, her thighs tensing against my face. The way she responded drove me wild. Yielding to me, bringing herself against my mouth. Gasping at the grittiness of my face on her skin. This felt nothing like it had with Inge, years ago. This wasn't closed eyes and make-believe. This was raw, real.

I took my mouth away. Stood to kiss her, and when she kissed back eagerly and sucked my tongue, tasting herself, I couldn't bear it. I pulled her toward the bed. My shirt came undone in her hands. We undressed each other, to panties and boxer briefs. This was the part

I'd never known how to imagine. How to deal with the fact that my dick was hard and I was wet at the same time. No silicone cock, no devices. Just me. However she saw me.

Tamsin pushed me to the bed beneath her. Our legs tangled, her breasts flattening against my chest. She kissed me, braced my wrists to the mattress, and I knew: my turn. She wanted to touch me the way I touched her.

It took all the willpower I could muster to relax.

To let her.

Her mouth moved down the ridges of my chest. This body I'd carved from nothing, from the wrong default template. Over the tattoos Vada had inked, the boy standing against Poseidon's rage. Along scars faded to ghostly lines, small male nipples, washboard abs, the dark trail of hair disappearing into my waistband. Tamsin looked at me across my body and I looked back. Everything between us felt balanced on the paper-thin edge of this moment. She held my gaze a beat longer, then traced the V lines leading into my underwear and slid the boxer-briefs off. Kissed the tight flat muscle of my lower belly. Pushed my legs apart. Her thick curls tickled my skin.

"Tam," I whispered. "You don't have to."

"Ren," she whispered back. "I want to suck your cock. Objections?"

I stared at her. Bit my lip. Shook my head.

"Good lad. Lie back."

I did.

Slowly, softly, she took me in her mouth, and it felt like lightning bursting in my belly, my spine plugging into an electric socket. I gripped the sheet, twisted. Groaned through my teeth. Felt her chuckle, her breath on my wet cock like a current surge. For a while it was pure euphoria, no nuance in sensation. Then it shifted and I felt my hardness in her mouth, fucking it gently, the way she ran her tongue up the shaft and circled the head. Every motion sent a shock of ecstasy through me. Intensity built endlessly on itself, rising and rising. I'd never done this with anyone after transition. Hadn't known how it would feel. When I looked down at Tamsin with her eyes closed and my dick in her mouth, I felt like a fucking god. Not half anything. Full man. My cock was iron hard, huge, and she looked so pretty as she sucked it. I was not going to last. Tried to stop her but she glanced up and the lust-drunk look in her eyes was too much. I thrust a hand in her hair, rocked into her mouth, all of my tension and strength radiating inward to one explosive moment of utter bliss, and when my mind drifted back down from the ceiling I stroked her hair, soft, slow, the way she'd started.

Tamsin climbed up to my chest, nestled against it. I cradled her face in my hands.

"Ms. Baylor," I said.

"Mr. Grant."

"You're fucking amazing."

She rose over me, her hair tickling my face. I took her breasts in my palms. Even though I'd just come I felt that rev of desire deep in my core.

"Your turn," I said.

"No." She kissed me. Firm, but she stopped before it became ardent. "Tonight is yours. You don't owe me anything."

"I want to make you come."

"You will." Her grin shone in the darkness. "But I'm giving you this. This is how it feels when a girl wants you so badly she'll suck your cock and not ask a thing in return."

My eyes shut. "You're killing me."

"You're killing me a bit, too. But I like it. So don't stop."

I wrapped my arms around her, and together we stared through the muslin curtains at the broken, falling sky.

––––––––

In the morning light she was unreal. Dark legs sprawling, draped in the cream silk sheet. Curls spread on the pillow in a thousand spirals

of ink. I propped myself on an elbow, admiring. My own body in-
tertwined with hers seemed impossible. This whole life seemed impossible. When she shifted I pulled her closer, her skin cool on mine,
and she turned in my arms. Fingers ran over my lips, my jaw. I let
her touch. Then she pressed my hand between her breasts, to the soft
thrash of her heart.

"This is how I feel," she said, "when I look at your face."

That deserved a kiss.

We both tasted like rum and sex. My scent was all over her, and
smelling it on her skin made me hard. She smiled lazily and pressed
her face to my chest and inhaled.

"God, you make me feel drunk," she said.

I held her down, my body flexing against hers. Tamsin ran her
hands over my bare back, sculpting the muscles with her fingertips.
Her hips rose to meet me but I pulled up. Nails carved the hard ridges
of my obliques.

"Torturer," she said.

I rolled off the bed, taking the sheet.

Tamsin squawked in protest.

I wrapped the sheet around my waist and went to gaze out at the
city. The snow had stopped, but white film lay on everything that
faced the sky. Out on the oil-blue lake the ice had split like cracked
glass, and the sun glanced off it in knives of pure light. A glittering,
beautifully wrecked world.

Tam came to stand beside me. I looked at her a long moment, and
she stood undaunted. No discomfort in her own skin. I slid my arms
around her, nuzzled at her neck.

"What do we do with the rest of our lives?" I said.

"Stay in this room."

We did, for a while anyway. Kissed each other raw and bruised.
Worked up a fire to fuck and then stopped, cooled, started over. I
kept the sheet on, still not comfortable being nude in full daylight.
She didn't seem to mind. We wrestled across the bed, again and again

returning to my body over hers, my weight pinning her down, and her eyes hooded and her legs spread and I knew she wanted to be fucked. I wanted to give it to her, but not like this. Not yet.

There were things to do.

A girl to confront.

A man to kill.

And whatever would become of me after.

Tamsin's phone vibrated on the nightstand. She sat up, and I watched seriousness spread over her face.

"It's Laney."

My heart squeezed. "What does she want?"

"To talk to you. Since you apparently blocked her number."

The magic of last night began to fade. "I'll talk if she's ready to come clean. If she'll do the right thing about Adam. Otherwise, she can go fuck herself."

Tam frowned. "Perhaps it's best I speak to her first."

"And say what?"

"Negotiate."

"I'm not negotiating, Tamsin. I will *not* compromise on this. I can't." I touched her hand. "She's out to ruin my fucking life. She's involving the man who hurt me. No fucking compromises."

Tamsin turned her back, pulling her bra on. "Let me bloody talk to her."

I watched her dress and tried my damnedest not to be a paranoid, hypersensitive asshole. But when she bent to kiss me before leaving, I leaned away.

"Right, then," she said flatly.

At the door she glanced over her shoulder.

"Good luck, Cress," I said.

———

Even though I had the key, I rang the buzzer. No answer.

Bell meowed hello when I opened the door. I scratched her head, my nose wrinkling at the staleness of old smoke. Fucking Ingrid and her cigarettes.

Where was she, anyway?

Empty sink, garbage neatly bagged. Everything in its right place. It was like walking through her mind, the rigidity and cleanliness crushing. Except for those toxic fumes.

I wandered toward her bedroom.

I don't know what drew me—maybe that sixth sense we had. Inside she sat at her vanity, a miniature red eye floating in the darkness beside her. She was so still my heart hurtled into my throat.

"Ingrid."

In the mirror her face was a pale blur, an eraser mark. She was watching me.

I moved closer. Reached out and snatched the cigarette from her hand, skimming her fingers. First time we'd touched since that fucked-up kiss.

I snuffed the cherry out. "These will kill you."

"Everything's killing us."

One of those Ingrid moods. As I straightened she grabbed my wrist, slim white fingers hard as bone.

"Was she good?" Inge said hoarsely. "Did she suck it for you?"

"Don't be like this."

"Why are you here?"

"To see if you're okay, creep."

She let go, laughing, humorless.

Then her smile fell. She said, "Someone's been watching me."

"What makes you say that?"

"Little things. There's always someone at the end of the block, wherever I go. I get goose bumps when I'm out in public." She stared at the embers in the ashtray. "Before you came, I heard footsteps in the stairwell. I turned out the lights to see if they'd come in."

My hackles stirred. "Let's get the fuck out of here."

"I think it's your girlfriend."

"What?" Instinctively I glanced into the hall. "That's nuts."

"Remember how I thought I'd seen her somewhere before that night with the bouquet? I was right. I've seen her everywhere—getting coffee, or on the train, or browsing a store with me. She's been following me for months, too. Like she did with Adam."

"Ingrid." Believe her. "Are you sure?"

"I'm sure. She's with *them*. Laney and her friends. They're trying to turn you against me."

"You're the only one who's turning me against you." I sighed. "We'll figure this out once we're safe. Let's just fucking go."

"She'll come back. Wait with me, and you'll see."

I started to tell her this was absurd. I started to use words she'd used on me: paranoid, hypersensitive, overreacting.

Then I remembered the nights I'd come home crying, battered. First by *him*. Later, by strangers.

How she'd believed my version of events. No question.

"Okay," I said. "I have an idea."

I left out the front door.

It was later than I realized, the snow-fringed streets empty. Brake lights splashed sudden blots of color on the asphalt, neon blood splatter. As if someone were wounding the city. My footsteps echoed too loudly in the L station, and the echo sounded uncannily like a chase. I kept looking over my shoulder. The Beretta was on me. Every now and then, as if quieting a racing heart, I touched it.

When the train came I got on and rode it for one stop, then walked back home.

In the alley behind the building small footprints dotted the snow.

It could have been anyone. But I didn't think it was.

I climbed the fire escape, remembering that first night. Silently lifted the kitchen window Ingrid had unlocked. Took my boots off, tucking them into a cabinet.

In the shadows two bright green discs flashed at me.

I stroked Bell's head, praying she wouldn't cry out. She rubbed against my palm, purring.

Voices in the apartment.

I crept toward Ingrid's room.

"What do you want?" I heard her say.

Tam *tsk*ed. "Some hospitality would be nice."

"You *broke into my apartment*. You scared the shit out of me. For all I knew, you were Adam."

"You knew I wasn't Adam," Tam said acidly.

"I don't like your tone."

"I don't like a bloody thing about you. Give me your mobile."

"I'm calling the cops."

Something clicked. "No, you're not. Give me. Your mobile."

My hand went to the Beretta again.

No fucking way. They might barely be able to stand each other, but Tamsin wouldn't hurt Ingrid.

Would she?

"It was you, wasn't it?" Inge said. "You're the one who's been following me."

"Well done. Ten points to Slytherin." A creak, floorboards shifting under weight. "We have everything we need. Except for one last jigsaw piece. Which I think you're daft enough to have saved on your mobile."

I pressed myself flat beside the door frame. My heart was so loud I could hardly hear over it.

"I don't know what you're talking about."

"Oh, I think you do, love." Another creak. "Now hand it to me. I'd hate to spoil that pretty face."

The gun slid out of my coat, cold in my hand. Shaking.

Was she really about to make me do this?

Tamsin, why?

No, not Tamsin. Cressida.

"Don't touch me," Ingrid said.

"Don't make me hurt you."

My pulse thumped louder. I flicked the safety.

"Get the fuck off of me."

"You really don't want to fight me, love. You'll lose."

I edged into the doorway.

Tam's back was to me, Ingrid towering over her, but willowy, lanky, no match for her opponent's strength. The gun was half-raised. Ingrid met my eyes.

Then jerked her chin up and said, "You're faking me out. You won't actually hurt me."

I could read that sign anywhere. Did she think I'd forget?

Fake-out play.

Instantly I knew what to do.

I holstered the gun and ran on tiptoe to the front door. Rattled the locks noisily, flung the door open and slammed it and called, "I'm back. Forgot something."

I gave them time to de-escalate. Pretended to stub my toe, knock books off a shelf. If I hadn't been listening I'd have missed the faint screech of the kitchen window, the flex and groan of wrought iron steps.

Ingrid came running into the kitchen.

Down in the alley, a shadow slid over the snow, vanished. Blood banged furiously in my ears.

"What the fuck was that?" I said.

Ingrid answered, "Betrayal."

———

In the hotel that night, Tamsin said, "Fuck me."

Something cruel kicked through my veins.

We kissed in the elevator. And the hall. And on the bureau, where I stripped her pants off and she unzipped mine. Half-clothed, my cock hot in my hand. There was enough light from the shining skyscrapers and the lingering snow to see my scars, my seams, my imperfections.

But she wrapped her legs around me, brought herself against the head, and I gave it to her, hard. We both bared our teeth, the relief of it also an anguish. I'd wanted this so badly. Since the first night we fought, our bodies falling into natural rhythm, violent grace. I slid inside and watched her hold me as I withdrew. Deeper each time, her wetness gleaming higher on my cock, until she stopped pulling me in hungrily and instead went soft, submitting. Let me fuck her. Let me fill her. She clutched my ear to her mouth and whispered, "Does it feel good?" and I answered by thrusting deeper, our hips touching, my abs tight and my thighs braced and every bit of strength in me surging to one point. I didn't feel the packer pressing on my real dick anymore. In my head, it was all me. All one whole. Just a boy fucking the shit out of a girl. Tamsin cried out as I hammered her and a small, vile part of me hoped it hurt. For what she did to Ingrid. For what she was doing to me. The first girl I fucking trusted, a liar. Betrayer. But when she came she held me deep, clawed my back, our movements aligned so tightly I couldn't tell them apart anymore. She rode me a little longer, grimacing but not stopping, and I couldn't look at her face without my heart going liquid. I couldn't hurt her, not outside the bounds of mutual consent. Whatever monster I was, it was not that kind. So I kept fucking her, tenderly, till the last aftershock faded and she went still in my arms.

We held each other, our skin polished with moonlit sweat. It felt like one unbroken act, from the moment she pulled the gun on Ingrid to this. One long, violent fuck.

Tamsin stroked my face. Shadows moved over those violet lips.

"Are you all right?" she said.

It was always this way. I cracked my rib cage open only to allow venom into my heart.

I said nothing.

"Lovely boy. You look so sad."

She kissed my face, my mouth. Pushed me to the bed and held me down, her body light on mine. Not long later we began again, insatiable.

It felt so real. From a distance, it would look just like the real thing.

A boy and a girl, falling in love.

But all of this was mere illusion. Like me.

———

For days I kept her busy. At her side, always. Not a moment to herself. Most of that time we touched, savaged each other, got off fast and rough and went back at it before our nerves had stopped buzzing. Later we wandered through the night-cloaked city, two restless ghosts. Drifting in and out of dark alleys, phantoms fading into the snow. I watched Umbra from afar and remembered a life that now seemed like someone else's. Somewhere Adam was walking free while I was in exile. It made my marrow seethe. Made me want to annihilate something, someone. That urge twisted into libido and Tam let me shove her up against an alley wall, her hands braced on the brick and the lights from passing cars mixing on our skin, moon silver, electric blood red. When she came I clapped a hand over her mouth, stifling her moans. Maybe I pressed harder than I needed to. It was only a matter of time until we parted. Until Black Iris made their next move against me.

If I had to face them all myself, I would.

I thought about telling Ellis to skip town. Miss this showdown. But that would tip my hand.

No. It didn't have to be like that. No one else needed to get hurt.

If Black Iris wanted to drag my carcass through their sordid little underworld, so be it.

As long as they let the girls I loved go.

———

"There's something I must do today," Tamsin said.

Her words filled me with dread. I sat on her hotel bed, listening to the shower hiss. She was in the middle of undressing.

Tam knew how to play a man. But I had eighteen years of not being utterly enslaved to my dick, and I knew how to avert my eyes.

"I'll go with you."

"It's a solo op, love."

If I pushed too hard, I'd give myself away. So I said, "Leaving me alone all day? I'll miss you."

She shrugged out of her tee. Bra and panties only, bright white. She sauntered toward the bed, touched my face with her nails, lightly. Her mouth hovered over mine. When the nails dragged I thought of tiny hooks.

"Join me in the shower," she said.

My whole lower body went tight, lifted toward her, but I said, "Got some errands to run, actually. Will you miss me?"

She kissed me, more a collision of lips than a kiss. That iron resolve in me melted, another hardness taking its place.

Then she pulled back, smiling. "Does that answer your question, Mr. Grant?"

"Sort of, Ms. Baylor. If you could just clarify some of your points—"

She glided into the bathroom with a laugh.

How could we be so good together, I thought, when it was all a lie?

As soon as she left eyeshot I grabbed my Beretta. Boots, coat, duffel bag.

I wouldn't be coming back.

"Renard," Tamsin called.

Reluctantly I walked to the bathroom.

She stood with a towel draped loosely over her shoulders like a stole. Naked beneath, beautiful in the soft light, tones of tobacco and clove glowing in her skin. Those large hazel eyes were full of irony and knowing.

"Are you quite sure you don't want to join me?" she said.

For the last time.

It hurt too much.

Through a clenched jaw I said, "Save your appetite for tonight."

"I will. And I'll devour you."

You are so lovely, I thought, when you're lying to my face.

Before I ducked out, I caught the hint of hard metal peeking out from the clothes piled on the sink.

Her gun.

————

Ingrid wouldn't answer her phone.

Days since I'd been home, but it felt like years. Out front the maple tree withered, stripped by winter to its dark skeleton, and the names on the mailbox—*Ingrid Svensson & Renard Grant*, a strip of Wite-Out beneath mine, where it had once read *Sofiya Khoury*—seemed unreal, like characters in some fiction. That white ink was my transition, the barrier between us. It had chipped away on one side, revealing the curved tail of the *S*, and I touched it, thinking, You're still here, aren't you? Just under the surface.

I rang the doorbell, waited. Nothing.

Unlike Ingrid to be completely unreachable. If they'd gotten to her—

I let myself in.

Bell wove eagerly around my feet, crying. Hungry. No one had fed her this morning.

I did a quick walkthrough of the apartment. Empty.

"Where is she?" I said, setting a food dish on the floor.

Her room was cold, the air clear. Felt like she hadn't been here in a while. On the vanity lay the empty T packets she'd flung at me, accusing.

I sat at the mirror, crumpling them.

Why did this have to mean so fucking much to her?

She'd agreed not to put up old pics, save one: the two of us at senior prom, both in dorky tuxes. *Solidarity*, she'd said. *They fuck with you, they're fucking with me.* The tuxes came off later in her parents' basement, under a scratchy wool blanket. Sweat turned our skin so slick we could barely hold on. It darkened her wraith-white hair, and

I gazed up at her, tucking it behind an ear. *I love you*, she said. I had never felt so needed by someone before. It made me want to do anything for her. Give her anything.

A year after that photo, I'd begun to take myself back, piece by piece.

My heart felt like the mauled foil in my fist.

I flung the packets into the trash beside the table. There were more in the basket, dozens. God.

I started to stand.

Then, impulsively, looked again at the tabletop.

Lined up among the vials of scent and tint were certain items that caught my eye: rubbing alcohol, hand sanitizer, superglue. All of which undoubtedly had cosmetic use—gluing nails on, removing polish, whatever.

As did the pair of precision scissors that stood in a jar.

And the bare razor blade.

And the unmarked bottle, filled with clear gel, sitting right there in plain sight.

I looked at the foil packets again. Pulled them out of the trash, spread them across the table. It took a minute to find what I was looking for:

The botched ones. The cuts that had gone awry, the edges that couldn't be glued back together seamlessly.

I leaned on the table, dizzy.

My phone rang. INGRID SVENSSON.

I sent the call to voice mail and pocketed the unmarked bottle.

Get out. Get out of here, get air. Think.

I staggered through the apartment, down the stairs. Wasn't sure if I'd shut the apartment door or not. Be a good girl, Bell. Don't run.

On the street the light was too intense, the snow blinding, a white scream in my eyes. There had to be another reason. This was just my paranoia. Nothing real, Ren. All in your broken head.

Someone was calling my name from across the street.

Someone with a voice that made me shrivel inside.

I stood fixed to the pavement as he came closer. His jeans were tight, clinging to his quads. Shoulders wide like a yacht boom. Snow salted his hair. Maybe this was it, a psychotic break of some sort. Maybe I'd OD'd on T and gone off the deep end.

He stopped a few feet away and said, "Ren?"

Adam Halverson, calling me by my right name.

I reached for the Beretta.

His hands rose, palms up. "I'm not going to hurt you. I just want to talk."

"All I have to say to you," I rasped, "is in the barrel of this gun."

"Listen to me. You're not safe."

If I hadn't been knocked so off-center I would've drawn and fired then and there, in broad daylight. Instead, like an idiot, I engaged. "No fucking shit, you bastard. I will never be safe in a world where you exist."

He stood there motionless, hands in the air. His eyes tracked rapidly over my face. I sensed him comparing images: the girl he'd last seen, the boy before him. The person he'd hurt and the person who was going to hurt him back, over, and over, and over.

"You sound so different," he said softly.

My teeth gritted. Otherwise I would shriek.

Adam's arms trembled, straining. "Look, there'll be time for this later. I came to warn you."

"Get the fuck out of my sight."

"Ren." My name in his mouth struck like a sucker punch. "You are not safe. She's destroying you."

I drew the gun. "Get the fuck. Out of my sight."

"Ren, listen to me—"

"Stop fucking saying that." Safety off. Raise and aim. "Leave before I kill you."

He took several hasty steps back. "Okay. I'm just going to—"

"Turn around. Walk away."

My voice was deeper than his now. It rang out over the pavement, hard as steel.

Obediently, he turned. Without another word he walked off.

I put the gun in my coat. When he was a speck at the end of the block, I turned in the other direction and ran.

———

In a blind fervor I crossed street after street, taking random turns through a maze of metal and stone. Lights flashed senselessly, devoid of meaning. There was nowhere to run that was safe but I kept moving anyway.

My phone was ringing.

Her.

"Thank fucking God you answered." Ingrid's voice was distant, windswept. Car tires crackled on pavement. "I need your help. Please."

I breathed deeply. "What happened?"

"I'm being followed."

I stopped in the middle of a sidewalk. Nearby a traffic light clicked from yellow to red, unsettlingly loud. "By who?"

"Who do you think? Your fucking psycho girlfriend."

"Where are you?"

"On my way home."

"Don't go home."

"No shit." She sighed. "What the fuck should I do?"

I clutched the bottle in my pocket.

Truth was like a kaleidoscope. With every twist, it looked totally different. All the bits rearranged themselves, some coming clear, others growing obscure. But in the end it was the same pieces every time. All that changed was how you saw them.

"Come meet me at Umbra," I said.

Long pause. "Black Iris is there."

"I know. And Inge?"

"Yeah?"

"Bring Norah with you."

————

Umbra, a place of undoings and endings. We always came back here to fall apart. The place where Laney had ripped Armin's heart out, where a blonde and a brunette had ruined me. It devoured its own.

The bouncers eyed me coldly.

That would change, I thought. In time.

As I moved through the crowd heads turned, whispers swirling. *It's him, it's him.* How damning it seemed, the pronoun I once longed for. I kept my chin up, refusing to be cowed. Let them see my face. Let them see me unafraid, standing against the lie.

Soon they'd understand.

On my way downstairs, my phone vibrated.

TAMSIN: **Here yet?**

I froze on the marble steps. My pulse clogged my throat.

REN: **Yes**
REN: **Is she with you?**

No answer. Then, a photo:

Ingrid, sitting in a pool of warm candlelight. Hair in her face as she glowered at the camera. Wrists and ankles taped to the chair.

REN: **Don't hurt her, Tam**

TAMSIN: **Oh, I won't**
TAMSIN: **We're saving her for you**

I took the steps two at a time.

At the bottom I sprinted, my heart gunning wildly. The door to the Black Iris meeting chamber was shut. I hauled it open, remembering Adam inside, defenseless.

How badly I'd wanted to hurt him.

How badly I wanted to hurt her now.

Tamsin turned, gun in hand. It hung at her thigh and she didn't raise it. Her face wore that wry, savvy expression I found so lovely. Ingrid's face was a total blank. A cipher, a zero.

I closed the door.

"Where's Laney?" I said.

"Upstairs, with the others. Waiting." Tamsin stepped aside. "This is yours, Ren."

Ingrid watched me approach.

On the court, when we stood side by side, people feared us. They knew how strong we were together. I'd spent years learning her: first her mind, when we were young, its inexorable clockwork, its sharp steel gears clicking, clicking. Then her body, in adolescence. The unrealness of its beauty, her paper-white skin, her boy-straight bones. Then, when we moved away from home, I finally learned her heart. That crag of cruel ice lying beneath still water, a thing that would shipwreck whatever came near it.

I had feared her all this time, too. Her power over me. Her cold, jagged love.

I still feared her now.

"Ingrid," I said, and it came out a croon.

She watched me kneel at her feet. Watched me draw the Beretta, lay it on the floor, and push.

Tam caught it beneath her heel.

"Don't let me use that," I said.

"She bloody deserves it."

"I know."

Inge smiled, bitter. Still silent.

I touched her leg. Wrapped my hand around that sinewy calf, as I had before. But now I kept squeezing till it felt like I could rip meat off bone.

"It hurts," she said finally. Satisfaction in her voice.

I let go.

"You have put so much pain into this world," I said.

"Oh, don't be so fucking banal."

I took the bottle out of my pocket. "Is this what I think it is?"

Her eyes glittered. No answer.

I rolled up her pant leg. Uncapped the bottle, dipped my finger inside. A whiff of alcohol stropped the air like a razor.

My hand moved toward her skin.

"Don't poison me with that shit," Ingrid said.

Something heavy tumbled to the bottom of my chest. A closing book, the end of a story. Of me and you, Inge.

I wiped the testosterone gel on my forearm. Rubbed it in.

Then I said, "Did you tamper with it from the beginning?"

She didn't answer. But she didn't pretend not to understand the question.

And that, in itself, was an answer.

SIX MONTHS AGO

PRIVATE VLOG: GASLIGHTING

REN: I'm not uploading this. This is for me. I feel like I'm going crazy and I just—

I need to get this out.

Ingrid watches these. I know she does. Pretends it's so disgusting, that she's grossed out by my beard and dick and all this boy stuff, but she's seen every single video. I test her, sometimes. Casually mention something I said in a vlog, and she'll know what I mean. I joke about my shitty memory so she won't suspect.

I think she's trying to change me.

Like, back. To a girl. The way I was.

I have this dread that someday I'll come home to a trans in-
tervention, and she'll be sitting on the couch where we fucked,
and my family will be there, my tyrant mother, my spineless
father, and Inge will say, "We care about you, Sofie. We want
to help you get well."

By "well," she means female.

I swear I'm not crazy.

My endocrinologist says my T levels don't make sense.
Sometimes they start to taper off, as if I'm lowering my dose.
But I'm not.

For a while he had me on shots instead of gel. Inge did
them. I'm squeamish with needles so she volunteered to help,
which was nice, I thought, until I started feeling strange between injections. Irritable, tired. Depressed. Low sex drive.

Signs of low T.

She marked the shots on a calendar. Every two weeks, on
the dot, was an X, but some of those were wrong. Days I wasn't
home, or days she was sick. The schedule was off by a day or
two here and there. I added it up and I was actually only getting
one shot a month. Half my dose.

She's not sloppy. This is Ingrid. Ingrid doesn't know the
meaning of that word. Everything she's ever done is precise,
deliberate. Like Laney.

There's no way she didn't notice the calendar was wrong.

I'm not saying it's intentional, but—

I don't know what I'm saying.

Anyway, I switched back to gel. Packets, not the pump.
They're foil, sealed.

I figure, remove the temptation, right?

Not that I think she'd ever *do* something like that. Not to
hurt me. Not to fuck with my health.

But if she thought it was helping, not hurting . . .

This is nuts. Can't believe I'm saying this. Even thinking it. It's paranoia.

I looked up my *feelings* online. I'm nothing if not an expert self-diagnoser. Every trans person is. This one word kept coming up: "gaslighting." It's from an old film where a husband lies to his wife over and over, telling her she's imagining things—that the gaslights in the house aren't really flickering when they are. When he's the one messing with them.

When someone gaslights you, they make you doubt reality. They make you feel like you're going crazy, being unreasonable, overreacting. It's a form of emotional abuse so effective that the abuser only needs to plant the seeds of doubt—your brain takes care of it from there, growing them, nourishing them. Feeding on them.

Poisoning itself.

Ingrid has been there for me through everything. Through *him*. Through so much other bullshit. I know she hates this, thinks I could be happy without hormones, but she'd never actually fuck with my body. She wouldn't.

Except.

Except sometimes, when she looks at me, I think she sees Ren the same way I saw Sofie. As someone temporary.

Someone she could kill.

–9–

Old friends don't need words. Everything in a glance, a touch. All the things that meant more because they were unspoken. Ingrid and I stared at each other, wordlessly.

To Tamsin I said, "Where's her phone?"

She handed it over.

It was there, just as I knew it would be. The video of the liar's face, streaked with mascara. Norah. Filmed by Ingrid. Orchestrated beautifully.

"She's behind it all," Tamsin said. "The blonde and brunette. Ingrid and Norah. This is the person who tried to ruin you, Ren."

I kept staring at that lovely pale face. The one I thought I knew.

"All of you were in on it. This whole time, you all knew Crito wasn't the real threat."

"Yes."

"What did Laney actually want with him that night?"

"A meeting. I was merely checking in with him till you twits showed up. I bound him to make it look like a mission, like I'd come to scare him straight. But then you wanted to take his gag off, so I had to bloody shoot him."

"Laney was working with Adam."

"Yes, but now you can see the big picture." Tam shook her head. "Adam went to Ingrid with a plea bargain for Crito. Crito thought she was involved with Black Iris's missions against him. He was wrong, but it tipped Ingrid off. She learned about us. She learned you were one of us. And she tried to turn you against us. But we're smarter, stronger, bigger. We let her watch us while we watched her. She was right about me following her—I've been surveilling her since summer."

"What did you see?"

"Everything. She met with Adam. She 'befriended' Norah, used her as a pawn. She manipulated you in so many subtle ways. I wanted to tell you—wanted to throw the whole thing, expose her, but Laney told me to wait. Armin had suspicions that someone was tampering with your medication. We needed to be absolutely sure before we unmasked her." Tamsin stared at Ingrid with a look of puzzled revulsion. "What I don't understand is *why*. Why did she tamper with your medicine?"

My knees burned on the freezing cement floor. "Because she wants me to go back."

"Back to what?"

"Sofiya."

Ingrid leaned forward, her face unsettling in its implacable calm. Those intense eyes, that softly fervent voice. "*His* life is ruined, not yours. You don't have to be *him* anymore."

It wasn't just my reputation. It was my fucking body.

Tampering with my meds. My bloodwork always coming back weird, the T levels too low. How good it felt when I "overdosed." How right.

She'd been trying to undo my transition.

"You are the sickest person I've ever known," I said.

Ingrid rolled her eyes. "So are you, Sofie. You used to be so pretty. And now look at you."

A spasm racked my body. I reined back the arm that wanted to hit her.

Do not. Do not fucking do it.

Don't prove her right.

"Show some fucking appreciation," she said. "I freed you from this. Your 'masculinity,' your delusions of gender. You're not trapped anymore."

"I was never fucking trapped, you lunatic. I'm not delusional. This is who I am."

"You were suffering." Her teeth met in a rictus between words. "You were miserable. I watched you writhe in agony every day. It was mercy to stop it."

"I was suffering because of *you*." I lunged, shook her till her head jerked, hair flying. "You were never fucking happy for me. You dragged your heels the whole way. You hated what I was doing but you wouldn't let me go." My jaw was about to drive straight through my skull. "You're the reason I dated Adam. So I could break free of your fucking Svengali hold on me. You're the reason all of this happened. You toxic fucking bitch, this is all on *you*."

Tamsin crouched beside us. Put a hand on me, an anchor to reality.

I let Ingrid go. Her hair was wild, a lash of blood snaking from her lip.

"You're in denial," Inge said. "I've seen your videos. I've seen how much you regret this."

"I don't regret it. It's just hard."

"You bailed on being a girl because being a girl is hard."

"I bailed because I'm not a fucking girl." I clawed the back of my head. "Want to talk about how hard being a girl is? Were you the one who was fucking raped?"

Saying it aloud tore something loose from me, left a raw place.

"You think it was easy for me, Sofie? Being the dyke, the fag?"

"It doesn't justify this."

"But you never gave a shit how hard it was. It was all about you and your fucking *gender identity*. My identity is always visible. I can't hide being a lesbian. But you pass now. If you didn't tell people you weren't born a boy, they'd never know. You could live without taking anyone's shit, if you wanted."

She was right. But it didn't make me wrong.

"You could have said this before taking matters into your own hands, Inge. Told me you were struggling with your identity, too."

"I'm telling you now."

"It's too fucking late."

"Sofie," she whispered. Her eyes were glassy, limpid. "I know you're still in there. And I still love you."

Something snapped. That last thread between us, finally breaking.

I reeled away from her, staring up into the light. Looking for something to burn away this feeling.

Tamsin stood, touching my shoulder. "We'll take care of this now."

"Just let her go."

"She's tried to ruin your life. She's no better than Adam."

"Let her go, Tamsin."

Tam exhaled, hard. "We've worked for months to gather evidence on her. We'll record her confession, clear your name. You deserve this."

"I don't want it. It won't fix anything."

"It's justice."

I flooded my lungs with cool air. "Then I don't want justice. Hurting her changes nothing."

"It stops her from hurting others."

"Nothing stops that."

"This will," she said, gesturing with her gun.

Our eyes locked. Hardness in hers, an unforgiving gleam.

I put my hand on the pistol.

"Tamsin," I said, "let her—"

We moved at the same time, in sync. Like always.

I grabbed the gun and Tam whipped an elbow at my chin. Part of me expected it and I held on through the pain, twisting till she dropped the weapon. It skittered between our boots and I kicked it away. Tried to pin her arms but she anticipated, slid free. She swept my feet just like I anticipated, and I braced. We knew each other too well now. How the other moved, thought. I was stronger than she was by far but also unwilling to hurt her past a point. So she pushed me to that point, again and again. We danced across the room, evading blows at the last second, taunting each other. She kicked a boot heel into my back and knocked me breathless. I slammed her against the wall, all my weight on her chest. Win passively, I thought. Wear her out. But she was wild, a demon energy in her veins. She jabbed my jaw and blood flew. I reeled and she tackled me, toppling us to the floor.

I knew what she was doing. Working me up, getting me to break through this final mental block. First I'd hurt her, a woman I cared for. Then I could hurt Ingrid.

"I won't do it," I gasped. "Just stop."

Tamsin seized my collar. "Then bloody let me hurt her."

"Why?"

"Because she hurt you, and I can't bear it. Because I'm in love with you, you stupid boy."

I stared up at her. Stunned, but no pain now. I worked a hand free and touched her face.

Tamsin winced. "Oh, hell. Oh, bloody hell. I've done a number on you."

"Ditto, I think."

Gingerly we sat up. Everything hurt. I felt bruised down to the bone. Tam dabbed the blood from my mouth, kissed my cheek, my temple.

"How sweet," Inge said dryly. "She hits you, so it must be true love. You like it rough, right, Sofie? You always did."

"Can I make that aggravating noise stop?" Tam said.

"Be good."

Ingrid snorted. "No offense, Tamsin, but you're simple. Sofie doesn't do simple. It's boring." She shrugged. "I'm fucked-up on a whole other level. You're about as complicated as *Harry Potter.* I'm *Ulysses.*"

"No offense taken. *Ulysses* is a crock of shite."

Inge actually laughed. "I knew I liked you."

"Now *that* is offensive."

I peeled my jacket off, and my sweaty tee. Tam raised an eyebrow.

"Tell Laney to come get her," I said.

Inge's eyes moved over my bare chest, tats, muscle, hair.

"You can still come back," she breathed. "It's not too late. Your voice, your clit, that's all you can't change. And I kind of like you with a big clit."

I twisted my tee into a rope.

"Ingrid," I said, looping it around her mouth, "shut the fuck up, you toxic bitch."

———

Two girls sat in front of the camera and the bright lights. Norah fidgeted, her gaze fluttering around the room. Ingrid stared into the lens stoically, her eyes empty and clear. Cold light cascaded off the high slopes of her cheekbones.

"State your names," Laney said.

—*Norah Grainer.*

—*Ingrid Svensson.*

"Are you here under duress?"

—*No.*

—*No.*

Norah did most of the talking. Eager to take the blame, do penitence, absolve herself. The world held no pity for a woman who'd falsely accused a man of rape.

I knew how hard it would be on her. They'd hold her up as proof that all girls were liars. They would hate her. They would say she should *actually* be raped, for lying about it.

Strange, how those so eager to punish girls for lying turned a blind eye to the boys. As if the real goal was merely to inflict hurt on female bodies. To punish femininity.

I knew these things. I knew exactly how hard it was to be believed after you'd been hurt. Even by yourself.

But believing was Black Iris's job. I needed my name cleared. My life back.

"How do you know each other?" Laney said.

—*Through my friends. Inge hooked up with some girls I know. It's kind of a small world. All the lesbians have slept with each other at some point.*

"Did Renard Grant ever assault you?" Tamsin said.

—*No. Never.*

"Why did you lie?"

—*She . . . well, everyone sort of convinced me.*

"Everyone?"

—*My friends said he'd played me. That I was nothing to him, just another slut. He's slept with every willing girl at Umbra. That's what they say.*

"They slut-shamed you?"

—*Yeah. Lesbians can be pretty judgmental of bisexuals. But Ingrid was always nice to me. Sympathetic. She said he'd played her, too, and she wanted to get back at him.*

"That convinced you to accuse him of rape?"

—*No. But she kept putting these ideas in my head. She'd say, "Are you sure you wanted it? Did you ask him to stop?" And she told me how sometimes, when she was with him, he'd keep going when she didn't want to. It made me question myself.*

"Do you feel the sex you had with him was coercive?" Laney said.

—*No. No, I wanted it.*

"Then why did you say it was rape?"

—*Because I felt slutty, okay? Everyone made me feel like shit about*

it, except Ingrid. She said I could make myself look better if I played the
victim. That I could fix my reputation.

"By ruining his."

—I didn't think it through that fully, but . . . yeah. That's what it was.

"Didn't think it through?" Tam echoed, anger in her voice.

—It's like . . . I know he's different, but guys do that kind of thing all
the time, you know? And most of the time they get away with it. Ingrid
kept saying that sometimes you need to make an example of someone to
keep the others in line. It sounds crazy now, but it made sense then. I felt
like such a pariah. I just wanted people to stop treating me like trash. I
didn't realize how much it would hurt him.

"Why did Ingrid want to ruin me?" I said.

—She hated that you became a man. She thought it was destroying
you.

"Why couldn't you let me be happy, Inge?"

No answer from her.

Softer, I said, "When did you start to hate me?"

Something wet and fractured glittered in her eyes. Breaking ice.
But still she remained silent.

The lights and the camera switched off, and everyone else left, and
the two of us remained, facing each other.

"I never hated you," she said quietly.

I crossed the room and sat in the chair beside her. Pressed my palm
to her cool marble cheek. Her eyes closed.

"Open them," I said.

She looked at me.

"This is why I had to get away from you, Inge. You're like my
mother. You will never see me as I am."

"I could try."

I let my hand fall. "Sometimes I wonder what would've happened
if I never transitioned. If I stayed the way you wanted."

Now she put a hand to my face, tentatively. Brushed my scruff.

"You wouldn't have been happy," she whispered. "But I would."

At least she didn't lie.

Something prickly scratched my throat. I stood.

"What are you going to do to me?" she said.

"I'm going to let you go."

At first she seemed to think I meant *go free*. Then she understood.

On my way out of the room she said, falteringly, "Ren."

I shivered once, hard. Turned.

Ingrid never apologized. That statuesque face never cracked. In another era, she would have marched unflinchingly to the stake to burn, head high. For all that her heart was a twisted mess, I admired the diamond hardness of it.

If only you'd been a better friend to me, Inge.

If only we'd both been.

We held eye contact for a long moment. Then she said, "Kill that motherfucker."

———

I kept you in the dark, Laney said, *because I knew it would hurt you. If you knew I was using him.*

Adam had been thinking about what happened between him and me. *What happened.* Like it was a force of nature, not man-made, not a brutality he inflicted on me but some unpreventable disaster our bodies had endured, a wreckage of limbs and skin. Well, he had been thinking, and he wanted to apologize. If *I* thought it was rape. Not because he did.

Amazing, that he managed to shirk responsibility even in his guilt.

Once Adam finished grad school, he moved back to Chicago, where he reunited with Jay, his old college friend.

Jay had always been a misogynist. The kind of guy who'd assign hotness numbers to girls straight to their faces, as if handing out compliments. The kind of guy who'd shame his best friend for not simply taking what was his by birthright, for not using my body the way it had been designed to be used by men. Without Adam to temper him,

Jay had become radicalized. He called himself Crito and harassed women on the Internet, with the help of a hundred or so of his cronies.

And someone very powerful had noticed, and was sniffing out his trail. One by one, Crito's "soldiers" had gone dark, scared silent.

I need a favor, Crito told Adam. *Remember that hot blonde your ex-girlfriend was all dykey with?*

Ingrid? Adam said.

Yeah. Remember how she never shut up about feminism? She's gone off the deep end. She's trying to ruin my life.

Adam had his own reasons to talk to Ingrid. She was his only link to Sofiya, and things had ended badly between them. So he went to see Inge.

He said, *How is Sofie?*

She said, *Sofie wants you dead. And I do, too.*

Adam expected as much. He said, *Jay says your vigilante friends are ruining his life. He wants a truce. And I want to talk to Sofie.*

Ingrid saw opportunity.

Maybe we can work something out, she said. *Tell me what you know.*

Unwittingly, Adam told her all they knew about Black Iris. She put the pieces together, realizing that I had to be involved, that she could use this to plant the seeds of doubt in my mind. Make me distrust my friends. Render me isolated and helpless, with her as my only safe haven. When Adam asked about me, she lied.

Sofie transitioned because of you, she said. *Because of what you did to her. You made her hate being a woman so much it pushed her over the edge. Now she thinks she's a man, and it's your fault.*

He was horrified. *What can I do?*

She said, *Help me bring her back.*

Adam knew this wasn't right. If someone felt like a man inside, he was a man. If his ex had gone down that path, then good for him.

Amazing, that an abusive asshole managed to be more accepting than a radical feminist.

Tamsin, of course, had been watching the whole time. Anyone who contacted Crito was suspect as far as Black Iris was concerned. Especially a notorious radfem blogger who should've been public enemy number one to the men's-rights creeps. When Ingrid didn't contact Black Iris for help, Laney realized something was off. Tam followed all four of us, and Laney gradually put the puzzle together:

Ingrid had been ruining my rep, systematically destroying me.

By following a male monster, Laney found the hidden female one.

My ex–best friend.

I had to use Adam, Laney said now. *I couldn't tell you. There was no way you'd accept it. He was our link to Ingrid—she didn't know we'd flipped him. Once we saw what she was doing to you, we built a case against her to undo the damage. And he helped with that. We've been behind you all this time, Ren. We've always been on your side.*

I told you to trust me, once.

Was I right?

For years I'd lived with the person poisoning my body and mind. The person turning me against myself.

And the man who'd hurt me was the one who freed me from her.

Too much. My mind couldn't hold the idea without feeling as if it would crack.

It's all over now, Laney said. *Her machinations. His usefulness.*

I can make them both disappear. If you want.

What do you want, Ren?

———

It was a small room without windows. White walls, white door, chair under a colorless lightbulb. When the man in the chair moved, his shadow split from his body and struck a random surface. He was not tied or restrained.

No camera. No witnesses.

Only me and him.

Like that night.

When I walked in, his eyes widened, and he looked at my body, every inch of it, unblinking. Then he swallowed.

I wore joggers and a tank, to show him there was no weapon on me but my own muscle.

I'd lifted a few sets before I went in, to heat my blood. To make me feel like I could take the whole world on, single-handed. But seeing him this close, feeling the air stir and eddy with his breath, made me shiver.

Over the years I had rehearsed this scene a hundred times in my head. Sometimes even recorded my part, watched the video again and again till I slammed the DELETE key. It became a letter I was writing to him, and the letter became a diary, and this thing, this evil thing he'd done became the great divider between *her* and *him*, Sofie and Ren. In some sick way it was an anchor point, almost a perverse comfort. It contextualized things. Gave shape, form, meaning to the pain roiling inside me. I hurt because he hurt me, not because I was messed-up before then, not because I was transgender. I hated my femininity because he used it as license to violate me, not because I had problematic feelings about being feminine.

I hurt men because he hurt me, not because I hated myself.

All the speeches I'd rehearsed focused on the past. What he'd done to me, how it made me feel. A darkness that had come and gone.

They were all wrong.

"Adam," I said.

His head rose.

Here's the face of a rapist:

He looks just like any other man. Nothing distinguishes him from men who don't hurt women.

This face was handsome, and once I'd thought, as I let him unbutton my jeans, *I wish I looked like you.*

Now I said, "Don't talk. Listen."

His expression didn't change, but the apple in his throat bulged. He glanced at mine as I spoke.

"You came here for forgiveness, and I won't give it to you. I will never give another thing to you."

Without touching him I leaned close, until our bodies shared one heat.

"But I'll do something else. Something better." I smiled. "I'm going to let you go. Live your life. Get married, have kids, buy a house. Build something for yourself. Put down roots. Find your place in the world, Adam Halverson."

Faint wrinkles lined his brow. I imagined that face aging, showing no sign of what it had done.

"Live the dream," I said. "The good life. What every man fantasizes about. And every time you start to feel comfortable, warm, safe, you'll pause. You'll shiver for no reason. Feel eyes on you in a crowd. See a shadow on the street, following." Closer. "I'll be watching you, Adam. To see if you're fucking up. If you're hurting anyone. And if you do, I'll drag you out of bed, or into an alley, and I'll hurt you the same way you hurt me. I'll make you feel what that felt like. Do you know how much I bled? You will."

The wrinkles smoothed away. He stared vacantly, as if he'd just been struck in the back of the head.

"You may live to be an old man, like I will. Or you may not. But you'll always be living on borrowed time, *my* time, and someday I'll come to collect. No forgiveness, Adam. Only fear. You'll always be looking over your shoulder. You'll never know when I'm watching." I laughed. "Better be a good boy."

I glanced up into the light, as if it sealed the promise. I felt it in my bones: the power he'd taken from me, returned. Now he would live with fear. Always on guard, alert, vigilant. Analyzing every situation for a threat.

Welcome to how it feels, I thought, to move through this world like a woman.

At the door I looked back. Still blank-faced but his eyes were wet and bright.

"Don't cry," I said.

TODAY

VLOG #406: FIVE YEARS ON T

[A party at Umbra. All of Black Iris is present, including siblings and significant others. Ren leans over a giant cake that reads HAPPY FIFTH BIRTHDAY.]

REN: I can't believe you guys are giving alcohol to a five-year-old.

ARMIN: Don't get my license revoked.

BLYTHE: For your information, I've tasted all of these drinks and none of them are remotely alcoholic.

ARMIN/ELLIS: [Simultaneously.] Aussies.

BLYTHE: Christ, they're getting along. I may vomit.

REN: That's probably got more to do with tasting all the drinks.

BLYTHE: Don't judge me, birthday boy.

TAMSIN: Laney's got that look. Watch out.

LANEY: A toast.

EVERYONE: Toast! Toast!

LANEY: To a very brave boy.

BLYTHE: And handsome.

ELLIS: And kind.

ARMIN: And genuine.

TAMSIN: And good in bed.

EVERYONE: [Groans.]

BLYTHE: Nice, mate.

LANEY: And a very dear friend. Here's to you, Ren. Happy birthday.

EVERYONE: Happy birthday!

———

[Ren and Tam drive to a house in the suburbs. Tam films Ren getting out of the car. He rings the bell and waits on the lawn until an older man emerges. The older man stops, staring.]

REN: Dad. Dad? It's me.

MR. KHOURY: [Approaches.] *Ya Allah, ya Allah* . . . [Murmurs in Arabic.]

REN: Hey. It's . . . been a while.

MR. KHOURY: [Clasps Ren's hand.] Hello. How are you—

REN: You can call me Ren.

MR. KHOURY: Ren. Hello. Can I call you my son?

REN: Y-yeah. Yeah, that's okay, too.

MR. KHOURY: Who is the young lady?

REN: My girlfriend, Tamsin.

TAMSIN: Hello, Mr. Khoury.

MR. KHOURY: Ahmad, please. So beautiful. What a lovely girl. Both of you, come inside, come inside.

REN: I can't. You know how Mom is.

TAMSIN: We're here to pick up the little ones.

MR. KHOURY: Yes, yes. But come inside for a minute and cool off.

REN: It's forty-five degrees out here, Dad.

MR. KHOURY: Ah, he sees through my tricks. Okay. I'll get the little ones.

[Mr. Khoury goes inside.]

TAMSIN: He called you "he" without a thought.

REN: Yeah.

TAMSIN: Are you all right?

REN: [Smiles.] Yeah.

———

[At the beach. Tamsin and Kari are playing tag near the lake, screaming with laughter. Ren and Mina, bundled in winter jackets, build a sand castle on the shore. The camera is propped beside them.]

MINA: Is Tamsin your girlfriend?

REN: Yep. Is that weird?

MINA: No.

[They dig a moat.]

MINA: Are you her boyfriend?

REN: Yep. Is that weird?

MINA: No.

[More digging.]

MINA: Do you love her?

REN: [Smiles.] Yep. Is *that* weird?

MINA: Yes!

REN: Why is that weird?

MINA: Because, love is stupid. It's a dirty trick played on us to achieve the continuation of the species.

REN: [Laughs.] Where did you hear that?

MINA: [Scornfully.] I *read* it in a *book*.

REN: I think you found it on the Internet when you were looking up "love is stupid." Because you have a crush on someone.

MINA: Shut up.

REN: Is it on a boy?

MINA: No.

REN: Girl?

MINA: No!

REN: Nonbinary person?

MINA: Huh? No.

REN: You don't even know what that is.

MINA: It's still no.

REN: Okay, I give up. Tell me.

MINA: [Sighs dramatically.] It's on a *fictional character*.

REN: [Starts laughing.]

MINA: See! This is why I never tell you anything.

REN: You tell me everything. You literally never shut up.

MINA: Well, it's not serious, because *A*: he's not real, and *B*: Mom would kill me.

REN: Mom wants to kill all of us. Why did she even have kids?

MINA: I *know*.

[They build a bridge over the moat.]

MINA: Are you going to marry Tamsin?

REN: [Raises eyebrows.] I don't know.

MINA: Don't you want to get married?

REN: I think so. Someday.

MINA: Well, why not her?

REN: She gets a say in it, too.

MINA: She'd marry you.

REN: Why do you say that?

MINA: I just know these things.

REN: [Laughs.] You're so wise, Mina. I'm not. I'm only twenty-four.

MINA: That is *so old*. You are ancient.

REN: You're only saying that because you're eleven.

MINA: Don't be ageist.

REN: [Laughs.] You just called me old!

MINA: That means you're *supposed* to be wise.

REN: What are you supposed to be?

MINA: [Flips her hair.] A princess.

REN: [Smiling.] Well, lucky for you, you are. Come on, Princess Mina. I miss the other royals.

[He kneels and offers his palm. She takes it and together they walk toward the water, dwindling against the sun, hand in hand.]

ACKNOWLEDGMENTS

There are two stories in each of my novels. The first story is fiction, and it plays out over three hundred or so pages. The second story, the true one, takes place in the acknowledgments. It's my story—a diary that's spanned four novels, first as Leah, now as Elliot.

This book is where Leah's story ends.

In this space I usually address you, my readers. All of you mean the world to me, and I'm beyond humbled and grateful that you've followed me on this journey through my books and in my life. Thank you. But there's someone out there I've never thanked properly. Someone who deserves to have her strength and suffering recognized. So this time, I'm doing something different in this space.

This time I'm writing to her.

————

Dear Leah,

The last image I have of you is when you were writing the acknowledgments for your third book, *Cam Girl*. It's late on a hot night in August 2015. Your boyfriend has gone to bed and you're alone on a futon mattress on the floor, a little tipsy on tequila, spilling your heart onto the page. You've spent the past year battling the paralysis of depression by writing a book about someone like you: a girl who's not really a girl.

That book is a step closer to your personal truth. Each novel has been both confession and acceptance: of becoming an adult in *Unteachable*, then your queerness in *Black Iris*, then your gender in *Cam Girl*. But the last one didn't go far enough, and you know that.

And you're terrified of the book you're going to write next.

Because this one *will* go far enough. It's going to drag you along, kicking and screaming and crying the whole way.

You already know the name you'll take. You first heard it as a kid, in the movie *E. T.* It sounded wise, knowing. Later you discovered a poet with the same name, who spoke to the darkness inside you, and something about his name resonated—a hum in the center of your chest, your rib cage struck like a tuning fork. You'll know it's your name, but not why. It'll come clear in time: *Leah* is contained inside the name *Elliot*. El-ee-et. Hear it?

You already know you'll take testosterone, too. You're terrified, trying to scare yourself off, but you know that without it, the body in the mirror will never match the one in your head. You've known this for years. You remember poring over your mom's Sears catalogs, staring entranced at boys' clothes and picturing yourself in that stuff, a self with short hair and straight hips and broad shoulders. You remember how much it hurt the day you beat R in a race, and M sneered, "It doesn't matter because you're just a girl," and you felt no one could see that you were the same as R or any other boy, because of the stupid body you wore. You remember being called "dyke," "fag," "queer" (the latter of which you embraced, eventually), and being upset not because they were wrong, but for some other reason you couldn't articulate. A "dyke" was a girl who liked girls. Only half of that was true for you. It would take years to understand which part of you those words were hurting.

You're scared of T. Of losing your hair (you won't), of getting teen-boy acne (you won't), of losing the ability to feel things as intensely as you do on E (you won't, but it *will* change).

You're scared of losing your boyfriend when you transition. You will in some ways, but not all. He'll surprise you, again and again, with how sensitive and accepting he is, how open to learning. You'll both cry your eyes out and the particulars of your relationship will shift, but that's why they say *it's a transition for you both*.

Deep within you, in a place you don't like looking because of the pettiness and vanity that dwells there, you're scared you'll find yourself repulsive once the changes start. That you'll trade in one body you hate for another you'll hate differently. From ugly girl to ugly boy. You're so wrong. There's nothing ugly about you—that's dysphoria distorting your image. You'd never believe me now, but at four months on T you'll share the first photographs of your face on Instagram. The response will be so kind and encouraging that you'll soon be sharing selfies of your body, undressed, without a second thought. People will say nice things about the way you look, and the miracle is that *you'll finally believe them*.

You already know you're a man. The word sits weirdly now—you still recoil instinctively, remembering all the ways men have failed you, hurt you. You want everything that comes with manhood—muscles, beard, pronouns, "sir"—without having to acknowledge to yourself that yes, you *are* a man.

You'll spend a lot of time trying to reconcile your

feminism with your masculinity. Spoiler alert: it's an eternal struggle. Like Ren, you'll constantly seek a delicate balance between the two while staving off bitterness and indignation. But you'll also find that people are surprisingly willing to listen. Men will tell you they've become aware of their own privilege when you discuss how society treats you differently as a man. Women will tell you they better understand the ways men experience emotion when you discuss how your emotional responses have changed.

What it means for you as a writer—as a human being— to have experienced both sides is invaluable. People will tell you, "You've opened my eyes," but really, yours will be opened just as wide.

You already knew all of these things at the end of last summer. When you finished writing the acknowledgments for *Cam Girl*, you collapsed into major depression. You knew beyond a doubt you were transgender. You stayed up till dawn day after day, watching video after video on your laptop—Skylar, Chase, Ty, all the trans guys you envied and idolized. You googled everything you feared: *permanent changes, transition regret, suicide.*

One day, while Alex was at work, you knelt on your bedroom floor and screamed. Just screamed yourself raw, for who knows how many minutes. You said things like *I can't do this* and *I wish I was fucking dead* and *I don't want to be me.* When you washed your face, your gaze lingered on the shower rod, judging if it could take your weight.

You'd tried that years ago, with a belt. Almost succeeded. Your chest was numb for weeks. You *would* succeed, if there was a next time.

But a voice inside you kept telling you to hold on.

That was me.

At the end, you were so tired. So fucking sad, worn down,

empty. You almost didn't make it. I wasn't sure I'd ever get to write this, to open my eyes and wake up as Elliot. But you carried us both here. You spent your whole life shouldering both of our burdens. I've got this now, Leah. You can rest.

Thank you for holding on until I was ready.

———

As always, my deepest gratitude to the two women in publishing who've made my dreams come true: my agent and adviser, Jane Dystel; and my editor, Sarah Cantin, whose guidance and allyship have meant everything to me. Three years ago, I self-published a romance novel called *Unteachable*—and if Jane hadn't seen the worth in it, and Sarah hadn't seen the spark in me, I don't think I'd be here today. Life is wild like that. Thank you both for helping me achieve my dreams as a writer, and in doing so enabling me to pursue the dream I never thought I'd realize: becoming the man I am.

Thank you to everyone at Dystel & Goderich and Atria Books for your support and sensitivity regarding my transition. It's an honor to work with people who truly care about me as a person, and who advocate for work by marginalized authors like me. I'm proud to be published by you.

Thank you to my family, who have come to grips with this each in their own way. Thanks to my sister, Bethany, who made me cry when she called me her brother; to my father, Masoud, who cheerfully wrote back *Dear Elliot* to my coming-out letter; and to my mother, Rita, who has always loved me unequivocally, however I identify. Thank you to my partner and Life Dude, Alexander, who is the man most important to me in this whole world. I love you all so much. You didn't lose me, and I'm so glad I didn't lose any of you.

Thank you also to my dear friends and online supporters, including Ana, Bethany, Fox, James, Matt, and every single one of you who's followed my transition journey under the Twitter hashtag #WakeUpElliot. Having a support network is critical when transitioning—and having you guys cheer at my victories and console me over setbacks is priceless.

And, of course, thank *you*. Yeah, you. The person holding this book. It's because of readers like you that I went from someone who hated herself and her life and who self-published an escapist romance without believing anyone would read it, to this guy. This person who is only now starting to find his true place in the world. Thanks for reading my stories, and for letting me tell my own, book by book, in these final pages.

Here's to Leah's story ending happily—and to Elliot's story, which is just beginning.

All my love,
Elliot Wake
Chicago, July 2016